THE DARK SORCERER'S PROJECT MANAGER

THE DARK SORCERER'S PROJECT MANAGER

GAVIN BROWN

Podium

Cover design by Mike F. Miller

ISBN: 978-1-0394-7561-8

Published in 2026 by Podium Publishing
www.podiumentertainment.com

Podium

THE DARK SORCERER'S PROJECT MANAGER

MAGICAL SECURITY AGENCY

SUPPLEMENTAL THREAT ASSESSMENT BRIEFING—TOP SECRET

TO: MSA DIRECTORS AND ABOVE

FROM: SPECIAL AGENT ANGELICA CRANE

The Magical Security Agency's arcanometrics monitoring services are reporting a notable new development. Observation stations worldwide have noticed statistically significant leaps in background levels of arcane energy. There is no historical record of such extreme, widespread, and consistent variation from baseline.

While other government agency resources are tied up with current global conflicts, disasters, and reports of compromised governments, the MSA is monitoring this situation closely.

This arcane phenomenon will not impact regular spellcasting activities, but it demonstrates that arcane energy is being deployed periodically for powerful magic use of unknown nature. While this level of arcane power has historically been associated with Zambrano, the noted dark sorcerer, intelligence gathering activities indicate that it is neither emanating from his residence nor his frequented locations. Additional surveillance information and contacts suggest Zambrano is not performing any spellcasting activity during these surges.

While we cannot be certain if the energy readings are related to the self-proclaimed demon king, it is nonetheless very concerning. I advise placing both MSA staff and US military resources on elevated alert.

CHAPTER 1

Some inventions are crucial to the advancement of civilization. The wheel, the plow, the printing press, electricity, the washing machine, antibiotics, the internet. And those are all worthy and valuable, and I hope the people who helped invent them were all richly rewarded, because without them, life would be lonely and dark, dirty and squalid. But at this particular moment, one invention looms above them all in importance: the cardboard cupholder tray that lets you carry a bunch of hot drinks all at once.

You don't think about them all that often. You take them for granted. They've always been there when you needed them. But when you don't have one, and you have an order of five hot drinks, six breakfast sandwiches, and one over-caffeinated HYPERDRIVE™ soda that you're trying to get home from your local deli, well, it feels about as important as the steam engine or crop rotation. Human hands can comfortably hold a grand total of one coffee each. If you line up the cups in the crook of your arm, you can get maybe one or two more in there—but that is courting disaster with each step.

I stand there for a few seconds, staring at the counter full of food and drinks that I've paid for. It's late morning, and this part of Queens is quiet, so the employee who sold everything to me has turned and walked into the back, leaving me here with a row of drinks. He could have done something to help, sure, but at least he's not standing here, judging me or trying to help another customer.

I guess I'm alone in here. The only other person around is the burly MSA agent, who's in a suit and dark sunglasses and standing outside, nonchalantly periodically peeking in through the glass to check on me. It's Derek today, the big Pacific Islander, who has become my favorite of the government guys who keep an eye on me.

Whenever I leave Zambrano's warehouse headquarters, Derek or one of his coworkers follows me around. At first they tried to be subtle about it, but by now we all know one another, so we make the best of it. It's not clear to me if they're here to protect me from the world or to protect the world from me. I'm not sure they know either.

I experiment for a moment, trying to pick up the hot cups in my hands, but it's not happening, it's just too precarious. I look around, wondering if there are cupholder trays somewhere obvious, under the coffee dispenser or by the stack of cups. Did I miss them? But I don't see anything.

I grab a paper bag and start opening it up, trying to figure if I can fill the bottom of it with the coffees in such a way that they'll hold one another upright. I get four of them in there, but it feels like asking for spilled food and a waste of a bunch of good drinks.

Why didn't I order delivery? That would have been so much easier. But we're getting our whole little group of misfit magical heroes together for the first time in a while, and I wanted to do something nice for the team. Also, Zambrano is being his usual annoying, pompous sorcerer self, and Seraphex has embraced even more of her haughty demon-trapped-in-the-body-of-a-duck identity than usual lately, and I wanted to get out for a bit to gather my thoughts.

Additionally, I don't have their magical powers or arcane knowledge, so I have to figure out how to contribute to our as-yet-unnamed small crew. Seraphex once offered to help unlock my potential to learn magic, but it would have required letting her transform back into a full demon. That was a clear no, if not an easy one. So here I am, fetching calories and caffeine for everyone.

The door opens, ringing the little bell above it. Derek pokes his head in.

"Do you, uh, need a little help, Mr. Alexander?" he asks.

"Sure," I answer. "Are you allowed to do that?"

Coming in, he steps closer. "Well, if anything happens that requires me to spin, I will have to immediately throw your drinks and food onto the ground. If you accept the risk, then sure, I'll give you a hand."

"Okay, great, thanks," I say. "I formally accept the risk of losing this extremely expensive investment of bodega snacks."

Derek is allowed to talk to me now. He was tight-lipped when we first met last summer, when he and the other MSA agents started tailing me any time I left the warehouse. Summer's long over now, and we're both wearing our winter coats.

I've just come back from Thanksgiving at home, where I had to be cagey about my job as an assistant of someone my parents consider a dark sorcerer. They don't approve, but they do see it as a step up from making protein shakes at Samba Smoothies, so they don't complain too much.

And while they worry that my current job is dangerous, I've let them believe I mostly do paperwork and supply-chain management type stuff. My mom is still proud I got promoted from intern to assistant a few months back, so she has something nice to tell her friends when they ask about me. And that's the most important part, isn't it?

Luckily, they don't have any idea about the frequent, intense, and frankly stupid levels of danger I'm subjected to. My parents would one hundred percent pitch a fit if they had any idea.

I'm not sure if Derek's more talkative disposition is because his orders have changed, or if he got a promotion, or what. But now we have careful, circumspect chats that don't reveal anything about his personal or professional lives, and in which he attempts to learn things about mine.

"How's it going?" he asks. "Is the world, uh, ending this week? Should I be sticking to my diet or go to Five Guys tonight?"

He is looking trimmer than he was a few months ago. I hope it's diet rather than the stress of the world's possible impending doom.

I glance down at the giant bag of greasy breakfast sandwiches in my hand. "Don't interpret our unhealthy nutritional choices as proof of the apocalypse, okay? Keep eating those vegetables."

"Sure thing, Mr. Alexander," Derek says. "But, an extra cheat day is probably fine, right?"

"Sure," I say. "Want an ice cream sandwich? I got the bulk package from Costco a couple days ago. I'll trade you a couple of those for a Javelin missile launcher?"

I don't say "for *another* Javelin" because there's a good chance the MSA is recording this conversation. And I don't want him and his boss, MSA Agent Crane, to get in trouble for the time they gave me one to use against Demon King Rex. It was a huge help, allowing us to rescue the sorcerer Liao Ling, who was frozen in time with him for fifteen hundred years.

I guess that's partly why we're friends now. We've got some shared lore. And Derek doesn't know the half of it.

"Don't have any cool hardware for you today," Derek says with a wink that I interpret as the Javelin thing not being a huge secret. But I don't know for sure. "Are you about to get into a situation where you'd need something like that?"

I shrug. "Nah, just a business meeting. No giant battles with the fate of the world at stake planned for today, thankfully. That I know of." What I don't mention is that my main contact in the MSA, Agent Crane, called me last night to let me know that some sort of movement was happening in the arcane energy readings around the world. But I'm not sure what Derek is supposed to know, so I don't want to get him in trouble with information that's top secret, or highly confidential, or whatever they call the big, classified info these days.

"You know," Derek says, stopping at the street corner and looking me in the eye. "You can ask us for help, if you need it." He has the tone of a friend reminding me that he has a spare bedroom if I need to leave a toxic and abusive relationship. Which is not *completely* off base. But things have gotten a lot better lately. Zambrano has started trusting me to make decisions—which is its own special challenge.

Living in a world where you have no control over anything is terrifying. A world where you can make decisions, but with terrible consequences if you get it wrong . . . is just a different flavor of terror.

"I'm okay," I say as we cross the street and walk up to the warehouse where Zambrano has set up our headquarters. Somehow, over the past six months, it's become my home too. We're both able to carry one hot drink in each hand, and I wedge my own drink in a bag and carry that, figuring if I spill a little bit at least no one else can complain.

"Well, it seems like mostly you're doing supply runs, so that should be safe," Derek says. "And now you have two sorcerers to help," he adds, referring to Liao Ling, who has become something of an ally since we rescued her. "You're supposed to be Zambrano's assistant, but you're still doing intern stuff like fetching coffee, so maybe that will keep you safe?"

He's clearly trying to bait me into talking, but I don't care. It feels dangerous to admit this, but I have to vent to someone. "No, I'm . . . I'm kind of important now. I called the meeting this morning. I need to make sure everyone shows up and is in a good mood, so I told them I'd bring coffee and breakfast."

"Ah," Derek says. I'm sure he's going to report this information back to Agent Crane and the MSA, but that's fine. I want them to know. "Well, that's a lot more responsibility. Does it come with a promotion and a raise?"

"Huh," I say as we stop at the fence outside the warehouse. "You know, that's a very good point. I'll be sure to take it up with my manager if the world doesn't get taken over by a giant demon bent on destroying all of humanity."

"Make sure that doesn't happen, okay?" Derek says as I precariously line up three of the drinks in the crook of one arm—it's a bit warm but I can take it for thirty seconds. He then helps me open the gate in the fence, whose defensive spells have been taught to recognize me and unlock. "I don't want eating all these vegetables to have been for nothing. See you later, Mr. Alexander."

"Have a good one, Derek," I answer with a laugh. Moving slowly and carefully, I carry my perilously-stacked load of food and drinks into the warehouse, and the door shuts behind me.

CHAPTER 2

Welcome back, Bryce." Ruffling her feathers, Seraphex hops over. "I would offer to help you, but tragically, I cannot. You'll have to attend to my needs on your own, as usual."

If I were a demon queen trapped by magic in the body of a duck like Seraphex is, I would be a pain about it as well. But still, I did just go out in the cold to get breakfast for her and everyone else. Rude.

"No problem, Sera," I answer, laying it on thick. "I live to serve, oh great queen of all demons."

The lower floor of the warehouse has changed over the past two months. The display case that used to hold the Sword of Wayland has been removed, since it was unfortunately destroyed in our battle against the Leviathan. It's been replaced with an additional lab bench and desk space, which Liao Ling uses when she's visiting. Sorcerers like space from one another, and she's already managed to set up her own base in the South China Sea.

The biggest change is a big new table in the center of the room, with plenty of space for five humans and one duck to sit around when we're all able to get together.

On the wall of teleportraits, the magical paintings that Zambrano uses to teleport to the location displayed, there are several new pieces. They show a courtyard in Liao Ling's new lair in the South China Sea, the closet in Mei Song's office in the artifact-collecting demon Slickwad's compound, and a quiet alley behind my friend Parth's dorm at the Indian Institute of Magic in Hyderabad. Although at the moment, the one for Parth's dorm is missing.

"He went to grab Parth?" I guess.

"Yes, the sorcerer has gone to fetch your internet buddy," Seraphex says. "Though why he gets to be part of this, I still don't understand. He's a first year magic-user-in-training, and he doesn't have your particular special ability to be invisible to magic. He's nothing but a peasant."

"And we're the Avengers, right?" I say, shaking my head. "Parth is here because of trust. Who else can we trust not to be a double agent or betray us at the last minute?"

"I understand your sentiment," Seraphex answers. "But what value is the word of a human? I've sworn an unbreakable promise of friendship to you and to Zambrano. Parth is, as you might say, 'just some guy.'"

"He risked his life for us in Merlin's Vault," I retort as I set out everyone's sandwiches and coffee around the table. "And he got badly injured for it."

"Very well," Seraphex responds. "And Mei Song, do you trust her in the same way?"

I shrug. "Mei? Oh, absolutely not. She's willingly taken admin jobs in the offices of demons—twice. I trust her as long as our interests are aligned. She doesn't want humanity to end in demonic hellfire, and neither do we. And she has connections and intelligence that we need. It's a risk worth taking."

"What's a risk worth taking?" Zambrano asks, having popped into the room partway through my sentence, with Parth in tow. Zambrano adjusts his usual snappy suit, while Parth's T-shirt, with the logo for some Indian metal band I've never heard of, looks like it could definitely use an iron.

"Letting you have the double shot of espresso you asked for," I answer.

"Don't worry, Bryce," Zambrano says with a friendly slap on the back that's a bit harder than necessary. "A little burst of caffeine isn't going to make me go insane and betray humanity."

"We could always hope for next time," Seraphex says with a sparkle in her eye. "Maybe a triple shot?"

"Let's not, please," I say with an annoyed chuckle.

"If you're going to go insane, Mr. Z," Parth says, "Blow me up first, okay? And make it a *big* explosion. I want to be remembered for something cool."

It's probably better to joke about these things than never talk about them, but it's a real risk. Every sorcerer in history has eventually gone insane from the sheer amount of their magical power, usually while trying to harness demonic magic or bring people back from the dead. You know, the usual smart and healthy uses for arcane power.

"Don't worry, I'll make sure you leave a mark on the world," Zambrano says with a smile. He's taken a liking to my friend, and he even taught him some magic that has helped him get ahead of his studies at the Indian Institute of Magic. You know, magic, the thing that I desperately wanted to learn from Zambrano, which led me to risk my life becoming his intern. Unfortunately, my magical nature has been locked away and will likely never be accessed. So my friend Parth gets to learn magic from the great dark sorcerer.

I'm not jealous. You're jealous!

But in reality, it's not that big a deal. Saving the world and trying to keep this ragtag team together has consumed all the brain space that used to be obsessed with magic. The only spell I want to be able to cast is one that will get this group to successfully work together.

The door to the upper floor opens, and Liao Ling and Mei Song walk down the stairs into the lab. Liao Ling is holding a few teleportraits in her hands, including one for the street outside the warehouse's secret magic entrance, a few blocks away. Zambrano painted them for her, and told me that painting teleportraits is a very subtle art that is going to take her some time to master. But I suspect he hasn't shared the secrets with her because he doesn't trust her. The same lack of trust also led him to only give her a teleportrait that leads to outside the warehouse, rather than letting her have one that brings her directly into the lab.

"Hello, everyone," Mei says, finding her spot at the table and taking a sip of her tea. "Thanks for doing the supply run, Bryce."

"Alix always used to make me pick up the supplies when I was the newest to the Sorcerers' Circle," Zambrano says. "Which lasted for a couple decades before Ilyas Rahmani joined us. So don't think this is a onetime thing, eh?"

It's nice to hear Zambrano speak casually of Alix LaFontaine, the sorcerer who discovered him and what can best be described as the love of his life, though he probably wouldn't phrase it in such a cheesy way.

"What's up, losers," Liao Ling says, dropping into her chair and eagerly opening her sandwich wrapper while taking a slurp of her hot chocolate. "Yeah, thanks for the food though." She has taken to modern habits quickly after we unlocked her from being frozen in time. I'm glad she mostly learned English from movies and TV shows, and not the latest social media brain rot.

Everyone takes their seats and digs in, exchanging small talk but mostly focusing on enjoying our preferred delivery mechanisms for caffeine and calories. They're all grateful, which is nice. It's funny, we've all got access to resources to get as many sandwiches as we want delivered to our door at the push of a button, but there's still something special about someone else buying and picking up food for you.

They're all mostly pleasant to one another, though Liao Ling occasionally gives Seraphex a sour glance. It's understandable, given that the demon duck killed her brother, and despite her unbreakable promise to be our friend, is still very much a demon. But it's annoying because we all need to work together since there's a demon king on the loose.

"Okay, I've got junk to do," Liao Ling says. "What are we here for?"

They all look at me, which makes sense because I organized the meeting and asked all of them to come in. Still, it feels weird to be in charge, even if it's only for one meeting.

"We've all been working on our separate projects," I say. "But I think we need to be coordinating better. We need a plan. I'm hoping we can review everything we know and figure out what to do. Agent Crane gave me a call last night. She wouldn't be specific, but she said something big is happening, some sort of magic pressure readings. We need to make our moves before it's too late."

"The Caesar Special is ready," Liao Ling says with a shrug. That magical demon-sapping dagger is our biggest advantage at the moment. "Mei and I got it sorted out with a little assist from the druids. It's got enough juice to weaken Rex, and then we can trap him. We did our part. What have the rest of you been up to while we were getting it set up?"

"We did kill one of the greatest mythic monsters of all time," Zambrano points out. "While you were on vacation in England."

"That was months ago," Mei notes with a snide smile. "How have things gone since then? Any way to get to Mars?"

Zambrano seems ready to burst out in one of his furies, but I jump in before he can escalate things further.

"Hold on, let's not get ahead of ourselves. We're all on the same team here, right?"

No one verbally objects, but I can see in their faces that they aren't all as sure of it as I am. Zambrano and Mei don't trust each other, Seraphex and Liao Ling hate each other, and no one takes Parth very seriously. He's been sitting here this whole time, watching as the sorcerers and the demon debate. And I'm getting more worried about Zambrano's sanity with each passing month.

We're definitely not a well-oiled machine. We're more like a rusty machine with random branches and debris in its gears. But we're the best hope for humanity, probably.

"How about we slow down and start from reviewing where we are?" I suggest. "Parth, you've been doing research on world events. What are you seeing?"

"Since the rockhide demons and the Leviathan that Rex attacked with, he's gotten much more subtle," Parth says. "I'm pretty sure he's behind a variety of famines, the war in East Asia, the weather anomalies causing everything to dry up in central Africa, and the big market collapses in India and Pakistan. India's economic crash especially took everyone at the university by surprise. It doesn't make sense with the fundamental numbers, at least that's what my professors say."

"He is intentionally acting in ways that destabilize the world but that are difficult for us to contend with," Seraphex says.

"It's absurd! How are we supposed to fight a drought? How do we battle economic sabotage? Or convince world leaders to stop fighting?" Zambrano gripes, tapping his fingers on the table in frustration. "Why can't he send more monsters at us, or raise an army of skeletons, or something like that?"

"Could he really raise an army of skeletons?" I ask, scared once more.

"I doubt it," Seraphex says. "Attempts at necromancy have been more the territory of sorcerers. It's one of the standard tropes they fall into as they inevitably lose their sanity."

"Watch yourself, duck," Liao Ling says with a glare.

"Offense was not my primary intention," Seraphex replies haughtily.

"And yet I suspect it was gleefully accepted as a side effect," Zambrano notes, though his tone is more resignation than anger.

"You can act prim and proper, but I know the monster that you are," Liao Ling says.

"Prim? I don't feel that any reasonable person would describe me with that word," Seraphex answers. "Perhaps I could recommend *regal*, *stately*, or even *majestic*?"

"So what's Rex's endgame?" I interrupt, trying to steer things back on course.

"He's quietly making allies," Seraphex says. "He's likely getting back to his full power, and with that he can win any stand-up fight. But to conquer the world, he will need vassals and servants. So he is playing favorites and making quiet alliances, and he's wreaking havoc on those who won't work with him. For now he will call it a covenant, but once he seizes control, it will be subjugation."

This statement seems to focus everyone a bit, though Liao Ling is staring at Seraphex, and Zambrano simply looks tired.

"But we have a plan to beat him, right?" I say. "We have the Caesar Special, that should weaken him. And then we can stuff him in the remaining half of the arcane conduit. He will be constantly teleporting with no destination, frozen there forever. Simple enough."

"Simple enough, if we can find a way to Mars to get the other end of the arcane conduit," Zambrano grumbles. "And we still need the spell that activates the damn thing."

"There's no way in hell it's going to be that simple," Liao Ling says, taking a loud slurp of her hot chocolate.

"Well, we haven't had any luck finding my birth mother," I point out. "She's the only one who knows the spells to control the arcane conduit." We've been hunting around for a clue as to her location, with no success. But part of me is relieved. I already have great parents, and I don't know what I would make of Zuzanna, my birth mother and a great sorcerer who locked away her magic—and with it, mine as well. She did it to save her sanity. And to save me from being raised by an unhinged and dangerous sorcerer. But I'm still pissed about it.

"But those are the core elements of the plan," Mei says, agreeing with me. "Pulling it off will be its own challenge. But first we need to get that conduit before the whole world falls apart."

"Which means that we need to get to Mars," I say. "But we don't have a good way to do that."

"I've been looking into that, but I don't think we can do it safely," Zambrano says, frustrated. "Dead end after dead end. A space launch is a delicate thing. If Rex got wind of it, one little push and we go down in a giant explosion. I've been trying to figure out how to hide it or make it safe."

"Maybe we could distract him?" Parth suggests. "Figure out how some of us can draw him out on the other side of the world while you hijack a spaceship launch. I'll challenge him to a fight. Taunt him until he comes out."

"Even if my former husband could be baited out of hiding like that," Seraphex chides him, "you are so very far beneath his notice. He is the king of demons."

"I may have an idea for getting to Mars," Liao Ling says. "Demons have occasionally been able to teleport themselves to and from Earth over the years. That's how Seraphex came here when she returned last century. Bent on sowing destruction and subjugating the human race."

We all turn to the duck, who has the good grace to look slightly embarrassed, turning her long neck to look around the room.

"How *did* you get here back then?" Zambrano asks. "I was always curious about that, but I didn't know much beyond that you appeared in rural Texas and started wreaking havoc."

"Well, I didn't do it myself. I couldn't, or I would have done it many centuries earlier. There was a sorcerer, Carmen Medina. She created what she called a *Vuelo de la Imagen* or 'Flight of the Image.' It was quite similar to how Zambrano creates his teleportraits, based on the same principles."

"I wasn't the first to invent this method of teleportation spells?" Zambrano says, outraged. "That hermit woman did it first?!"

"Surprise, surprise, Zambrano is not quite as brilliant as he thought," Liao Ling says, giving the other sorcerer a friendly pat on the back. "But the question is, why would any sorcerer be such a complete nimrod that she would want to teleport you to Earth?" Liao Ling asks, dropping the last bit of her mostly-finished sandwich into the foil wrapping in annoyance.

"I think I know," Zambrano says.

"Don't tell me you hooked up with her," I say, glaring at the sorcerer relaxing calmly in his dapper suit with his magically perfect bronze skin and white hair.

"No, no," Zambrano protests. "In those years I was only involved with Alix."

Then almost apologetically, he adds, "Along with a brief fling with your birth mother."

"Damn, I hate you," I say with an honest-to-god eye roll.

"I knew Carmen Medina, but no one knew her very well," Zambrano continues. "She was quite powerful but kept to herself and rarely left her home in the forest of the Lost Pines of Bastrop. At the time, it was said that the loneliness and isolation had driven her mad, but I think by now we know that it was the power of the magic she used. Though I managed not to be driven insane when I invented teleportraits, so I guess I'm ahead of her on that count . . ."

"So that arcane madness led her to seek out demonic power," Seraphex says, ignoring Zambrano's egotistical ranting to continue her explanation. "She crafted a spell to communicate across the solar system, and I was the one who picked up on the other end. It wasn't hard to make some cleverly worded promises to convince Carmen Medina to harness the power of the Galveston Hurricane to teleport me across space to your trifling little planet."

"Global domination, raising the dead, or demonic power," Seraphex chides us. "It's always the same clichéd goals with you mad sorcerers."

"If I go mad, I'm going to do something original," Liao Ling remarks. "Like using my magic to create a larger-on-the-inside stomach so that I can eat fifty hamburgers a day." She's now picking every little crumb out of the bottom of her foil sandwich wrapper. I should mention that her "breakfast sandwich" order was a triple hamburger. Though I guess in the time zone where she's made her hideaway in the South China Sea, it's late at night. Still, that's a mighty big burger for a very petite woman. Gotta respect the game.

While we're talking, I notice that Mei is on her phone, texting with someone. Her face is twisted up in concentration and concern, so I let it be.

"Okay, so with enough power, we can teleport to Mars and back," I summarize. "Sounds straightforward."

"Not exactly straightforward," Zambrano grumbles, "But I have a few ideas."

"And we'll need the spells that Carmen Medina used to teleport Seraphex from Mars," Liao Ling says. "According to my research, no one ever found her secret home in the Lost Pines. Is that true, Zambrano?"

"To my knowledge, yes," the sorcerer says.

"From the descriptions," Liao Ling continues, "I think she may have used some cloaking spells that I'm familiar with. I'm going to head there to see if I can find her spellbooks."

"Should we go with you?" I ask. "In case you need backup?"

"I can go," Parth volunteers. "I don't have any more classes this week."

Liao Ling gives both of us meaningful glances, clearly communicating how little she thinks of our offered help.

"It's possible Rex could have agents there," Zambrano points out. "He has surely been covertly observing us, and—"

"I think we may need to deal with something else," Mei interrupts.

"What's that?" I ask.

"Your birth mother," she says. "Rex has put out a bounty on her capture."

"Oh, shit," I blurt. "We have to stop him. But we haven't had any luck finding her, and we've been looking for months. We don't even know where to start."

"We do now," Mei says with a sigh. "My boss has identified her. Luckily, I'm copied on the emails. He's sending a team to 'acquire' her now."

"God damn it. That horny seaweed bastard Slickwad again," I say with a groan.

"Where is she?" Parth asks.

"A nursing home not too far from here, over in Hoboken."

"New Jersey? Wait, really?" My mind is racing. Until I got involved with Zambrano earlier this year, I lived on the north side of Jersey City, just south of Hoboken. Was my birth mother really living a mile or two away from me?

"Yeah," Mei says. "She's at Hudson View Senior Living. It's a transitional assisted living facility. The information is solid; Slickwad's research department is very good and finds things and people who don't want to be found."

"Do you have a photo? What name is she using?" I ask. My pulse is starting to speed up. Am I finally going to meet my birth mother?

"Sure, one second," Mei says. She pokes at her phone for a moment, and I fidget as the Wi-Fi takes its time to load up the information. "Here you go."

She shows me the image, and my breath catches. The photo is a bit out of date and displays a woman a decade or so younger, but there's no denying who she looks like.

"Oh my god," I say, recognizing her immediately. "That's Susan. She used to come twice a week to the Samba Smoothies I worked at. One of my nicest and most consistent customers."

"Zuzanna is the Polish version of the name Susan," Zambrano notes. "How did you not notice that connection?"

"How was I supposed to guess she was my birth mother? Or even think about that? She was just a nice old lady who bought smoothies and would occasionally make inappropriate comments about how things got spicy at her nursing home."

"Yep, that's Zuzanna, all right," Zambrano says. "She was always a randy one."

"Ugh," I say. "Can I go to the Lost Pines, please? Or fight a demon?"

"She's your birth mother," Parth admonishes me. "And it sounds like she's been keeping tabs on you. You should go—you might need to convince her to come with you or help with the spell."

"Okay, okay, fine," I say. I really want to meet her, but also really, really don't. It's a lot to process.

"I need to get back to my office," Mei says. "This is an important operation, and they'll expect me to be monitoring things. I'll see if I can throw them a few red herrings to slow things down a bit. I won't be able to contact you, and I won't be able to help too much without giving myself up."

"Thanks," I say. I always forget how much more Mei is risking right now than the rest of us. One misstep and her boss, Slickwad the seawater demon, will lock her in one of his slow-time cases, or worse.

"I'll take Mei back and then head to Lost Pines to search for Carmen's spell," Liao Ling says. "I'm worried that something is happening with this magical pressure that Agent Crane reported to you. Rex is making moves, and we don't know what they are. We need to get our plan in motion."

"You'll need someone to drive," Parth points out. "And maybe boldly risk everything to help at a crucial moment."

Liao Ling shakes her head but shrugs. "It's going to be a lot of driving," she admits. "But you have to drive and let me lie in the back and listen to my podcasts, okay?"

"Sure thing," Parth says.

"Great," I say. "Zambrano, Seraphex: we should get to this retirement home and grab Zuzanna before Slickwad's goons make it there."

"It will be good to see the old firecracker again," Zambrano says.

"It would be nice to meet this sorcerer at a time when a whole crowd of you aren't hurling spells at me and ruining my life," Seraphex adds.

"Great. Zambrano, do you have a teleportrait for anywhere in New Jersey that would help us?"

"Why would I have a teleportrait for New Jersey?" Zambrano asks. "When has anyone ever wanted to go there?"

"I'm from there, it's great! I visit all the time to see my parents."

"Name one good thing about New Jersey that's unique to it. Other than your parents living there. All three of them, as we have discovered."

I open my mouth to argue, then shut it. We'll have time to fight about this once we're on our way.

"Ugh, shut up," I say. "I'll order a car."

CHAPTER 3

"Welcome to Hudson View Senior Living," the lady at the front desk says. "How can I help you?"

The place's name is appropriate—we can see past the desk into the main dining room, which has a nice view out across the river and to Manhattan. It can't be a cheap view—based on that and the size of this lobby, the regal-looking building, and the location on a hill in the pricey waterfront district, Susan lives in one of the most expensive retirement homes in the city.

"We're looking to see Susan," Zambrano says. "Is she in?"

"Susan Czarowska," I add, reading from the screenshot on my phone that Mei forwarded to me. With everyone else off on their other missions, it's down to Zambrano, me, and Seraphex. Sera is perched on my shoulder, but she's wearing an illusion prism on a necklace around her neck that Zambrano enchanted to keep her invisible. That hasn't stopped her from annoying me with her whispers the whole ride over.

In my backpack, I have the magical gauntlets that give me invisibility to demons. Mei told us that Slickwad probably wouldn't be sending demons after us, but these days it seems like demons crop up unexpectedly.

"One moment, let me check," the receptionist says, stepping into a back room to use the intercom.

"She's going by the name Susan *Czarowska*?" Zambrano hisses.

"Yeah, what about it?" I ask. "Is that Polish or Russian or something?"

"Czarowska is literally the polish word for 'sorcerer' with the suffix meaning it's a woman's last name," he answers. "She's not putting that much effort into hiding!"

"Well, we couldn't find her for the last two months," I point out. "So she must have been doing something right."

"Stay focused here, boys," Seraphex reminds us in a whisper.

Before Zambrano can respond, the receptionist returns.

"I'm sorry, gentlemen," she says. "Ms. Czarowska is out at the moment. She's in our independent living wing, so she comes and goes freely. I believe she's almost always out on Sunday afternoons."

"Do you know where she is?" I ask. "Or where she usually goes?"

"I'm sorry, sir, I can't tell you her location if you're not listed in her file in my system," the receptionist says.

"Can you tell us her cell phone number?" I ask. "We need to get in touch with her quickly."

"Sir, we take privacy very seriously here at Hudson View," the woman replies crisply. "If you want me to take a message, I can give it to her when she returns."

"You will help us find her," Zambrano intones, holding out a hand and drawing an invisible line in front of himself. "It's very important that we speak to her."

The woman shakes her head. "Ms. Czarowska is very private. If you're yet another pair of her jilted lovers who want to hold a boom box toward her window from the indoor courtyard, I must inform you that we have strict noise regulations and a very good relationship with the local police precinct, which is right around the corner."

Zambrano and I glance at each other.

"Threaten her! Boil her blood until she gives you the information," Seraphex whispers.

"No, that's not how we do things," I shoot back. "We're supposed to be the good guys, remember?"

"Because you're cowards!" Seraphex replies, but I turn and motion for Zambrano to come out with me.

"Thank you for your help, we'll come back another time," I say as we leave.

Outside, I stare at Zambrano.

"What was that?" I ask the sorcerer. "Were you trying to use a Jedi mind trick? Is that a spell you have?"

"It's a thing Liao Ling does," Zambrano answers. "Though now that I think of it, it doesn't appear to work for her."

"Does she have a Jedi mind trick spell?" I ask.

"Oh, no," Zambrano says. "There's no magic that can plunge into someone's brain and rearrange it to convince them of something. Can you imagine how complicated and subtle that would be?! She said it's something you non-magos use when you try to convince people of things."

Liao Ling did learn English and modern culture from watching TV, so I suppose she would have no way of knowing that the Jedi mind trick isn't a social thing that we do.

"What's a non-mago?" I say, though I'm pretty sure from context I know exactly what it is. "Did you invent a new slur for people who don't use magic?"

"Um, yes, I suppose so?" Zambrano answers. "It's just something she says."

I sigh. "Is Liao Ling a bad influence on you?"

Zambrano shrugs. "I haven't had a friend in quite some time." He pauses for a long moment. "Other than you two, I mean. You know, a friend who's my peer. Er, in magical power specifically, that is."

I glare at him. "*Are* you two even friends? You don't act like it."

"It's nice to have someone around here who understands what it's like to have the responsibility of great power."

"I would be so very deeply insulted if I cared about the opinions of mere humans," Seraphex says, "but we don't have time for that sort of emotion. How are we going to track down Bryce's birth mother?"

"Could we wait until she gets back?" I say. "It's already three p.m. How late do old people stay out? She should be back in a few hours."

"In a few hours, she could be tracked down and bagged by Slickwad's goons," Zambrano points out.

"Let me see if Mei can help," I say. I text her, and we wait a few minutes, but there's no response, and it looks like she hasn't even read the message.

"She must not be able to get to her burner phone right now," Seraphex suggests. "Who else can we call for help?"

I think about it for a few seconds. Then I dial up Agent Crane.

It rings several times, and I'm about to give up when she finally picks up.

"Hi, Bryce, how are things going?" Agent Crane says. Thankfully, her voice is cheerful, so hopefully she's in a helpful mood.

"Good," I answer. "Or, well, interesting at least. Look, we're in a hurry and trying to track someone down. Is there any chance you could help with that?"

"Maybe," she answers. "Who is it? And why are you looking for them?"

"It's someone who has information on a spell we need. I can explain more later," I say.

"Okay, fair enough. Happy to do a favor for you," Agent Crane answers. "Who is it?"

"Susan Czarowska," I say, and I spell it out.

There's tapping for a few seconds. "I see one in here, the S. Czarowska who lives at Hudson View Senior Living? I guess that's where you're calling from, so that would make sense."

"Yes, that's her," I say, skipping over the fact that Agent Crane immediately knows where I'm calling from.

There's tapping for another few seconds. "I've got her location from her phone GPS. She's been at 1329 Jefferson Street for the past two hours. It's a live ping so she's still there. It's only a ten-minute drive from your current location."

"Wait, you can look anyone up like that and get their live location? It's that easy?" I say, suddenly alarmed.

There's a pause on the line. "You're welcome," Agent Crane finally says cheerfully.

"Um, thanks," I say.

"Think of it as everyone in the country being subscribed to Find My Friends with their grand old friend, the United States government," Agent Crane says.

"Okay, okay, I'll stop asking questions," I say. "I appreciate the help. Thank you, Uncle Sam, you nosy creep."

CHAPTER 4

A slightly musty-smelling car picks us up, and we're on our way. It's only a short drive to the new address, but we're quickly into a much less ritzy neighborhood. This area has chain businesses, garages, warehouses, and empty streets. We roll past two competing auto lube places on opposite sides of the street. Why they can't just call it an oil change, I don't know. No need to be gross about it.

"Shouldn't we have a cool magic way to get around?" I ask. "Like a flying carpet, or broomsticks, or a giant soaring eagle, or whatever?"

"I would like an ornate carriage pulled by a team of bronzed and oiled servants," Seraphex says. "Humans, finally put in their proper place."

"We do have teleportraits, you know," Zambrano points out. "Have you ever tried to hold on to a magic carpet flying through the air? It is absolutely freezing, the wind knocks the breath out of you, and balancing is not easy. Olujimi had one, and it was terrible. Every time it took a turn, you felt like you were about to fall off, throw up, or both."

"Okay, I guess. But we spend an awful lot of time in cars," I say, enjoying the sorcerer's annoyance.

"Is it not magical enough for you," Zambrano counters, "that we drain the blood of ancient creatures from the Earth itself, float it across the ocean, store it in the belly of a mechanical beast, and at the slightest press of a foot, it rolls like a chariot at speeds an order of magnitude faster than you can run at a dead sprint?"

"Yeah, but this particular magical chariot smells like an armpit," I say.

Zambrano shrugs. "It was the cheapest option on the app. I wasn't going to spring for one of the fancy black cars."

"You do have essentially limitless money," Seraphex notes.

"Yes, certainly I could afford it, but I'm not going to get ripped off!" Zambrano says as we pull up to the address.

1329 Jefferson Street is a small, squat building. There's a tiny parking lot with a fence around it, a single neon sign on a pole, and all the windows are blacked out.

The sign has a picture of a dancing woman, with her body in pink and her hair in bright white neon. The name below says SILVER HEELS ENTERTAINMENT CLUB.

It's a strip club.

The car drives away, and we stand there for a second, staring at the building in front of us.

"I didn't bring a stack of ones. Did you?" I ask.

"Don't worry, these places always have an ATM with outrageous fees," Zambrano says as we cross the street.

"I'm going to need you to get me a nice thick wad of them," Seraphex says.

"I thought most demons weren't attracted to humans," I reply. "Suddenly, you want to see some twerking?"

"It's not for my titillation," the demon duck answers. "But I do like to reward hard work. It's rude to go to a place like this and not support the employees."

"Okay, thanks, Karl Marx," I say.

"Let's keep this quick. Our goal here isn't to support New Jersey's finest erotic performers. As noble as that may be. We're on the clock and here to save Zuzanna from Slickwad's goons," Zambrano says. "If we have to pull her out of a lap dance or whatever she's getting into, so be it."

I desperately don't want to watch my birth mother Zuzanna—and my friend Susan—give a lap dance. Or receive a lap dance? It's unclear.

Finding her at the strip club she frequents weekly is weird enough. But after we step inside, pay a cover, and get frisked by the imposing bouncer, the next surprise is waiting in the main room.

She isn't getting a lap dance or making it rain in small bills from the edge of the stage. She's up in the spotlight, strutting her stuff.

Okay, I don't know exactly how to say this. She is my birth mother and biologically fortyish years older than me and chronologically hundreds of years my senior. But she is really working it onstage, for an older lady. And her sparkling outfit, which I feel is unnecessarily revealing, shines like a thousand diamonds in the spotlights. She's still got it, and there are a number of older gentlemen around who agree and are throwing bills at the stage.

I look away, horrified,

"Why is she onstage?" I ask. "Is that normal?"

"Welcome to Silver Heels," the bouncer says with a wry grin. "New Jersey's finest, and only, erotic dance club for quality vintage women and their admirers."

"I guess we should have googled this place before we showed up," I say.

"No refunds on your cover charges, boys," the bouncer says. "Why not go in and try it out? You might have a better time than you expect. It's okay to embrace your interests, even if they're embarrassing."

"We need to talk to her," I say. "The woman onstage."

"Good, isn't she?" says the bouncer. "I'm sure you can pay for a lap dance after her set. Grab a table, and I'll make sure she stops by. But if you cause any trouble, you're out, got it? No refunds."

"Yes, got it," I agree.

"It is quite urgent that we talk to her," Zambrano says, slipping the bouncer a couple bills from his wallet. "Thanks for your help."

"You got it, boss," the bouncer says with an appreciative nod.

We walk in and sit down at an empty table. I can feel Seraphex, invisible on my shoulder, bopping to the DJ's beat.

"People like this?" I ask.

Zambrano shrugs. "When you've lived as long as I have, you've learned that there's someone interested in everyone and everything. Besides, you've seen the ads on the internet. The advertisers wouldn't keep buying them if they didn't work."

"Oh, and where do you see those ads?" Seraphex whispers.

"You're not going to shame me, duck," Zambrano replies. "I know about that pond you go to sometimes out in the Brooklyn Botanic Garden."

"That is for *platonic* duck companionship, and only once every few months," Seraphex shoots back. "There are some classy gentleman ducks there. It's not like the hoi polloi over at Prospect Park. That is a collection of savages."

"Well then, we all have our peccadillos," Zambrano concludes with satisfaction. "So let's not begrudge these gentlemen their tawdry entertainment," he adds, gesturing to the patrons raining ones down on Zuzanna as she finishes her set with, honestly, some very impressive pole work for someone her age. Certainly, I couldn't turn myself upside down and kick my legs out like that.

A couple minutes later, Zuzanna comes out of the dressing room. She's wearing a modest-looking robe now, which I appreciate. She clearly knows exactly who we are, approaching with a tight smile and much less of the performative air she had onstage.

"I figured each of you might show up sooner or later," she says, sitting down at the table with us. "Though I didn't expect it would be the two of you together. You've made an . . . interesting choice there, Bryce."

"You've fallen off from your glory days as the greatest practitioner of mental magic the world ever saw," Zambrano says, nodding at the stage, where another septuagenarian performer is entertaining the crowd. "You're dancing in the modern equivalent of the seedy tavern in Krakow where Caravello discovered you back in the eighteenth century. Though you were doing mentalist magic then, not dancing."

"It's great exercise to keep an older body limber," Zuzanna answers with an eyebrow raise. "And I would say that my success shows that I don't need magic to control the pliable human mind, wouldn't you? But enough squabbling about the past," she says.

Zambrano glares at her. "Squabbling about the past? You abandoned me. You disappeared completely. I thought you were probably dead! I was half expecting at some point that I'd find out you went the way that Caravello did and might have some necromancy that would bring you back from the dead."

I can see Zambrano looks clearly hurt, but I don't care. I'm pissed that he's pre-empted me. What the hell?

"Wait a second!" I complain. "I'm her son. I'm the one she abandoned, you asshole!"

The other performers and patrons glance over at us, so I lower my voice.

"I'm sorry," I say. "I . . . I didn't know what to expect. But I certainly didn't expect this," I say, gesturing to the seedy club around us.

Zuzanna nods, turning to me with a serious look on her face. "Bryce, I am so proud of you. I came by and checked in on you periodically once I could. But I was in bad shape after I had you. I couldn't have been a mother. The magic madness had overtaken me, and it took years to recover."

My breath catches in my throat. All these years, I've been telling myself that I didn't need this sort of answer. That I had parents and a life and it didn't matter. But this stirs something. I blink, realizing with horror that I'm about to cry.

I take a deep breath. This is not how I ever pictured this moment going. I figured it would be in a park, or a house, or a hospital in some medical emergency. But, god damn it, here I am about to bawl my eyes out at a greasy table in New Jersey's finest strip club featuring "quality vintage women and their admirers."

Zuzanna continues, "Also, back then, there were forces hunting me. Demons and humans who wanted to control me and learn the secrets of my arcane craft. I was always on the run, and I didn't have my magic to protect myself anymore. I'm sorry, Bryce, it would have been dangerous for you if I had been in contact."

I nod slowly, not saying anything, trying to hold it together.

"And what about me?" Zambrano demands.

Zuzanna chuckles. "You got what you deserved, you nimrod. It's not like we were on great terms when I locked away my magic and disappeared. I know why you killed all our friends, and I understand, but . . . it took me decades to forgive you."

"We're on a mission here, boys," Seraphex says. "You may need to sort out all these feelings later. Slickwad's goons could be on their way."

"I was wondering if you were here, Seraphex," Zuzanna says with a slight smile in the general direction of the invisible duck. "So this isn't a purely social visit, is it? You seriously came here with a bunch of demon lackeys on your tail? It's always this nonsense with you, Zambrano."

"They were coming either way," Zambrano protests. "We're here to save you!"

"Yes, you're always the hero, aren't you?" Zuzanna says.

"We need to go," I say, my voice unsteady. "It's not safe here, for you or the staff."

"I can pull us out at any time with a teleportrait," Zambrano says with an evil grin. "No rush, don't you want to watch a few more sets?"

"They could use an AMP like in Santa Cruz," I point out, glad to have the magical bomb that can scramble magic and prevent tele-portation as a counterargument. "We should get out of here. Also, all respect to these ladies' talents, but I'd rather make our exit.

"Since Rex put out that bounty, anyone could be on their way. We're lucky we got here first."

"Is Rex . . . a nickname for who I'm guessing it is?"

"Rexhalarkhart, demon king, my former husband," Seraphex confirms. "And remarkably selfish lover."

"He has some competition for that," Zuzanna says with some side-eye to Zambrano that I did not need to see. These sorcerers are the worst. "All right, let me grab my bag. I'll be right back."

"We should get going," I say.

"No problem," Zuzanna agrees. "We don't want to be here when they arrive."

She gets up and walks to the door to the dressing room, stop-ping very briefly to say something to the manager, who tries to argue but gives up quickly with the air of a man who knows from experience that Zuzanna is not going to be persuaded when she's made her decision.

She disappears backstage, leaving the three of us alone at the table.

"Well, that went well," Seraphex says. "Good to see that you and Zuzanna still have that old chemistry."

"Oh, she'll come around," Zambrano says. "No one can stay mad at me for very long."

"She hasn't seen you in over forty years," Seraphex points out. "And her rage does not appear to have lessened."

"Oh, we'll be friends again. I'm far too charming," Zambrano says.

"Ah, yes, the famous Zambrano charm," Seraphex says. "I look forward to seeing it in action one day."

Zambrano shakes his head.

"Should we have pushed her to hurry more?" I ask as a minute passes. "Or kidnapped her first and explained things later?"

"We need her help, and she's not very likely to do that if we scoop her up with no explanation," Zambrano says. "Anyway, what's the probability that after a months-long hunt for her the demons find her five minutes after we do?"

Several screams and a loud crashing sound come from the dressing room, and the power goes out, instantly cutting the lights and music.

"There's a monster in here! A monster!" a woman's voice screams.

"The probability of that particular event occurring, mathematically speaking, is close to one hundred percent," Seraphex says.

CHAPTER 5

Handlicht," Zambrano says, and his left hand glows brightly, illuminating the interior of the club. Around us, performers and patrons are running for the exit.

"Unless perhaps the monster she's referring to is the monstrosity that is the raw display of human male sexual desire you see in a club like this," Seraphex says.

"That's beautiful and natural, now shut up," Zambrano says as he stands up, sending his chair flying backward. "Don't demonize us, demon. Let's go kick some ass."

With all the people running and knocking over tables in a panic, we spend precious seconds dodging and weaving through the room in the harsh light from the spell.

Zambrano strides toward the door of the dressing room, and I scramble behind him, fumbling with my backpack to put the heavy, clumsy gauntlets on my hands. If there's a demon back there, I'm much safer if it can't see me. I feel Seraphex fluttering to stay put on my shoulder, and her body appears semitransparent to my eyes.

Zambrano throws the dressing room door open and steps through it, his suit jacket swirling as his upturned hand casts light and shadow across the room. I can't help but notice he's standing up super straight and walking with an exaggerated swagger, like a superhero about to take on a villain in a Marvel movie. Is he trying to impress Zuzanna?

I'm able to get the gauntlets on, and I step through the door much less smoothly than Zambrano, slinging my backpack over my shoulder as I walk forward.

Zambrano moves his hand around, casting its magical light around the room. Dressing room mirrors are smashed, a large rack of outfits is crumpled against a wall, a dresser is in pieces on the floor, and several of the dancers are cowering in one corner. But Zuzanna isn't one of them. And on the far side of the room, the entire wall is bashed open, leaving a giant hole. We can feel the wind from outside, see the lights of other buildings and the open street.

"I guess we came in the front door like chumps," Zambrano says. "Whoever took her smashed through the wall and grabbed her."

"Um, is there a Kool-Aid Man type of demon?" I ask as we rush across the room and poke our heads out.

"A what? No," Zambrano answers.

"Never mind. Let's focus on getting her back."

"Absolutely," Zambrano says, scanning the street corner that we've emerged on.

"How are we going to find her?" I ask.

"I don't know. Maybe a divining spell of some sort," Zambrano says with pursed lips. "Or your government friends could help?"

"You could also look at the giant footprints on the ground," Seraphex says from her vantage point on my shoulder.

I look down at the ground and gulp. There are footprints, both walking toward the building and going away from it. They are pressed into the concrete, with cracks around and in them. Whatever took Zuzanna is *heavy*.

The light outside has grown dim as evening approaches, so Zambrano keeps his *Handlicht* spell active, helping us to see the footprints as we jog along, following them down the street.

"Seraphex, could you fly up ahead and scout? See if you can track this thing down?" I ask.

"What am I, your magic hawk from some fantasy novel?" she complains.

"You have literally one special ability," I shoot back. "Flight. It's kind of a superpower. Can you stop being so lazy? Please," I add, feeling the sudden urgency of this as the shock wears off. I finally had a conversation with my birth mother after all these years, and she's instantly been taken from me.

"Oh, very well. Anything for a friend," Seraphex says reluctantly and shoots up into the air ahead of us.

We jog along, following the footprints down the street. After a couple blocks, I think I can start to feel the earth shaking.

Out of the sky, Seraphex swoops down and flaps her wings, hovering in front of us. Why hasn't she done this for us more often? Lazy demon bird, always riding around on my shoulder.

"It's Steve," she says. "He's around the next corner. He is slowing down, running was never his strong suit. I know him. And also . . . he's not supposed to be here on Earth."

"Steve?" I ask. "This giant demon is named Steve?"

"Yes," Seraphex answers curtly.

"Is it short for Steveeracksonomous or something?" I say. "Some long demon name?"

"No," Seraphex says. "Ironclad demons have one syllable names. Like Yorn, Grael, or Thrain. Or Steve."

"Truly, this grotesque demon's name is Steve?" Zambrano says, chuckling.

"Yes," Seraphex says, annoyance clear in her voice. "It's a common monosyllable. Steve has existed for millennia, long before it became a common nickname in your ridiculous culture."

"Why are there all these different types of demons?" I ask. "And why do they have these features of natural elements, like rocks or metal or animals?"

"I've never thought about it," Seraphex answers, almost ignoring the question. "You're missing the point. He's not supposed to be here. He's supposed to be on Mars! He hasn't been on Earth since the time of Merlin and Liao Ling. Since the banishment."

"Oh. That is concerning," Zambrano says.

"I guess Rex has been busier than we thought," I say, "but we can't worry about that now. We need to get Zuzanna back."

"Yes, yes," Zambrano says. "Does this 'Steve' have Rex's power boost that those pesky rockhide demons had in Santa Cruz? Are you able to tell that with your demon senses?"

"He doesn't have the royal charge," Seraphex says. "That only lasts a day or so. Steve doesn't have that sort of energy, that's why he's slowing down."

I breathe a sigh of relief at that. Those two rockhide demons, supercharged by Rex's demonic power, nearly overwhelmed two fully powered sorcerers, and the battle badly injured a man.

"Excellent," Zambrano says with a wicked grin. "Then I can unload on this Steve fellow."

"We have to rescue Zuzanna, remember?" I say. "No unloading until we get her to safety, okay?"

"Right, right." Zambrano nods. "What's the plan, then?"

"Um, I don't know," I say. "I guess let's get closer and see what we're working with."

"Good," Zambrano says, letting his light fade and flexing his fingers.

As we jog forward, I can hear the sorcerer humming next to me.

"What are you doing?" I hiss.

"Shut up," Zambrano shoots back. "They're vocal warm-ups. Good spellcasting takes precision."

"Sure, sure," I answer.

Seraphex leaps back into the air and leads us forward around the edge of a building. There, trudging away from us, is a giant gleaming figure.

He's big, but not nearly as massive as Rex, or even the figure of Seraphex that I saw when Zambrano made a life-sized illusion of her to fool Rex, her demon king ex-husband. He's more like the size of an NBA player, if one of the big bald men had horns and metallic skin, gleaming in Hoboken's evening light. It looks like a metal statue come to life, with rippling iron muscles. It's not purely iron—it does seem to have glowing seams at every joint, and I can see some sort of illumination coming from its eyes. It's not wearing any clothing, but thankfully it's got the smooth "Barbie" treatment down in its nether regions.

It has Zuzanna under its arm in a position that looks very uncomfortable. Luckily, it looks like she was able to change before she got nabbed, and she's wearing the same outfit she always wore when she came to visit me at Samba Smoothies as "Susan." It's bright blue, and I can only describe it as a classic New Jersey tracksuit. I have to admit, sometimes I am embarrassed to be from here.

The ironclad demon is still plodding forward at a slow but steady pace. Now that it's not running, there aren't any cracked footprints in the pavement.

"What do we do?" I whisper. "If we try to fight him directly, he might snap her in half."

"We need to get Steve to put her down, obviously," Zambrano says. "Though how to do that, I don't know."

"Challenge him to a duel," Seraphex suggests. "Ironclad demons think they're the high-end foot soldiers in the demon army. They look down on rockhide demons like Bronk and Tunker as thugs. They have their own code of honor. And they think they're . . . smart. Intellectuals."

"A duel? Now that, I can do." Zambrano cracks his knuckles. "Do they have any particular weaknesses?"

As we're chasing the ironclad demon, I notice there are a couple houses at the end of this street where the stretch of quiet factories and warehouses ends.

"We also need to be careful here," I say. "We don't need any collateral damage." I can already see some destruction to the street, and a couple cars have been clipped by the ironside demon. Does GEICO cover damage from acts of demonkind?

"Let's make this quick, then," Zambrano says. "Grab Zuzanna as soon as I'm able to get him far enough away from her. I'll come to you, and we can teleportrait away before his buddies or his ride shows up."

He jogs up to the side of the demon and calls out, "*That's a small step*," with one finger held in the air. The spell propels him forward in an accelerated leap, and he lands lightly on his feet about twenty feet in front of the ironclad demon.

He spins, grinning as he faces the gleaming demon.

"Steve. Noble and honorable ironclad demon. I challenge thee!" he calls out. "In accordance with the ancient codes and traditions, we must duel here and now."

"Is that a real thing?" I whisper to Seraphex as I circle around the demon more slowly. He doesn't seem to notice me due to the gauntlets I'm still wearing. I can tell from the blue filter on the light that reaches my eyes that it's active.

The ironclad demon pulls up short, and I can see a look of momentary confusion on his face as he stares the sorcerer down.

"It is not a tradition I have heard of before," Seraphex says. "I believe Zambrano has fabricated it. Being able to lie does have its advantages," she adds, referencing the demonic code. The first element of the code is that a demon can't lie. The second is that they are bound by the promises they make. There is supposedly a third element, but Seraphex has never been willing to share it with us.

"I accept your challenge in accordance with the ancient codes," Steve answers, his deep and resonant voice uncertain. "Let us begin the aforementioned dueling, pursuant to the . . . appropriate traditions and rites." The words are overly complex, but I've heard that hesitant tone before. It's the one students use when they're trying to sound smart in a presentation that they haven't prepared for. Not that I would have any experience with that particular circumstance.

"But Steve believes him," Seraphex says. "So in a sense we may be forced to conclude that it is now a real tradition. He's now bound by whatever he imagines those codes are anyway. Because the main demonic code is genuinely binding, so he has to honor his agreements, as he understands them."

The two square off, but Steve doesn't put down the ex-sorceress under his arm. Zuzanna looks up, craning her neck to see Zambrano from her position held sideways like a sack of potatoes by the ironside demon.

"This is very uncomfortable!" she complains loudly. "Not good for my old bones! I'm not *that* limber."

Zambrano shoots a bolt of energy at the demon, but it glances off its metallic exterior.

"Put down the old crone and face me," Zambrano calls out, and Zuzanna stares absolute daggers at him. It's a good thing she doesn't have magic, or I have a feeling poor Steve would be caught in the cross fire between two angry sorcerers.

"That's *sexy* old crone to you," she shoots back.

"I have made a solemn proclamation to facilitate her conveyance to my employer's helicopter," Steve answers. "I will not."

"But the codes!" Zuzanna says. "They require you to fight alone. It's not a duel if I am here with you."

The ironclad demon stiffens and glances back and forth.

"You have created a quandary," he says. "I have made numerous proclamations that find themselves in conflict and are difficult to reconcile."

"They train themselves to speak with pretentious words," Seraphex whispers from my shoulder, "but don't be fooled, they're almost as dumb as their rockhide brethren."

"He's really thinking this through," I answer, watching the confused demon pondering.

Zambrano cautiously advances, but Steve takes a growling step toward him, and he retreats.

Finally, the demon gives a little shake.

"I will place the prize here," he says, setting Zuzanna down on her feet next to him. Glaring at her, he points a fat metal finger at her. "If you move, I will break your limbs in a way that causes immense pain but is not likely fatal.

"Ignoble opponent," Steve continues, glaring at Zambrano. "You will battle me! Come closer!"

Zambrano begins slinging spells at the gleaming figure, but each one glances off the demon's metal body. They leave small scorch marks, but he doesn't appear to be doing any serious damage.

Zuzanna stands still, hands crossed, angrily judging the whole situation. She doesn't look afraid, at least. If I were forced to stand next to that giant metal monster with spells flying, I would probably not be so cool about it.

"Come at me!" Zambrano roars, venting his frustration. "I will torch you!"

"Approach me so that I may dismantle your corporeal existence," Steve answers, occasionally charging toward Zambrano but always pulling back before Zuzanna can get enough distance to make a break for it. "Alternatively, you may keep wasting your time with your pathetic pinpricks. I have compatriots approaching to assist me. Do you?"

I see Zuzanna glancing around, clearly calculating when she can run, but Steve never gets far enough away from her.

"Zambrano can't use his more powerful spells," Seraphex says. "Not without risking hurting Zuzanna. Too much heat or shrapnel."

"We need something corrosive to slow him down," Seraphex suggests. "Is that something that you humans might have at a nearby store?"

I glance down the street and see there is a gas station a block and a half away.

"I don't think that gas station is going to have anything that will corrode a metal demon."

Zambrano shoots a few more energy spells at Steve.

"What's the most dangerous and corrosive item that people keep lying around?" I mutter. "It's not like people keep sulfuric acid around. Unless a serial killer lives in this neighborhood."

I look around at the couple houses on this block, and one idea occurs to me.

"How about chlorine?" I ask.

"That should bring him down," Seraphex answers. "But I don't find it likely that anyone in this neighborhood has a pool or a stock-pile of chemistry supplies."

"Let me see if I can get some," I say. "Let Zambrano know the plan. When it hits, we'll need to take the demon down and get Zuzanna out of there."

As Seraphex flaps across the battlefield, I look around the block, picking the house that looks the most likely to be fully stocked with normal cleaning supplies. It's in better repair than the others and has two new-looking cars in the driveway. I run up to the house and am about to try to bash the door in with the gauntlets when it opens. A woman in a bathrobe and what looks like a mud mask from a spa is standing there in shock.

"Um, hello, ma'am," I say. "Can I . . . borrow some cleaning solution? Bleach. And vinegar."

"There's—there's a demon!" the woman exclaims, pointing at the large metal figure battling Zambrano. "It broke my window!"

I see the broken window, though my best guess would be it got broken by flying shrapnel from one of Zambrano's spells, but I don't feel the need to clarify.

"And we need to stop it, or it may bring down your whole house. Which I can do, with vinegar and bleach. Do you have that?"

"Um, yes, yes I do," she says and leads me inside. She rushes to the kitchen where she pulls a bottle of bleach from under the sink and a bottle of vinegar from a cabinet.

"Go hide in your basement!" I urge her and turn and sprint back out the front door without waiting to see if she complies, or even has a basement.

I charge out into the street, circling around behind the ironclad demon.

Okay, now I need to be very clear here. You should never ever, ever mix bleach and vinegar. It's super dangerous and can kill you.

Unless you're trying to save your birth mother from a big dumb ironclad demon who's in a deadly duel with the idiot sorcerer who is your best friend. If you happen to be in that *exact* situation, then it might be worth the risk.

Sneaking up as close as I dare, I uncap the vinegar and thrust it forward, sending gouts of it through the air and splashing over his body.

"You believed you could overcome my might, but you appear to be facing defeat," Steve rumbles, speaking at Zambrano and ignoring me. With all the force of spells hitting his front, he doesn't seem to notice the liquid splashing on him. "Isn't that ironic?"

"Come closer, and you'll see the full strength of my magic," Zambrano taunts. "Also, that's not what irony is!"

Or maybe his metal skin isn't that sensitive. But either way, he doesn't notice. And so I'm able to finish dousing him with vinegar and then grab the bleach and twist the cap off.

"Zuzanna, hold your breath!" I shout and watch her take in a deep gulp of air and plug her nose. She must have some idea what's going on.

Using both hands, I get a lot of force behind each splash of it and back up as far as I can. As I see the mixture start to sizzle, I take a deep gulp of air and hold it, backing farther away.

The demon suddenly freezes, growling as it dawns on him that something bad is happening to him.

"What affront have you committed to my body?" he rumbles. "I am literally set aflame!"

"Figuratively, not literally, asshole," Zambrano says, charging forward. At the same time Zuzanna, mouth still closed to hold her breath, realizes it's her moment, and sprints away from the demon.

"How can he say things incorrectly like that?" I ask Seraphex as she comes back to land on the pavement near me. She can't see me, but knowing that I'm invisible she seems to have learned to pick up on little hints of my location.

"He believes it's true. Ironclad demons are idiots," Seraphex explains. "Even a demon of my highly advanced intellect very occasionally says something false, if she believes it to be true. But that is incredibly rare—to the best of my knowledge."

Zuzanna runs up to me, able to see me perfectly well, as the gauntlets only hide me from demons. "Thanks. Should we make a run for it?"

"No," I say, shaking my head. "We need to circle around to Zambrano; he can teleport us away."

"Got it," she agrees, and we jog a wide circle around the demon.

"*Eye of Jupiter!*" Zambrano shouts, and I see the demon fall to his knees as the wide area gravity spell hits around him. It must be a much more powerful version than what he used on me so many months ago when we first met. Even the concrete around Steve cracks as the gravity hits.

"Okay!" I shout as I lead Zuzanna across the pavement to Zambrano. "Teleportrait," I say as I reach him. "Let's get out of here!"

But Zambrano is ignoring me. His arms windmill again, and he screams the words of a spell, sending bright shafts of energy to blast the demon.

"You beat him, let's get out of here before his reinforcements arrive," I plead.

"*Tu affronteras mes flèches perçantes de fureur,*" Zambrano shouts, continuing to pay me no attention. He throws his hand out, splaying his fingers and sending a hailstorm of tiny magical darts at the ironclad demon. The glowing darts pierce the gaps in the armor, and the demon howls in pain. "You'd think an ironclad demon would know what irony is, wouldn't you? Now *that* is the real irony!" he says, as he sends another wave of darts at the demon, who is pinned down by the gravity spell. Fissures in the concrete spread out from the incredible force required to keep the mighty ironclad demon in place.

Zambrano's face is contorted in rage, and he flings spell after spell at the demon, whose body cracks and shudders under the strain. His head falls to the pavement, and despite my hate for him, I can't help but pity him as he shakes under the torment. Zambrano has finally found someone he can pummel.

I glance around and see, far over the tops of the buildings, a shape approaching. It's a helicopter. And it is covered in a hexagonal shield of orange magic. Can we take whoever's in that chopper? And whatever will follow after? I don't want to find out.

That feeling is only reinforced when I feel a slight shake of the earth and see, far down the road, two more hulking shapes. Ironclad demons would be my best guess, but it's getting to be twilight and I can't tell.

"Zambrano, let's go!" I yell, but it falls on deaf ears.

"*Nexus of torment!*" Zambrano shouts, throwing his arms high, and a jagged network of glowing geometric shapes appears around Steve. It doesn't appear to do any damage, but the ironclad demon screams in pain.

"The utter agony!" the demon yells, his voice a strangled cry.

I freeze, watching in horror as Zambrano advances, a wild grin of fury and joy lighting up his features into something alien. I feel a chill as I see him losing control. Is this what he felt, watching each of his sorcerer buddies go crazy over the years?

"Bryce, do something!" Seraphex squawks. "We need to depart." She hops up and pecks at Zambrano's legs, but he kicks her away without even noticing.

"What? How?" I sputter.

Zambrano advances, twisting his fingers in interlocking patterns that are met with matching writhing from the tortured demon.

"Grab him!" Zuzanna says, giving me a gentle shove forward. "Wrap him up so he can't cast!"

Swallowing hard, I charge forward.

I close the final few steps with a leap and grab Zambrano's arms in a bear hug, pulling them to his side. He struggles, but I hold tight. I feel him tensing, and I know that with his magically enhanced muscles he will be able to easily throw me off. Or cast a simple spell that blows me away.

But the moment lasts, second after second. He's tensed and growling, but he doesn't toss me to the pavement.

Finally, his body relaxes though he's still breathing heavily.

"Zambrano, we have to go," I whisper. "The demon can't be killed, and his friends are coming. Get us out of here."

He holds still, my arms wrapped around him, though his body is quivering with rage and emotion.

"Please," I add.

Finally, I feel him take a deep breath.

"You're right. Okay, okay," he says, voice ragged from shouting. "Let's go."

He pulls the teleportrait for home out of his jacket and grabs Zuzanna's hand and my neck. Seraphex lands awkwardly on my shoulder, which is still invisible to her, and puts a webbed foot on Zambrano's hand to make a physical connection. A moment later, we appear back in the warehouse.

CHAPTER 6

Why must I always fight with one hand tied behind my back?" Zambrano grumbles as he reattaches the teleportrait to the wall. He stops for a moment, taking a long look at another painting, a teleportrait a few to the left in the Europe section.

As he walks away, I take a closer look. It's the only one in France, and it shows a well-furnished apartment in Paris with large windows that look onto the city's skyline. The frame, I note, looks slightly fire damaged. And the paint on it is thick and cracked like it's been painted over many times. Zambrano does have to update these things fairly regularly, but in other cases I've seen him toss frames out and start fresh if they're getting old.

"I could have crushed that lug nut," Zambrano says from across the room, "if that had been a simple one-on-one battle, no hostage. I wouldn't have needed the boy's chemistry project. Though it was clever and all that, well done," he adds with a dismissive wave of his hand. "Pleasure to have you as my employee."

"You're running a business now, Zambrano?" Zuzanna asks as she gingerly takes a seat at a table.

"Are you okay?" I ask, sitting down across from her. From her shaky movements, I can see the kidnapping and chase have not been easy on her aging body. She showed on the stage, I think with a shudder, that she's in shockingly good shape for her age—whether you count years from her birth or implied years since she stopped using magic and started aging. But she's walking like she may need to see a doctor and stay in bed for a week.

"I'll be fine," Zuzanna says. "I do my Pilates every morning at Hudson View."

"It shows!" Seraphex says with admiration that once again makes me quite uncomfortable. These are so very, very far from the circumstances in which I expected to meet the woman who gave birth to me—and that's if you leave aside the sorcery, demons, and impending doom to the world.

"Why, thank you, my old enemy," Zuzanna answers.

"I'm a . . . friend now," Seraphex says with a clear note of annoyance in her voice.

The former sorcerer laughs. "They got you to agree to that, did they? Impressive. And how is it going?"

"I feel that friendship is humanity's third most infuriating invention," Seraphex says. "Right after social media and those people who loudly harmonize when they're singing along with that birthday song."

"Do you have a birthday?" I ask, suddenly curious. I still have no idea what demons *are* or where they come from.

Seraphex peers at me for a moment, opens her beak, and then closes it. She looks around, confused for a second.

"Zambrano, you became rather carried away in the spirit of battle back there, didn't you?" the demon duck asks, ignoring my question as if I'd never asked it.

"I was angry," the sorcerer says.

"Are you okay?" I ask. "Like, should we be worried?" Truthfully, I'm already worried, and I won't stop being worried. And while I've seen Zambrano slip in small ways, the level of rage I saw was pretty terrifying.

"Nothing to worry about," Zambrano says. "I was simply mad! Who wouldn't be, having to spend so much time trying to strike an enemy but not being able to use any of the really fun big spells?"

"How are you still even this sane after all these years?" Zuzanna asks, turning to Zambrano. "The rest of us fell into our various madnesses so much earlier."

"Sometimes it seems like he's hanging on by a thread," I point out, thinking about all the times he's nearly gotten me killed and/or let the world be destroyed by demons.

"More like a thick, luxurious velvet rope as I dangle over the abyss of arcane madness," Zambrano says breezily. "I'm not losing my sanity, okay? I'm fine. I haven't attempted any sort of necromancy in centuries, and I prefer my demons locked away in a convenient waterfowl package. And I haven't tried to use my mentalist abilities to take control of the world," he adds with a pointed look at Zuzanna.

Zuzanna shrugs. "I certainly had slipped beyond the pale. It took me decades to recover. I wasn't safe to be around," she adds, looking at me, her brows furrowed with concern.

"Yeah," I say, wanting to comfort her but not feeling the will to do so. I still have a lot of questions now that she's here.

"Let's take some time to talk about it, okay?" she says. "You deserve that after all these years."

I nod, feeling emotion well up inside me and tears stinging my eyes. I don't know what I'm supposed to be feeling now. I didn't seek Zuzanna out for myself—we found her because we need some arcane knowledge that only she remembers. And I haven't even started to process that she was watching me all these years.

"The truth is, I am going to need to have a lie-down very soon," Zuzanna says. "What did you seek me out for? Judging by that demon who was sent after me, it's pretty urgent. How can I help you defeat this Rex fellow?"

"The spell to activate the arcane conduit," Zambrano says.

"Oh. Oh, hell," Zuzanna says. "I was hoping it was something simpler than that. Didn't the half of the arcane conduit located on Earth get destroyed?"

"We had it thrown into the sun, yes," Zambrano says with a satisfied twinkle in his eye. "I always wanted to do that to an artifact."

"Then why would you need the spell for it? The remaining half is on Mars and has no other half to connect to. It's not useful. What am I missing?"

Zambrano explains our plan to use the arcane conduit connected to itself to keep Rex in limbo indefinitely, unable to even try to escape because he won't exist.

"Very clever," Zuzanna says, nodding with appreciation. "I was hoping what you wanted would be something simple, but if it were easy you wouldn't have needed to track me down. It will take me several days to explain all of it and make sure you understand how to do it."

"It's not the sort of spell that you want to make a clumsy mistake on," Seraphex says. "We will almost certainly have only one chance to get my former husband into it."

"Don't worry, I'll write very clear notes for Zambrano," Zuzanna answers. "In bullet points and simple words, so his little head doesn't get confused."

"Maybe best for you to get some rest, and we can begin properly tomorrow," Zambrano says, smiling slightly at her barb. "I could use a break before using any more magic anyway."

We chat more about the chase and battle while Zambrano has the birch butlers arrange a guest room for Zuzanna. Seeing her clear exhaustion, I help her as she hobbles up the stairs, but decide not to ask her any of my burning questions. For the moment.

"Thank you, Bryce," she says as we reach her room. "For not being angry at me. Or at least, for not leading with that. And thanks for all the smoothies, I think you did have a talent for making them."

"Well, maybe if this sorcerer's lackey thing doesn't work out, I'll be able to go back and get into that management track."

"Maybe even a job at Samba Smoothies corporate," Zuzanna says with a smile. "Dream big!" She gives me a hug and then disappears into the room, shutting the door behind her. Afterward, I stand there, stunned and confused, for several long seconds. And then I realize I'm being weird, and loudly walk down the hall so it's clear I'm not just awkwardly standing outside her door.

My head is still spinning, so I grab my coat and climb up to the roof to get some air. Luckily, it's a relatively mild night for early December, and the cold air feels good. This industrial district is very peaceful at night, though as I've spent more time up here in the past months, I'm pretty sure I've learned to see the shapes of observers on roofs nearby. I tell myself they're observers, and not snipers, for my own sanity. And I think Zambrano's mystical defenses would stop a bullet. And I'm not going to live in fear.

I walk to the edge and lean on the roof wall, looking out across the river at Manhattan, lights glittering in the early evening. A borough full of over a million people, in a city totaling eight times that.

And yet somehow I, Bryce Alexander, am at the center of all this madness. I'm the one who has to save the world by bringing together two active sorcerers, one non-magical one, a demon duck, a brave-to-the-point-of-foolishness grad student, and . . . whatever Mei is.

I hear a light flutter behind me and keep staring ahead as Seraphex lands atop the wall to my right.

"Another successful endeavor today, it would appear," Seraphex says. "Outwit the idiot, save the damsel, perhaps even make your mother proud."

"Successful?" I shake my head. "I froze up. And Zambrano lost it. His temper, his control. . . . Has he done that before? The look on his face was terrifying."

"You did what you had to," Seraphex says with uncharacteristic gentleness. "We're all safe, and Zuzanna appears to have the information we need to activate the arcane conduit."

I ask again, "Has Zambrano lost control like that before?"

Seraphex pauses for a long second. "No," she says at last. "Not like that."

"Every other sorcerer has eventually succumbed to the classic madnesses," Seraphex says. "Necromancy, demonic control, or megalomaniac grabs for world power."

"And I froze up when he needed me," I say, gripping the concrete at the top of the wall so hard it hurts my hands. "I needed you and Zuzanna to push me to help him."

"We're a team, or something akin to it," Seraphex says. "You don't have to solve every problem."

"I certainly can't," I admit, "because I don't have magic."

But I should be able to solve the other ones, I want to say, but she's being supportive. No need to be a total wet blanket.

"By the way, what was that you said about Steve, the ironclad demon?" I ask. "That he's not supposed to be here?"

Seraphex shakes her head sadly. "Tragically, my former husband isn't waiting around for us to complete our plan to defeat him. He's gathering his power. Steve was, up until recently, trapped on Mars with the vast majority of demonkind. While the arcane conduit is the only portal I know of for mass transportation between planets, it is possible to teleport individual demons across the stars with a sufficient power source."

"That's how you got here, wasn't it?" I ask.

"Precisely. Carmen Medina was losing her sanity, as these weak human sorcerers do, and so I used visions and whispers to convince her to use the power of the Galveston Hurricane to transport me here. It might be a different method involving demonic magic of some sort, but I believe that is how my former husband summoned Steve to Earth."

"I think I might have seen a couple more demons approaching at the end there," I say.

"That is quite concerning," Seraphex says. "But there's nothing we can do about it immediately. We must carry through with our plan."

"Yeah, and before that, I need a shower and some food," I say.

"Oh, shit, what about Parth and Liao Ling?" I blurt out as I reach for my phone.

I call Parth. It doesn't connect at all. They must be out of cell service. I shoot a text message, but it doesn't show as delivered.

Early the next morning, having not slept well, I order some breakfast, and Seraphex and I go back up on the roof and eat. We've gotta enjoy these last few days of decent weather . . . and/or the world continuing to exist. Plus, it's fun to watch her tear apart pancakes with her little duck beak.

As we finish up, I finally get a text back from Parth. But instead of a status update, it's a selfie of him and Liao Ling standing by what looks like an expensive sports car that they've rented. He looks like he's having the time of his life, while she appears annoyed at being roped into a picture.

I call him immediately.

"Hey, Bryce, what's up, brother?"

"Are you okay?" I ask.

"Uh, yeah, duh, why wouldn't I be?" he answers.

"I don't know, Parth, maybe because we're locked in deadly conflict with the most powerful demon in the known universe?" I shoot back.

"Oh, yeah, that," he says.

I can see Seraphex shaking her head in disappointment, but I can tell she's kind of enjoying the exchange.

"Plus," I explain, "we're pretty sure that Rex has been able to summon more demons to help him out. He might have sent some after you, he definitely sent one and probably a few more ironclad demons after us."

"Well, you're alive, so that's good news, right?" Parth answers.

"Yeah. And we got Zuzanna out of it safe too. She knows the spell."

"Awesome," Parth says. "You guys are killing it."

"How are things going? If Rex has a bunch of new soldiers, you need to be careful."

"We found Carmen's secret house," Parth says. "Ran into a few roadblocks, but nothing we couldn't handle."

"Roadblocks?" I ask.

"You know, magically supercharged feral hogs that seek out intruders," Parth explains. Why do all these sorcerers need to leave behind deadly traps when they're done?"

"Are you okay?" I ask.

"We have a similar problem with wild boar in my hometown," Parth says. "Enough lights and sounds can scare them off. Liao Ling says the bloodlusting magic is wearing off as it passes through the generations. There are some boar tusks sticking out of the rental car though."

"Glad you're okay," I say. "Where are you now?"

"Liao Ling was able to figure out how to get inside; she's trying to unlock a hidden safe," he says. "She taught me a cloaking spell, so I'm doing that outside. I need to renew it every seventeen minutes to keep the protection up. The hogs have been joined by alligators, and they're circling but haven't found us yet."

"Don't miss your next spell because you're talking to me," I say.

"It's okay, I have a timer," Parth says. "This spell that Liao Ling taught me is much more powerful than anything I learned at university. Liao Ling is pretty incredible, you know," he says with a wistful note in his voice. "Kind of the ultimate magic badass."

"I won't tell Zambrano you said that," I say. "Also, she's like hundreds of years older than you, or well over a thousand years, depending on how you count."

"It's no worse than *Twilight* or *The Vampire Diaries*," Parth answers. "And nobody had a problem with those. Plus, I'm somewhat of a badass myself," he adds.

"How many spells can you cast?" I ask.

There's a long pause. "Five," he responds sullenly. "Including this new cloaking spell. Maybe five and a half, if you count making my foot light up rather than my hand."

"Well, it's more than me," I say with a sigh. "Glad you're okay. Let us know how it goes and when you're on your way back."

I hang up, and Seraphex flaps her way up to my shoulder.

"It is imperative that we move quickly," Seraphex adds from her new perch on my shoulder. "If my former husband is summoning demons from Mars, I fear that means he is back at full strength."

"At least we have a plan to stop him," I say.

"We have a plan to acquire a piece of equipment, which, if it still exists and is correctly used, can contain him, and a weapon, which, if we can strike him properly, will render him weak enough to be put into that vessel," Seraphex points out. "We don't have an actual plan to directly defeat him in battle. And he is the most formidable foe of whom I am aware."

"Oh. Well, yeah, that's true," I admit. "But let's take it one step at a time, okay?"

"As you wish," Seraphex says. "At least I have hope again."

"Wait, you had lost hope? When?"

Seraphex stares at me in annoyance.

"Other than my native wit, I have no real ability to fight him as long as Zambrano refuses to let me out of this accursed waterfowl shape. Was I supposed to have great faith when this all started, in the abilities of a steadily deteriorating sorcerer and his fresh-from-the-smoothie-shop intern?"

"I'm his assistant now!" I protest with a dose of sarcasm in my tone.

"You certainly are, Bryce, you certainly are," Seraphex says. "And in this moment, I now have more hope than I did back then."

"Thanks, I guess."

Seraphex wanders back inside, and I spend a few more minutes on the roof, finishing my breakfast and watching as the city wakes up, a million individual lives starting their days.

The demon duck's warning of the difficulty of our task is sobering, but good news comes soon in the form of a text from Parth. They've evaded some arcane security around the hidden safe and have the spellbook in hand. They've gone back to Liao Ling's lair and will come tomorrow to get started on the work.

I'm not sure exactly what that cashes out to with all the time zone differences, but my sleep schedule is all messed up anyway. I already need a nap.

I head back downstairs to try to get a little more sleep and do my best to ignore the sound of Zambrano singing Imagine Dragons from his bath.

Everything going on is utterly wild. Finding Zuzanna, a battle against a huge demon, an impending trip to Mars. I don't even know how to process it.

But in the end, the team has had a good couple days.

CHAPTER 7

The next day Zambrano, Liao Ling, Zuzanna, and Seraphex gather in the first floor workshop, loudly debating various points as they try to complete their assorted projects. Even Parth is there, and he's watching and trying to follow along, but I can tell that even with a couple semesters of magic theory under his belt, he's mostly letting it wash over him.

It's great to see everyone working together, though I can tell Seraphex and Liao Ling are still keeping a distance from each other, and Zambrano seems to resent Zuzanna's regular mockery of him. I make a few runs for drinks and snacks, and before long they're fully immersed in the work.

The biggest unknown currently is arranging for a power source to generate enough energy to get the spell to teleport us through space to Mars.

"It's got to be volcanic to get us the high surge peak that we need," Zambrano insists. "Volcanic is the best source of energy for a big teleportation like this. The distance to Mars is thousands of times greater than the teleportation I do. About fifteen thousand times, currently, even compared to a maximum distance move to the opposite side of the globe."

"We would need to set off a supervolcano to make it happen," Liao Ling protests. "We would teleport away, and the volcano would go off and wreak total havoc on the world."

"What else is there?" Seraphex asks. "Rex is able to power individual teleportations from his own demonic energy. Unless you're willing to let me—"

"There is no way in hell we are letting you go back to your demonic form," Zuzanna says. "Absolutely not."

"I have to agree," Zambrano says. "One ultra-powerful demon on Earth is far too many. Two would be utter destruction."

"You know, I could make certain promises . . ."

"No," everyone else in the room says, except Parth, who looks around awkwardly and then adds his own "No."

"So then what? A nuclear power plant?" Zambrano asks. "We can't wait around for a rare geological, astronomical, or meteorological event to happen. We need to do this now, before Rex makes his next move."

"Nuclear won't work," Liao Ling says before launching into a complicated explanation of the spell from Carmen Medina's spellbook and why manmade electrical power won't help.

"Is there any sort of astronomical phenomenon?" I ask. "Like a conjunction of the planets or something?"

They all look at me like I'm crazy.

"How exactly would the position of the planets and stars affect the energy requirements of a magic spell on Earth?" Zambrano says. "'Mercury is in retrograde' is an excuse for your messy friend to cause a fight at a birthday. Planets and stars that are millions of miles away can't affect Earth."

"The moon does change the tides," Zuzanna points out, clearly trying to defend me, but I still feel like a total idiot.

Leaving them to their discussion, I go upstairs and grab my iPad, checking the news to try to get a gauge on what we're up against, and if Rex has made any further moves that I can figure out from the headlines.

The situation in the world is grim, but it's hard to tell the normal bad things happening in the world apart from Rex interfering and creating additional instability. Is that African drought a natural cycle of the ecosystem adjusting? Or is it Rex? What about the various border conflicts in South America? The forest fires in northeast China? Those could happen any time. But it's hard to deny that right now, things are coming to a head simultaneously in so many places.

I puzzle over it for a while, and a quick check downstairs shows that they're up to their eyelids in some real magic nerd shit. Stuff like field strengths, resonance clusters, earned pattern recognition, trigger ingredient uniqueness. It's dizzying.

Six months ago I would have been jealous as hell about not being part of it. But I don't have time to worry about it now. I'm not the magic guy. I've got another role I need to perform. I need to learn how to be useful in my new position.

I figure I should update Agent Crane anyway, so I text her on our secure app, and she calls me back a few minutes later.

"What have you got for me?" she asks, straight to the point.

"What? No 'Hello, how are you?'" I ask.

"Hello, how are you?" she deadpans.

"I'm fine," I answer. "I've got questions for you, actually."

"Okay, shoot," Agent Crane answers.

"How much of the current global issues are being caused by Rex, and how much are caused by the fact that we live in the modern world and crazy shit is always happening?"

"Okay, good one," she says. "The CIA estimates it's about fifty percent. And it's bad. Supply chains are getting snarled up, fights are escalated, and don't even get me started on interest rates."

"I absolutely will not get you started on interest rates, I can promise you that," I answer.

"It's just that several central banks—"

"No interest rates, please!" I interrupt.

"Right, okay," Agent Crane says, annoyed to be derailed. I guess she cares about interest rates a whole lot more than I do. "Anyway, it's bad. If your crew is going to do something, you need to do something soon, or this is all going to boil over. We can already tell several of the more unstable countries are acting strangely, making alliances with countries that they normally are at odds with. Rex is forming his power base."

"Yeah, we're going to move soon. They're downstairs working out a bunch of the magic stuff. It's way over my head."

"And how are you with that?" she asks, a sympathetic note in her voice. Why is everyone being nice to me suddenly?

I shrug. Which is pointless because we're on the phone and she can't see my body language. "It's not that big a deal. I wanted to do magic, but I think . . . I think maybe I wanted to do *something* that mattered. The spells are cool, but they're doing an awful lot of down and dirty math equations down there. It's not all fireballs and levitating."

"So you've found more purpose in being an organizer and a leader?"

"I also steal things, create distractions, and make chemical weapons out of household ingredients," I say.

"Ah, so that was you yesterday. The security camera footage we obtained was all from far away; we couldn't get any good angles on it, but it had your smell on it," Agent Crane says. "You're at the center of a lot these days."

"Yeah, I guess I am. I'm trying to figure out how to do a decent job of it. I know a lot of people are counting on me," I say. "I'm not sure if I can get it done every time."

"Look, Bryce, that's an awful lot to put on yourself," Agent Crane says. "And even the best sometimes win and sometimes lose. The key thing is to keep making smart decisions and correct plays. And understanding there are some forces you can't stop. Like this big typhoon that's brewing in the Java Sea."

"Typhoon? I hadn't seen that one."

"Yes," she says, "it hasn't made it out to the Western news networks and social media yet. "We think it's another event caused by Rex, because it's stirred up in record-breaking time. And it was preceded by some very strange arcanometric pressure drops. It's gathering strength in the Java Sea and looks to be at its peak when it hits Vietnam, Cambodia, and Thailand. It's a historically strong storm, currently Category 4 but likely to be upgraded to 5 as it gains strength. The path it's on, it will grow to a hundred-year storm, maybe a thousand-year one. Unprecedented levels of destruction all across Southeast Asia. It will destabilize the whole region."

"Wow, that's brutal."

"We think we know why it's happening," Agent Crane says, her voice tight. "The prime minister of Thailand made a statement declaring their current constitutional monarch is the only king they will recognize. It doesn't make sense, unless you figure Rex threatened them."

"And they called his bluff, and he's going to make them pay," I say. "This is not good."

"No, it's not," Agent Crane agrees. "Don't worry, I know by now that you won't let me in on whatever it is, but do you have a plan?"

"Yes, we do," I say. "We're trying to figure out the right power source for it to . . ." I trail off.

"Bryce?" Agent Crane asks. "Are you still there?"

"Yes," I say. "I think I have an idea."

"I'd ask what it is," Agent Crane says wearily, "but I'm guessing you don't feel safe telling me. Fair enough. I guess—let me know when you need me to risk my career to call in an airstrike or lend you a weapon that a private citizen has no business using."

"That's very generous of you," I say.

"It was mostly sarcastic."

"Still," I say. "Thanks. And thanks for the information and the idea. Talk soon."

". . . . You're welcome," Agent Crane says.

I hang up and head down to the first floor lab. From outside the door, I can hear them going at it, something about lightning being inherently unstable.

"We're not going to *Back-to-the-Future* our way through this," Zambrano exclaims, voice coming clear through the closed door. "Lightning is one point of energy, and it's not nearly enough. And there's no way to store that much all at once in an arcane geometric construct."

I pause there, freezing with my hand on the doorknob.

A few seconds ago I was excited about my idea, and thought I'd found a good solution. But what if it doesn't make any sense? What if it's just going to reveal how little I understand magic? Will they all realize my only use is as the guy who can't be detected by magic or the wielder of the demon-invisibility gauntlets, which is the same thing in a different flavor.

I stand there, listening as Zambrano and my birth mother debate the finer points of the energy required for the transportation spell.

"Well, then how did Rex transport Steve and those other demons?" Zuzanna asks.

"He likely tapped his own personal energy," Seraphex says. "Which could be another reason why we haven't seen him in person yet. He probably has human wizards doing demonic magic, using his own energy to transport demons here one by one."

"Human wizards are helping him?" Parth asks. "Why would they do that?"

"There have always been fools who betray their own kind and work with demons," Liao Ling says sourly. I can only imagine her accompanying accusatory glances at Zambrano and Seraphex.

"The noose around this planet's neck is tightening by the week," the demon duck continues, ignoring Liao Ling, "and governments are sleepwalking into disaster. Everyone is waiting for someone else to do something."

Surely they would have thought of my suggestion by now, right? Though they don't know the key piece of information, which is that a major storm is brewing right now on the other side of the world. It was the energy of the Galveston Hurricane that was used to bring Seraphex to Earth.

I stand there, waiting as they debate various other options. Drain the entire power grid of the US East Coast. Set off a volcano. Wait around for a big hurricane, but hurricane season recently ended in the Atlantic. Minutes pass as I uncertainly linger at the door.

Finally, taking a deep breath, I open the door and start down the stairs. I have to try, at least.

I reach the bottom, and Zambrano, Seraphex, and Zuzanna turn their attention to me.

"Hey, Bryce," Parth says. "What's up?"

Behind them, I see Liao Ling is sitting with her chair leaned back and feet up on the table, looking at her phone with half a Twizzler dangling out of her mouth as the others debate.

"What do you want, Bryce?" Zambrano asks.

But before I can say anything, Liao Ling pulls her feet off the table, and her chair comes forward, its legs landing on the floor with a loud *clunk*.

"There's a big Typhoon building in the Java Sea," she says. "Just saw some news about it online. That would give us the power we need."

"Is that true?" Zambrano exclaims. "It could be the perfect fit for our needs."

Damn it.

CHAPTER 8

I walk across the room and sit down, letting out a heavy sigh. I was right about the typhoon, which is great. But I wish I had been more decisive. Why did I wait, wondering if they were going to judge me?

Before I can mention something about having had the same idea, they're all already pulling up weather maps and forecasts and talking about what it will take to use the atmospheric energy of the typhoon to teleport to Mars.

"We will need steady ocean for the spell," Zambrano says. "If it's anything like my teleportraits, you have to be standing still to use it relative to your local frame of reference."

"According to Carmen Medina's spellbook," Liao Ling says, "The *Vuelo de la Imagen* must be performed from the eye of the storm. From there we can harness the power of the surrounding storm symmetrically."

I immediately hate how risky that sounds.

What happened to me? When I made the decision to risk everything and force my way into Zambrano's warehouse, or what I thought of then as the lair of the dangerous dark sorcerer, I didn't hesitate. I saw an opportunity and went for it.

But back then I didn't have the fate of the world on my shoulders. Sure, if I died it would be sad for my friends and family. I guess I felt like it was my life to throw away. If I wanted to take risks with it, so be it—I didn't have kids or a wife or anything. Now, I need to make sure this ragtag band of psychos doesn't botch the plan and let the demon king bring a thousand years of torment or whatever he's got planned. No more hesitating like I did with the typhoon idea.

"So, maybe a stupid question, but how do we get back after we go?" I ask. "There are no typhoons or hurricanes or anything like that on Mars."

Zambrano looks at me appraisingly. "Not a terrible question. But did you think we would not have a plan for that?"

"No, no," I admit. "I just want to know what it is."

"Understandable," he says. He pauses for a moment, and no one jumps in to explain. Finally, he looks over to Liao Ling.

"Would you like to explain the plan?" he asks.

"You don't know, do you?" Liao Ling says with a smirk.

"Well, I naturally assumed that you had a plan for that," Zambrano says. "You do, don't you?"

"Yes, of course I do," Liao Ling says. "There is a version of Carmen Medina's *Vuelo de la Imagen* spell that allows for the mystic connection to stay in place between the pattern of the material that is sent to Mars and a chunk of material that replaces it. Then, with only a modest amount of energy, it can be reversed back."

"That is awesome," Parth says. "It's sort of like rolling a boulder up a hill is hard, but then rolling it back down is easy?"

"In the most vague and crude sense, sure," Liao Ling answers. "But it's the tension of displacement between the two items of roughly equal mass that matters. Essentially, we won't fully complete the transportation spell. So we can use the connection to snap things back. And be warned, while you can lose a few objects, or bring a small item like the arcane conduit back, the more change there is to you and your vessel, the more energy it will take to return the vessel back to Earth."

"The vessel?" I ask.

"The ship," Zuzanna chimes in helpfully, "that you'll be traveling in."

"Where are we going to get a spaceship?"

"No, no," Zambrano says with a shake of his head. "We're going to the eye of a hurricane. We're going to need a seafaring vessel."

"Oh," I say, this convoluted plan starting to come together in my head. "So we're going to use another yacht? Are we going to destroy it like the last one?"

Zambrano smiles. "I do not expect the vessel to endure being teleported to the Martian surface, crashing there, and being thrust back across space to Earth and still be seaworthy. We are hard on our things, aren't we? But Liao Ling has assured me that she has access to the necessary vessels."

I pat my pocket. "At least the ironclad demon didn't smash my phone," I say. "Unlike the last however many adventures we've been on." At this point I've lost count of how many new phones I've needed to buy after we get in some magical conflict or another. I've started carrying a backup with me.

"Parth, we will need you to stay behind and lead the rescue vessel to pick us up when we return. It's hard to say exactly what will happen out there, so we'll need someone we can trust ready to pick us up."

"Really?! I don't get to go to Mars?" Parth complains.

"I'll teach you a powerful locator spell in order to find us," Liao Ling offers. "This is an important job."

"Sure, LL, whatever you need," Parth says, immediately folding to her request. I smile to myself. He seems smitten with the sorcerer. Which I guess makes sense because she's cute and looks about the same age as us—but as far as I'm concerned she's some mysterious alien god who can kill with the flick of a finger.

I guess I don't trust sorcerers that much. An attitude that I feel they have fully earned.

"Should I stay with Parth?" I ask. "Or stay here at the warehouse to monitor things?"

Seraphex laughs, shaking her little duck head.

"Bryce, you think you get to sit here and order takeout while we perform this task? We need your natural undetectability to magic plus gauntlet-enhanced invisibility to demons for a crucial part of the extraction process. I set up many of the army safeguards myself, so I know them very well."

"Oh," I say. "All right."

I was looking forward to not being on the front lines here, but getting to go to Mars is pretty cool. If I can make it back, at least.

With the new plan set, there are now reams and reams of math and diagrams for the sorcerers to work through. Parth seems enthusiastic to follow along, but it's all Greek to me. Especially the two component spells that in fact are in Ancient Greek, early displacement spells invented by Archimedes.

I need to update Mei, so I text her and head upstairs. She gives me a call a few minutes later when she's able to get somewhere private.

"Wow," she says after I've filled her in on the plan. "You're really going to Mars? Home of the demon horde, the Torrid Red Wastes, all that?"

"It's not my first choice, but I don't see another way," I admit. "I'd rather stay home. I went to the beach a bunch this summer, that was nice."

"You're not going to pretend it's no big deal and you're some sort of action hero who is going to defeat the bad guys and look good doing it?" Mei asks.

"Um, am I supposed to?" I ask. "I don't expect I'll get a lot of credit for this."

"Why are you going, then?" she asks. "What's in it for you?"

I pause for a long moment.

Why the hell *am* I doing this?

"I don't know," I say. "I guess I'm going because someone has to do something. And I'm the someone in a position to do this particular thing."

"Weird," Mei says. "But it's your life to risk, I guess!"

"You're also putting yourself at a pretty big risk, aren't you?" I point out.

"You're right. I guess I am," Mei admits. "You know, Bryce Alexander, things in my life were a lot simpler before you came along."

"You're welcome!" I say cheerfully. "At least we're having fun, right?"

"Sure," she says with a rueful laugh. "We can call it that if you want to."

After we hang up, I go back down into the lab to see where things stand. But they're still speaking in math and ancient languages. Despairing of ever understanding it all, I take the rest of the day getting ready. *Clothes for a trip to Mars* is not a question my phone can answer, so I have to improvise. So I go for basic athletic wear that's easy to move in. I get a second backup phone just in case. There won't be service on Mars, sure, but I want to make sure I have a working one when we get back. I also fill a backpack with water bottles and protein bars because I have no idea how long it'll take to find and retrieve the arcane conduit on Mars.

I'm hoping it'll be a quick milk run, in and out, a smash-and-grab type of situation. Somehow, I don't think that's likely.

At the end of my shopping spree I'm standing in the kitchen, staring at the open backpack that I've filled with all the supplies I can buy in Queens on short notice. NASA has all that special astronaut food, and I've got my old backpack from college filled to the brim with water, Gatorade, and Clif Bars.

"Mars, huh?" Zuzanna says, walking into the kitchen.

"Yeah. I guess so," I answer. "Wait, you're not coming with us?"

"Oh, no, Bryce," she says with a sad smile. "I can barely walk after getting roughly carried for a mile by Steve the ironside demon. I don't have magic, and this creaky old body is not suited for adventuring. I've taught Zambrano everything he needs to know about the arcane conduit. We've worked out all the necessary spells."

"Will you be staying behind?" I ask, suddenly feeling very protective. "Is it safe with Rex and Slickwad and all their cronies hunting for you?"

"Don't worry, dear, I won't go back to Hudson View or Silver Heels. I have places I can hide. I was able to hide from Zambrano and the other wizards and mages for all those years, wasn't I? I still have some tricks up my sleeve."

"Why do you have to go at all?" I ask. "Can't you stay here and help out?"

"I need proper medical care after what that demon did to me, and frankly, being around all this active magic is making me . . . uncomfortable. I've spent decades keeping certain urges buried, and I'd rather not test my resolve while you're all gone and can't stop me if I make a mistake."

"But you can't do magic!" I object.

"I can't cast spells," she corrects me. "That doesn't mean I can't find other ways to use magic, or to direct its use. You know what they say . . . once an addict . . ."

I swallow hard, feeling some emotional bottom drop out from under me. She wasn't just hiding from Zambrano and other wizards all those years.

I don't even have to say it. She can read it on my fallen face, and I can see hers fall as well.

"I'm sorry about that, Bryce. I wasn't safe for myself back then, let alone for you. I barely was able to convince myself to lock my magic away. Then for years, I regretted it and made a bunch of mistakes. One of those mistakes turned out good though," she says, smiling weakly. "I didn't think it was possible. After all those years of magically enhanced life and then a couple decades of normal aging. But I was able to have you."

"Who's my dad?" I ask. "Biological father," I correct myself. I have a dad already. A good one. Using that term for someone else feels disrespectful.

She looks down. "I was in a haze for all those years," she says. "I don't know for sure. I'm sorry. I wish I could tell you a nice story about it. I wasn't keeping track of days, weeks, or months. By the time I realized what had happened, you were already very well along."

I nod. That feels unsatisfying, but I went from not knowing either of my birth parents to getting to actually meet one. And she's a legendary former sorcerer. That's pretty cool, I think, but my emotions are confused, somewhere between sad and lonely, and I'm not sure why.

"I checked in on you periodically. I chose a sweet family. You had a good life, didn't you?"

"Yeah," I say, tears welling up in my eyes. "Mom and Dad are good. You chose well. I guess . . . it would have been nice if you'd stopped by sometime. They would have been fine with it, I'm sure."

Zuzanna sits down heavily, tearing up as much as I am.

"I should have. Once I got things under control. But . . . what would I have said? How would I have explained it? 'You're the son of a several-hundred-year-old sorcerer who locked her power away, was insane and murderous, and also is in permanent hiding because powerful beings might want to torture her for information.' I would have had to lie to you. And I didn't think I could do that."

"You did lie to me!" I say, sitting down across from her. "You came into the shop twice a week for a year, pretending to be some nice old lady. Maybe you never literally said a lie . . . but we both know that doesn't mean you were not being deceptive. You must have learned that art from demons."

"That's true," Zuzanna says quietly. She puts her hand over mine. "I'm sorry, Bryce. I did the best I could. But you would have had so many questions, and—I was ashamed of it all. Especially how things got at the end. How I locked away my magic in the first place."

"What happened?" I ask.

She gives a long, low sigh. She's quiet for a moment, and all I can hear is the humming of the refrigerator.

"My flavor of insanity was world domination. I thought I could run everything better. I tried to influence global leaders, I did charity work, I cast spells to purify water, to improve agriculture, to cure diseases. But it never seemed to help. When I made an infinite well of purified water in Turkmenistan, the locals started a war over controlling it. When I increased crop yields in Angola, the colonial government immediately raised taxes on them, and the conflict over that was part of what led to their brutal civil war. So I decided I needed to go further. With all my mentalist powers, I had always respected others' autonomy. But I got more and more frustrated. I decided I needed to learn how to control minds. To force world leaders to submit to my will, to do things the way I thought they should be done."

"And did it work?" I asked.

"No," she answers. "Forcing a mind to act against its nature is incredibly difficult. I ran experiment after experiment. And each of the subjects died. I used willing volunteers at first, but then I got impatient and started experimenting on prisoners. None of it worked. I was obsessed with the magic at that point, and not even remembering why I started. I decided that the only way to control minds was to implant the seeds of it early in their mental development."

I feel an icy grip on my spine, hearing this grim story. She genuinely lost her sanity. This is not the sweet woman who stopped by twice a week for smoothies. "What happened?" I ask.

"I experimented on children. It's my greatest regret," she explains, shaking her head. "And I failed. And they died, all three of them. I tried to use my trigger, to test if it worked. Kara, Maurice, and Richard. The magic went wrong, and their brains fought it, and their minds shut off. They collapsed and died within minutes. Standing there, staring at their bodies, it brought it all into focus for me. Cut through the madness of the arcane fire that had torched my faculties. Not that I'm blaming the magic. I'm responsible in the end. But I had clarity for one moment. And so I reached into my own mind and cut the magic off at the root. I burned it away, cauterized it, breaking it out of my mind, my genetics, everything. I don't even know how I did it—it was a desperate act of someone at the absolute limit of her sanity."

She looks suddenly very sad and small. All the energy of the friendly woman at the smoothie shop, the dancer at the club, the elder store of arcane knowledge—it all has drained out of her.

"You've lost a lot," I say. "It couldn't have been easy."

She shrugs. "I deserve it. I had three hundred years of glory. The spellcraft, the parties, the battles, the friendships. The lovers. Even that idiot," she says, pointing downstairs to where Zambrano is still working, with occasional snatches of his raucous voice drifting up the stairs. "Don't worry, he's not as good as he thinks he is," she adds in a stage whisper.

I laugh despite everything I'm learning.

"I deserved it though. Everything that happened to me. I fell for the same madness that we had all been warned about. I thought I was safe because I never cared about demonology or necromancy, and I certainly didn't want world domination. Not in the clichéd and selfish way like when Rodney Wint tried to take control of the League of Nations in the 1930s to get himself declared emperor of the world. That twat."

"You wanted to do good," I say.

"I did the calculation," she says, shaking her head forlornly. "What are a few lives lost if I can stop wars and end famines?"

"Those ethical rules are in place for a reason," I say. "If you find yourself in a 'trolley problem' where you have to make impossible choices between saving one life or five lives, sure. But it's dangerous if you start making every decision that way. You're not supposed to set out to create new trolley problems in order to save people."

"You're a smart one," Zuzanna says with a smile. "And a good one. I paid for my hubris in decades of suffering. After I cut off the magic, I wandered the world lost, self-hating, slipping in and out of a semblance of sanity."

I nod. A part of me wants to comfort her, but how can I tell her what she did was okay? It's easy to forget in the excitement of all the magical adventures, the real human cost behind mistakes that we make. Like Larry from Larry's Lasers, who got badly injured. Or the US Navy sailors who died fighting the Leviathan.

"Since I finally came back from the madness and gained a relative sense of normalcy and peace . . . every day is a gift. This old body is still kicking for a bit longer. I have the best genetics magic could create, but biologically, I'm in my sixties."

"That's young!" I protest. "My grandmother on my mom's side is seventy-five. And her father, my great-grandfather, made it to ninety-two."

"Not many years of dancing left, though. But I'm sure Hudson View will save me a seat at the bingo table, if it's ever safe for me to go back." Her hand is still over mine, and I find myself gripping it tightly, tears welling up. I don't quite know who this woman is to me yet, but I know I don't want to lose her so soon after getting her in my life.

She says, "I'm glad Zambrano will have you to keep him sane, for as long as you can."

"And . . . how long do you expect that to be?" I can't help but ask.

From the open door to the workshop floor below, Zambrano's voice rings out, "It was a simple arithmetic error! One more word of your mockery, and I will roast every wing off your body, duck!"

Zuzanna shrugs. "Maybe he is insane already, but not in a way that will destroy the world?"

"Do you think?"

"No," she says with a heavy sigh. "The magic burns us all out in the end. But let's hope he also has some years left. Maybe we'll see who goes senile first. . . . I would be worried much more about him at this point than me."

We keep talking for several hours. I tell her stories about my life, and she shares some of the adventures she's had in the past couple decades since regaining a measure of sanity. We stay up late into the night. At the end of it she says both goodnight and goodbye, for now. And in the morning, her room is empty.

She does leave behind a little note on her dresser.

So long for now, Bryce. I'm sorry I can't go to Mars with you, but I'm afraid I would only slow you down. I wish I was young enough for swashbuckling adventures across the world fighting demons. It's a shame that sorcerers can only slow their own aging. The rest of us have to keep getting more wrinkles and creakier knees. Kick some demon butt for me. I've put a few numbers for burner phones that you can use to get in touch with me in the future. And tell Zambrano that if the two of you are going to interrupt me at work again, CALL FIRST.

Love,

Susan

And I guess I'm going to be calling her Susan, not Zuzanna. The new identity she's assumed, away from all the magic and the madness. The kind woman who visited me and kept an eye on me during my smoothie shop days.

So let's leave it there, because you don't want to hear about the confusing cry I had after that.

CHAPTER 9

Two days later, after a marathon of frantic prep and some final sleep that may have been aided by many over-the-counter pharmaceuticals to help me get some rest, we're out at sea again, this time not with one yacht, but two. Though after getting to the general area of the growing monsoon, Parth peels off, left in charge of the smaller of the two vessels.

I have my backpack filled with food, water, some climbing gear, and my invisibility-to-demons gauntlets. We also have some conventional weapons like guns on the yacht, but they're more for if we run into any human adversaries on our way to the hurricane. Liao Ling's Chinese-made AK-47s won't do much to a demon beyond annoy it, though she did give me a quick lesson in how to use one. We're planning to try to be stealthy on Mars anyway.

How and why does Liao Ling have a small arsenal of black market weaponry after only months in our modern world, one might wonder? I don't know the answer, but it is a very good question.

I'm standing on the deck, feeling the wind pick up as I strap an amber nexus onto my body. It's a large circular slab of amber, containing a harpy feather for pressure resistance, a piece of Norwegian coal for heat, a tiny ship in a bottle for airtightness, an evergreen sprig with druidic magic for oxygen, and iron for weight. It will allow me to breathe and stay warm in any environment, from the depths of the ocean to the surface of Mars. Thankfully, Zambrano has deactivated the iron, so I should be able to move well under the lowered Martian gravity.

I can see around the ship; there are various glowing glyphs, one placed on each major structural element. Zambrano explained that the glyphs are to tie the ship together and keep the spell activated so that it will be able to easily reverse the spell and pull us back to Earth.

"Good luck up there," Parth tells us over our radio earpieces as his ship turns away, still in radio range but heading away from us to chart a course that stays parallel to the oncoming storm. We've brought back the radio earpieces from our last sea voyage, not only to communicate while in the storm, but also to eventually talk on Mars, where there's very little atmosphere to transmit sound. I would never dare tell this directly to her, but I have to say Seraphex once again looks very cute with her earpiece on her tiny duck head.

I can see Parth outlined against the gathering storm clouds, standing on the deck of the other ship, waving at me. It's a smaller and less impressive yacht, not a giant superyacht like ours. "Bring me back a Martian rock or something."

"Thanks for doing this for us," I say. "I know you'd rather be coming along. But it's good to know you'll be there to pull us back."

"No problem," he says. "Wish I could come with you all, but I've learned a couple cool new spells. I've gotten more out of a few hours with Liao Ling than a whole semester at the IIM," he adds.

If I had to choose between school and our wacky adventures, I would . . . well, I don't know. School may be boring, but he's learning interesting things and, crucially, not frequently in situations where being pulled apart by metal demons is a possible outcome.

Parth, maniac that he is, is pumped at the possibility of more danger and adventure. I feel like I've hit my quota of thrills for the year. Once you've faced a few situations of impending doom, you've seen them all, right? But I'm gritting my teeth and dealing with this. It's too late to back out of my obligations now.

The plan is for Parth to remain on one of the vessels, armed with locator spells and the phone numbers of various officials from the local nations' navies who Liao Ling has bribed or threatened to be helpful.

This time, at least, the crew appears to understand what's going on. Unlike the battle with the Leviathan, before which the entire crew fled as soon as they learned where we were headed. It was quite reasonable, given that the ship ended up scattered in pieces across the North Pacific Ocean.

This group seems to be hardened sailors from the Philippines, China, Vietnam, and elsewhere around the South China Sea. We don't know exactly how Liao Ling won their loyalty in the past months, but they show her absolute obedience. They're heavily tattooed, look hard as hell, and while they avoid me and Zambrano, I get the sense that if the situation ever called for it, they wouldn't think twice about gutting either of us. I'm not sure who looks more out of place, Zambrano in his bespoke suit amid all these pirate-looking sailors, or the rough sailors working on what is very much a typical rich guy's sporting yacht.

We don't ask Liao Ling about them, given the old sorcerers' doctrine of not asking too many questions when an ally brings a valuable resource to a fight. And I'm not saying Liao Ling somehow has collected a crew of pirates of the South China Sea—but if that's what you're picturing, you're picturing the right sort of thing. None of them have actual peg legs or parrots, but one of them is definitely missing an eye. No cool eyepatch though, just an ugly scar.

The pirates are crewing two yachts, speedy and modern vessels that don't match their unkempt demeanor. But they operate them skillfully. Liao Ling and Zambrano spend the first several hours casting various enchantments on the boats. While Zambrano has the Polynesian boat-stabilizing spells that he used before our battle with the Leviathan, it's clear that Liao Ling has much more experience in the matter of nautical magic. I see Zambrano try to help at first and then mostly stand back and watch her work, paying close attention and helping out with smaller pieces. It sure is nice to see his abilities shown up once in a while.

Though, frustratingly, he doesn't seem to take it as a blow to his ego. He's eagerly following along and is learning as he goes. I guess you can't get to be one of the best in the world at something without being willing to learn and practice. You can still be a gigantic prick, mind you, but there has to be some learning happening there.

"What was Liao Ling like, back in the day?" I ask Seraphex as we watch the crew and the sorcerers do their work on the boats. "She seems to know her way around this sort of boat-focused magic very well. The way she tells it, she was a great and pure hero, and Merlin was a greedy traitor."

Seraphex laughs. "She does make it sound that way, doesn't she? There's a reason she wasn't beloved by any of the authority figures at the time. Banditry, piracy, forgery, various rebellions—she kept stirring up trouble. And she was the greatest thorn in the side of Merlin, who tried to control and lead the magic users of the time. I can't say for certain, but I suspect the island she's using as her headquarters now is the same one she used to direct a piracy operation fifteen hundred years ago. She only decided to pursue the more, shall we say, 'ambitious' goal of exiling demons from Earth after the death of her brother."

"After you killed her brother," I remind Seraphex. "At least according to Liao Ling."

"It was a very long time ago," Seraphex says wearily.

"In a sense, you caused all the demons to be exiled, didn't you?"

"An argument could be made," Seraphex answers. Or, rather, non-answers.

I don't push the issue because her reluctance to debate the issue is evidence enough for me. I've developed a real fondness for this dumb evil duck, but I have to always keep in mind that she is, at her core, an alien creature, a demon. She is bound by her promise to be friends to Zambrano and to me, but how effectively that constrains her behavior and forces her to protect us and our world is unclear.

The boat chops through the water, and the clouds that were on the horizon are soon around us. As it gets stormier, the boat begins to sway back and forth with more urgency, even with all the stabilizing spells on it.

"If you're not crew or a sorcerer, get inside!" Liao Ling yells. "I'm not fishing you out of the sea if you take a tumble, and neither is the crew."

I'm not sure if they understand the exact meaning, but the crew's looks at me indicate they certainly have no interest in helping me out if I fall overboard.

I don't need to be told twice. Seraphex and I head inside to the glass-enclosed observation lounge.

I go to the ladder to climb up to the bridge, but at one questioning glare from a crewman up there, I come back down, and the demon duck and I watch the action from inside the yacht's lounge.

The swanky interior of the yacht was clearly designed for some rich jerk to impress his friends. It would be a lovely place to relax for a day, maybe have some champagne, pop our collars, and debate who the greatest lacrosse player ever was while our pretty girlfriends tan out on the deck. I currently can't name a single lacrosse player, but I assume if I hung around on a ship like this, I would pick it up quickly enough.

Unfortunately, this isn't that type of voyage. We are headed straight into a giant typhoon, not a mimosa-filled sunset cruise. Pity.

Through the glass, we can see the waves getting taller and wilder, and the rain starts. At first it's a few drizzling drops, but a moment later, the rain comes down in sheets, rattling the windows.

Out on the deck, I see Liao Ling and Zambrano begin casting spells. They are outlined in glowing flashes against the stormy sky, Zambrano in his suit and Liao Ling in her brightly colored casual clothes that could be called "power clashing" but with the strength of a nuclear power plant.

Before the rain gets overwhelming, a shield of greenish-blue energy forms above the top of the boat. It crackles with power, holding both the rain and the raging waves back. The boat jerks and sways, but vastly less than the furious sea wants it to.

Around us, the crew yells and occasionally runs through the lounge as they make various adjustments and repairs. At one point the engine shudders to a stop and goes silent. It's several long minutes of cursing and shouting in various languages I don't understand before they're able to get it running again.

The storm is hundreds of miles across, and even at top speed with magical acceleration and protection, we have to settle in for a few hours of transit. Once the protective spells are settled and working properly, Seraphex and I are able to go back out onto the deck.

The yacht, protected by the swirling and glowing green-tinted shield, plunges through the storm. The crew doesn't have much to do, but even their weathered faces look tight and stressed. Around us the waves thrash and roar, and the raindrops explode on the shield like so many tiny artillery shells.

It's a terrifying sight at first, but the mind can get used to things very quickly. Before long, the fear of it fades, and I can look up and take in the beauty of it. The typhoon rages around us, spray and mist obscuring more than a few feet away. Occasional breaks show farther beyond the immediate turmoil, with soaring clouds and whipping winds.

And then, after a few hours of the sound and fury of the typhoon, we shoot through a curtain of mist and emerge into an open area of calmer seas. The transition is complete and abrupt, and we're suddenly out in gently rolling water.

"Welcome to the eye of the storm," Liao Ling says, making a circular motion with both her hands, which causes the greenish-blue shield above the boat to dissipate.

Zambrano leans down to the ground, pressing his hands on the deck and sending one more pulse of energy into the stabilizing spell. It does still seem to be in effect, as the swells of the sea toss the boat around far less than I would expect.

The sun has long since set, and the moon shines down brightly on a stretch of open ocean. The wall of the storm that we emerged from rises behind us, a vastness of towering height that goes up into the darkness. It slopes gently outward and extends all the way around us in a full circle, though the far edge is hazy and difficult to see even in the bright moonlight. I've never seen anything like it.

In a few quick trips, Liao Ling uses a pair of teleportraits to take the sailors back to wherever they came from. I assume it's some sort of secret island where pirates are free to roll around in piles of gold doubloons or whittle their peg legs into cool shapes or whatever. We can't take them all to Mars with us.

Meanwhile, Zambrano is setting up the various ingredients and incantations for the transportation spell. As the expert in teleportation, this is his wheelhouse. He holds a giant metal staff in both hands, closing his eyes in concentration. As the spell begins, the staff glows a bright orange, and I can feel my hair stand on end as static electricity builds up. Looking at the storm, I feel like it's moving slower as Zambrano pulls energy from it, but it could be my imagination. The wind and waves immediately around us, at least, seem to calm down as he draws power from the mighty typhoon.

While they're doing their spells, like any proper modern person, I pull out my phone and take a video of the whole scene. I'm not an idiot; no one would believe this if I told them. Parth *needs* to see this. And I bet Mei would enjoy it as well.

I get a little carried away, zooming in on the storm walls around us, the crackling orange spell that Zambrano is casting, and the contrast between the calmer sea around us and the closest part of the storm, where I can still see the thrashing water and rain. I keep at it for about ten minutes, recording every bit that I can. I have no idea what the transition to Mars will look like, but I'm pretty sure it will look impressive as hell.

Finally, I'm turning my camera to zoom in on the far side of the eye, distant and hazy, the wall barely visible many miles away. I pull the zoom back and suddenly see a swirling disturbance in the water.

Something rears up out of the swells. For a split second I have flashbacks to the Leviathan, with its scaly snakelike body. But this object, while it gleams in the moonlight, doesn't have the sinuous body of a snake. It's long and smooth, a cylinder with one end rounded and with a tower at the midpoint. It's a submarine, popping up above the water with a roar of rushing water.

But as it fully surfaces, I see there's something else beyond the tower, a lump of something clinging on to the metal. A figure with horns, claws, giant rippling rocky muscles, and a barbed spike tail.

Oh, shit.

This was not supposed to happen like this. We were so close to getting off the entire planet!

He stands up, first looking in the opposite direction, then finally turning to see us. His glowing blue eyes fix on us, and he roars with fury.

"You pathetic little worms," Rex's voice booms out across the eye of the storm. "Did you believe I was not tracking your movements, uncovering your little plans, and waiting for you to make your pitiful attempt to defeat me? How could you think you would win against a vastly superior foe such as me? You may think consorting with my treasonous harlot of a former wife will help you, but it will only lead to your doom!"

The demon king splays out one of his clawed hands, and a wave of barely visible magical energy distorts the air as it rushes at us.

Liao Ling raises her hands and, shouting a spell, creates a yellowish shield that deflects most of the blow, but the boat rocks violently, knocking me off my feet onto the deck.

And there goes my phone, flying into the air, sailing in a high arc, and disappearing over the rail into the churning waves.

Luckily, I've got one in my other pocket and a couple more in my backpack.

Still . . . god damn it. I'm gonna have to sign in to so many freaking apps once we get back into service.

CHAPTER 10

The giant demon perches atop the submarine, glowering at us as the submarine slowly turns to face our yacht. He sends a few more spells at us, bolts of energy that sizzle over the ocean. But Liao Ling raises more magical shields, which deflect the blows.

Liao Ling thrusts a fist forward in a martial arts–style punch, and a magenta burst of energy blasts the demon king, but he simply laughs as it is absorbed into his rocky armor without the slightest visible impact.

They trade a few more spells back and forth, but none of it causes any damage.

"His magic is fairly limited compared to a sorcerer," Seraphex explains. "Demons don't have the variety of spells available to a human magic user. But his body is almost impervious to harm, and those claws can cut straight through any defensive spell."

"Is he stuck on the submarine?" I ask. "He can't fly or swim?"

"He could probably propel himself through the water with magic," Seraphex says, flying up to the rail and peering out at her nasty demon ex-husband. "But a modern submarine can go much faster."

"What do we do?" I ask, looking to Zambrano, who is standing in the center of the deck with his metal staff. "Should I get out the guns? Will that help?"

"Bullets will simply bounce off him," Seraphex answers. "That won't do anything useful."

"I need more time!" Zambrano shouts. His white hair whips in the wind as energy crackles around his metal staff, drawing power from the massive storm that swirls around us, huge cloud banks rising up on every side of the eye of the storm. "Bryce, we need to move the boat—you have to take the helm!"

"What? Me?" I suddenly panic. I have no idea how to drive a boat. Or pilot it? Navigate it? Helm it? Why is my brain focused on this unimportant point? I need to focus on the task at hand.

"Yes, we need to get the vessel moving to avoid him," Liao Ling says. "I can hold off his spells, but once he reaches us, I won't be able to do much."

"I'll help you," Seraphex says, leaping into the air and toward the bridge.

I take a deep breath and turn and sprint back into the observation lounge and then up the narrow stairs to the helm. Seraphex follows behind, fluttering through the air with urgency.

The controls look devilishly complicated. If this were some little motorboat with a steering wheel and throttle, I could handle it. But there are touch screens, radar displays, camera feeds, rows of glowing buttons, and levers.

"What do I do?" I ask. "How do I steer it?"

"You can handle this," Seraphex says, hopping up onto the controls. "Sit in the chair and take that joystick to the right. That's both throttle and steering. You'll need to press the button right there to disengage the autopilot." She indicates the button with her beak.

"How do you know how to pilot a yacht?" I ask, complying with her instructions and sitting in the pilot's chair.

"I've seen it done before. These systems are all very similar."

"You learned just from watching?"

"I'm not a human, Bryce. I'm a demon. I'm smarter than you. Now, you can push that joystick left to turn us left. Gently at first, don't make sudden movements. It takes a moment for the ship to respond."

Zambrano's voice crackles over the headset, "She's always observing everything we do. It's nice when it plays out in our favor and not one of her plots."

Seraphex guides me through the basics of the yacht operation, and I'm able to get us moving forward and peeling off to the left. She shows me the radar readouts indicating our position and the submarine's. It also shows the storm raging around us, a giant oval of bright red spots surrounding the more muted eye that we're in. We're off to one side, having recently crossed into the center of it.

I accelerate, but the submarine turns to match course, coming at an intercept angle.

"They're going to ram us," Liao Ling's voice comes over the headsets. "Whoever is driving that sub doesn't care if the damn thing sinks us both."

Looking at the screen and trying to estimate the two courses, it appears as though Liao Ling is right.

"You can make it," Seraphex advises, "if you max out the throttle."

I immediately push the joystick to its maximum.

"It looks like they're coming right at us," I say nervously, watching the icons on the screen on a collision course.

"Ramming is much harder than one might think," Seraphex assures me. "These vessels aren't maneuverable the way a demon or a bird is. Push it a tiny bit to the left."

I comply, trying to keep breathing calmly as I see the submarine get closer. Looking out the window, I can see it aiming for us.

"What if he jumps?" I ask. "They may not need to collide with us. What if Rex only needs to get the sub close enough that he can leap aboard?"

"That would be very unfortunate," Seraphex says. "There's nothing more we can do from here; let's get back down there."

We rush back down the narrow stairs and out onto the deck. Rex has stopped flinging magic at us, probably realizing that he can't win at that, and he is perched on the bow of the submarine, crouched and ready to leap. He has a wicked grin on his face.

"The sub isn't going to hit us, but Rex is going to try to jump over!" I shout.

"What do we do?" Liao Ling asks. "I can't push him back alone."

"I need to keep the staff in place, or the spell will fail entirely," Zambrano yells.

I look back and forth between the two of them, Liao Ling at the rail and ready to cast spells and Zambrano holding the staff, which is now glowing and receiving periodic lances of lightning from the sky. The various glyphs around the ship are also glowing, far more brightly now that the transportation spell is powering up. I can see the air compressing and bending as the ship pulls energy from the vast storm around us. They are both looking at me as if expecting me to come up with a solution.

I freeze for a long moment. How am I supposed to know the answer here? Why can't I come up with a solution when they're all looking to me?

"I'll hold the staff, and you can help Liao Ling fight him off," I suggest.

"You can't hold the staff, Bryce," Zambrano shouts. "It will electrocute you. You have no ability to absorb and redirect the magic."

We stand there, watching as the submarine closes in on us.

"The gauntlets!" Liao Ling shouts.

Right, of course. "Will that work?" I ask, but I can already see Zambrano nodding.

"The gauntlets are powerful artifacts, their magic will serve as a barrier," he explains over the roar of the ocean and the crackling of the power.

I twist my backpack off and unzip it in a desperate hurry. I pull the gauntlets out, stumbling across the deck as I shove them on my hands.

"Humans, prepare to experience the brutal truth of your mortality," Rex's voice booms across the ocean. "Former wife and current treacherous jezebel, you will be served an infinity of torment."

I grasp the staff in gauntleted hands, and Zambrano lets it go, shaking his hands as if they've gone numb from the energy.

"I'll come back in a moment, the arcane power will get unstable without me to hold it in place," he says. "Stay strong!"

And with that, he dashes across the deck to stand next to Liao Ling. They exchange a couple quick sentences as the giant demon king tenses, horned head lowered in excitement.

As Seraphex predicted, the submarine is missing us, its path crossing behind our yacht. As it reaches the closest point in its path, the massive demon launches himself.

As he sails through the air, Zambrano and Liao Ling strike at him.

Streams of bright purple energy blast out from their hands. It doesn't seem to be a damaging spell, but I can see it hitting Rex as he flies through the air, washing over him with pure physical force.

He raises his claws, creating some sort of red magic that meets the purple, partially dispersing it. Still, the energy pushes him back, altering his trajectory.

The demonic form falls from the sky, arcing back down. For a moment, I think he's going to fall into the ocean, but he somehow manages to stretch out a single claw, sinking it deep into the metal of the yacht deck.

Liao Ling and Zambrano advance, sending a continuous blast of the purple energy at the demon. The strength of it pushes him back and keeps him flailing horizontally in the air. Though he tries to swing his other claw in, for a moment the sorcerers' combined magic holds him back.

"Seraphex," I say quietly to the duck, who is nervously lingering behind me. As if I'll be able to protect her. "I doubt they can keep that up long. Use your voice! Distract him somehow."

"With what?" she asks.

"Merlin," I mouth, turning around to say it silently, hoping that Rex's demon senses can't detect that.

"Merlin?" Seraphex asks.

"Liao Ling is here. Why couldn't he believe that he secretly survived?" I whisper, hoping that it's enough for her to get it and her ex-husband Rex to not notice.

The duck nods seriously, flying into the air and diving down below the side of the ship at a moment when Rex looks away as he struggles to advance through the waves of crackling purple energy.

I hold on to the staff, and what started as a light vibration has become a furious rattling in my hands. I grip as tightly as I can.

A moment later, I see the duck soar back up into the air behind Rex.

"Savage beast!" A voice rings out across the ocean, bright and confident and with a noble tone. "The guardians of this earthly realm do not welcome you!"

Just as the phrase finishes, I see Seraphex dive into the waves.

In a panic, Rex turns his head around, looking for the nonexistent ancient sorcerer.

As he does, a powerful blast of magic from Zambrano and Liao Ling hits Rex, sending him flying through the air. He splashes down in the ocean, like the biggest kid at summer camp doing a full-power cannonball, sending sheets of water up.

The staff in my hand is humming and rattling now, an unstable shaking fury.

Rex disappears below the waves, then comes up roaring in anger. I watch in horror as he puts his arms back, and a trail of black and red shoots out behind him, propelling him forward through the water. But true to Seraphex's prediction, our yacht, moving with the throttle stuck on full speed, is too much for him. He falls behind as we accelerate across the eye of the storm.

"Don't let go!" Zambrano calls as he sprints back, grabbing the staff and mouthing spellcasting words. He places his bare hands on the staff alongside my gauntleted ones, and within a few seconds the vibrations calm somewhat.

"Okay, you can let it go," Zambrano says. "It's still fairly unstable. We can't try that trick again." He closes his eyes, focusing intently as the staff grows calmer.

"How long?" I ask.

"We need another fifteen minutes or so to gather enough energy for the transit," he says. "Let me focus, Bryce."

"Okay," I say, forgiving his snappy tone because, well, this is a life-or-death situation and we just pulled off an unexpected win.

Unfortunately, the celebration doesn't last long. We are speeding away, but the submarine has swung around, and Rex is climbing back up atop its bow. Liao Ling rushes to the rear deck, preparing to repel any spells that the demon king sends our way. For the moment, however, he seems to be occupied getting back onto the submarine and glaring at us menacingly.

Seraphex and I climb back up to the bridge of the yacht and start looking at the various displays.

"The eye of the storm is about ten miles across," Seraphex says, pointing with her beak at the main radar display, which shows the elliptical shape of the eye, a darker oval inside of a bright and pulsing mass of nasty weather. "It will take us about twenty minutes to get across, and Zambrano only needs fifteen. We should be able to outpace the submarine and make the transit a bit before then."

"Okay, great," I say. "So we monitor the speed and keep well ahead of him, and we're out of here?"

Seraphex flutters to the other side of the console where rear-facing cameras show the submarine in pursuit. "There's no way it's going to be that simple. I feel certain that my former husband will have some way to threaten us."

"Volcanose was able to use magic to speed up his spaceship," I suggest. "Could the same magic work on a submarine?"

"It could," Seraphex says. "But," she adds as we see the submarine slip below the surface of the water, "we may not find that out immediately."

Almost as soon as it is swallowed up by the ocean, the wake of the submarine dissipates in the choppy water.

Other than the distant rumbling of the storm, there is only silence around us.

We check the heading and speed of the yacht, positioning it to give us exactly the runway we need to let Zambrano finish his spell. We also switch to a slightly different heading, though the probability of that helping against a naval submarine seems to be nil.

"Should we try zigzagging?" I ask.

"There's nothing a civilian vessel can do to confuse the sensors of a military submarine," Seraphex advises me. "Moving back and forth would make it easier to catch up to us."

For several long minutes, the ocean is still around us. Zambrano is deep in concentration, and his staff hums. And in the distance, the moonlight shines on the giant sloping cloud banks that form the edges of the storm's eye.

The silence is broken when the deck suddenly rocks. To the rear of us, a massive blast of water shoots into the air. Then the entire ship shudders as two more impacts rock us.

"We didn't have vessels like this in my time," Liao Ling says as she jogs out and joins us on the foredeck. She's grinning, which makes my pulse calm down ever so slightly. "But we did have explosives and projectiles, and I've got enough shielding on this thing to stop whatever they're shooting at us."

"They're torpedoes," Seraphex supplies.

"Ah, right," Liao Ling says. "I've got to get a hold of one of these submarine things; they seem very useful. Projectiles that shoot under the ocean! So much fun."

I am simultaneously reminded of two things: The first is that Liao Ling has only been in modern times for a few months, and despite magically accelerated learning and acclimation, she still has blind spots about current society. The second is how dangerous sorcerers can be, and that we have no idea what exactly we may have unleashed on the world in helping Liao Ling to return from the prismatic prison's glacially-slowed time.

What comes next is a lot of nerves and not a lot of action. The submarine sends a few more torpedoes our way, but Liao Ling's shielding is able to detonate them at a safe distance. Zambrano's staff hums louder and louder, and lightning regularly crackles down from above us and around the ship, but the staff absorbs the energy.

Seraphex and I speculate about what Rex is planning, but we don't come up with anything that seems likely.

We got a good lead when we sped past him. But how much of a lead do we still have? What will his next move be?

"Do you know what type of submarine that is?" I ask. "Is it faster than us? And by how much?"

Seraphex shakes her head. "I know a lot of things, but I'm not one of those human military buffs. I don't spend my days memorizing all the different hardware across all the different militaries. I don't get upset when a movie shows a gun with a seven-shot magazine shoot eight rounds. I'd guess it's Russian, because they would be the easiest to bribe."

"Okay, okay, that's fair," I say. "So it could surface at any moment? Or ram us?"

"It could appear at any moment," Liao Ling says. "I wish I'd had one of them back in my privateer days."

"How much longer?" I ask Zambrano, who's gritting his teeth and sweating as the staff continues to draw energy from the storm.

"I need a couple more minutes," the sorcerer says, the coattails of his suit jacket whipping in the wind, "and we'll be out of here."

I pull out one of my backup phones, turning on the stopwatch and watching as it counts up. When it gets to ninety seconds, my stupid heart starts to hope. Rex has no way to know exactly what amount of energy we need, does he? How much of our plan does he know, beyond the fact that we wanted to harness the power of a typhoon to enact a spell? What if he is too late? Another minute or two, and we will disappear. And he can play around with his submarine all he wants, but we'll be on another planet.

Unfortunately, that's not the way things work out. That's never the way things work out, is it?

Ahead of us there's a roar as the submarine explodes to the surface. Rather than catching up to us, it has had enough time and speed to circle fully around us. It bears down on us, churning through the water on a direct collision course. And this time Rex is poised on the rear of the submarine, glaring at us as his improvised battering ram, the ocean-churning submarine, approaches.

Yelling with fervor, Liao Ling flings spells from the prow of our yacht down at the approaching submarine, but that barely slows it down. I sprint up to the control room, cursing myself for not having been there already. I leap into the chair and pull on the joystick.

It alters our course slightly at the last minute. It's just powerful enough and sudden enough that the submarine, instead of hitting us straight on, impacts off-center.

Metal strains and groans as the submarine's bulk careens off our yacht's hull. I can't immediately tell how bad the damage is, but a *lot* of lights are suddenly flashing.

I can see the submarine is rolling onto its side, though it appears less damaged than the yacht, which has a massive dent and is starting to buckle and sink as water rushes into the hull. Rex had been tensed to jump again, but the uneven impact has knocked him off-balance, and he's clawing his way up to the top of the submarine again. Liao Ling, holding on to the railing, is thoroughly soaked but gamely casting some sort of spell that sends a thin line of yellow energy drilling into Rex. It appears to be keeping him off-balance.

"Thirty seconds!" Zambrano's voice booms out over the storm.

The controls flicker at me, and then all the screens around me go dead. I try to move the joystick, but the ship doesn't respond.

I rush down to the deck, not sure what I can do to help but prepared to try whatever it takes. Why can't I still have the magic

Sword of Wayland like I had last time we were fighting at sea? That thing was badass.

As I reach the deck, I see Rex is preparing to strike.

"The spell will activate in ten seconds," Zambrano shouts.

"We must keep Rex off the ship," Seraphex squawks, "or he'll be transported to Mars with us!"

For a second I wonder if that would be a good thing, but I know that it wouldn't help. Rex would slaughter us easily, and with his power, find a way to get back to Earth to wreak havoc again very soon.

I run to the rail and see Rex has regained his footing and is about to leap from the submarine onto the yacht.

Farther down the rail Liao Ling glances at Zambrano, who is clutching the staff as showers of sparks fly from his body, and the air itself pulsates around him, distorting the light as it passes through. Then she looks back to Rex, who is grinning as he sees the panic in both our eyes.

Giving a wild war cry, the ancient Chinese sorcerer steps back and, taking a running start, leaps off the ship. She puts her arms out, and they shoot gouts of flame behind her, accelerating her as a bright orange shield of hexagons forms in front of her.

The demon king lashes out with a clawed fist, slamming it into the shield with a roar of delight as the small sorcerer careens into him.

The shield dissolves, and Liao Ling's momentum is fully absorbed. She drops into the water in front of the submarine, splashing helplessly. I throw the fire extinguisher, hoping to hit Rex, but it falls pitifully short, splashing uselessly in the water.

"Pitiful mortal!" he crows, reaching a long arm out into the water, claws ready to snatch Liao Ling up.

But then, a streak of white slams into his face, and his claws pull back, swatting at it.

"You were a lousy husband!" Seraphex screams as she leaps out of reach of his grabbing claws, turning and soaring back into the air.

Down in the water, I can see Liao Ling swimming with one hand and fumbling with her shirt with the other. And then, as Seraphex swoops down and lands on my shoulder and Rex reaches down with his claws to finish off Liao Ling, the sorcerer pulls something out of her shirt.

The yacht, slouching into the sea as it takes on more water, begins to vibrate violently, and bright crackling white light suffuses everything around me.

Down below, I see Liao Ling has pulled a teleportrait out of her bright pink shirt and is treading water as she stares at it.

"Thank you, Seraphex," Liao Ling's voice comes over the headsets, sheathed in static as the energy around us comes to a peak. "I still hate you, you know," she adds.

And then she disappears from the ocean in a *whoosh* of teleportation. A moment later, so does the rest of the ocean, the sky, the storm, and the demon king.

I close my eyes as blinding white light explodes around me, the deck shakes once again, and the air buzzes with electricity.

Beneath me, I can feel the ship shudder and crack as it settles onto a new rocky surface. The sounds of popping and cracking fill the air, and I'm glad my eyes are closed as shards of glass bounce off me, wincing as a few give me stinging little cuts.

I grip the rail tightly, and metal screams as the structure collapses around me. But although I tense, I don't end up squashed between broken bulkheads.

With a grinding finality, the ship comes to a halt, broken around us but with the deck still mostly intact.

And there you have it, we've wrecked another perfectly good yacht. Frankly, I'm proud of us. Striking a blow for the common folk against the rich jerks who sail these things around the world. Not that I would turn one down if someone wanted to give me one. One day I'd like to be on a boat that wasn't currently or about to be utterly wrecked in an apocalyptic battle.

But beyond the metal and glass, there's a new horizon. The sky is pinkish red, and a small sun blazes down, bluish white through dusty red haze.

The dull roar of the storm and the sounds of battle are suddenly completely silent other than a ringing that lingers in my ears. Close by, rocky red hills rise, and beyond that, a gigantic red mountain.

We've made it to Mars.

Holy shit.

CHAPTER 11

I have a brief moment of panic as my body processes that there's something *different* about the environment around me. After noticing the silence, for a second, there's a tingling on my skin, like being stabbed by a thousand small pins. At the same time, my upper half suddenly feels painfully warm as the sun above blazes me. Meanwhile, my legs are shaded from the sunlight by the part of the yacht's hull that has been ripped up out of the deck, and they are freezing.

For a moment my relief at having escaped is replaced by another surge of adrenaline. Did we mess up? Am I going to pop like a balloon here on Mars as all the moisture tries to escape from my body at once?

But the amber nexus around my neck hums and grows warm on my chest, and the sensation subsides as its "airtightness" and "heat" protective enchantments activate.

I realize I'm holding my breath. Tentatively, I try to pull some air in through my nose—and despite the total lack of atmosphere around me, air comes in, magically recycled and provided by the amber nexus strapped to my chest.

I take some slow, deep breaths, letting my body calm and my pulse decelerate from the desperate battle we narrowly escaped.

As I do, I look around the yacht and speak into my earpiece.

"Zambrano? Seraphex? Are you okay?" I ask. It's a strange sensation, speaking normally but having my voice resonate in my body and come out thin and tinny to my own ears. There's barely any atmosphere on the Martian surface, so sound doesn't travel here.

"I am here," Zambrano's voice comes through my earpiece. "I fell down into a hole in the ship, but I'm not hurt."

Seraphex squirms out of the wrecked vessel and waddles over next to me. "I'm essentially immortal, no need to worry about me. But as you can hear, the earpiece is still intact," she says, her voice coming through clearly. We do have spare earpieces and other supplies in the ship, but with how badly the ship is wrecked, it might be hard to track it all down. "Unfortunately, I can't fly in this thin atmosphere," she says. She leaps up into the air, fluttering her wings in a fury, far faster than a normal duck would be able to. She's barely able to make it to my shoulder, plopping down in her usual spot. "This is infuriating. The low gravity helps, but even with that, I am barely mobile."

"I'm not releasing even a tiny bit of your transformation," Zambrano says as he climbs up out of the lower regions of the ship. "We both know that would end poorly."

"We both expect it would end poorly for *you* and your silly little species," Seraphex points out. "I imagine it would go swimmingly for me. Or flyingly, at least."

Knowing they're okay, now I get to do the part I've been looking forward to, from the moment we decided we had to come to Mars. The rest of it is terrifying and stressful. The fate of everyone I care about hangs in the balance. The fate of the jerks who bullied me in middle school also hangs in the balance, so there is some slight consolation there if we fail. Still, I want humanity not to die or be tortured indefinitely or whatever.

But there's one spot of joy.

I take one quick test hop. It feels great. I'm light on my feet, easily bouncing up into the air. Every part of my body feels free and strong.

Throwing caution to the nonexistent Martian wind, I crouch down and leap into the air.

I soar a full three times higher than I would be able to jump back on Earth. I stumble slightly on landing but steady myself and leap again, soaring off the yacht and onto the rocky Martian surface. I take a few more bounds, flying high into the air with each jump.

Eat your heart out, LeBron James. Put me on the court up here now, and I will *dunk*.

Leaping one more time, I take a moment to look around the area. That's why I was jumping the whole time. For visibility, not because it's insanely fun.

The ship is utterly wrecked. The impact of the submarine would have sunk it within minutes, but now the bottom of the hull has collapsed underneath the deck. I also notice that it's sitting in a hole on the surface of Mars, a jagged depression in the red rock.

All the seawater inside the boat was transported along with the ship and has drained out onto the rocky Martian landscape, leaving dark patches around the edges of the ship along with pools where the water hasn't been absorbed into cracks in the rock. Hopefully, we haven't upset some delicate biological balance or introduced our nasty Earth pathogens to Mars. Though I guess the place is infested with demons, so it probably wouldn't make things worse.

We're on a shelf of solid red stone, and I can see that down-hill from us the surface is more broken up, with smaller rocks and powder.

Zambrano swings over the railing of the ship, bouncing to me and clearly enjoying the low gravity and the light and easy movement that it allows. I'm still testing it out, a little unstable, but enjoying how freeing it is.

"It appears the teleportation spell sent back a solid chunk of Martian rock," Zambrano says, nodding at the big hole in the ground underneath the ship. "That was intentionally targeted so that when we're ready to reverse the spell, the stone should swap back neatly."

"Won't the ship sink to the bottom of the ocean?" I ask.

"Sure, but no need to worry, we've got these," he says, tapping the amber nexus on his chest, though his nexus is hidden, strapped to his chest under his dress shirt. "And we won't need to swim back up. As soon as we've returned to Earth, I can use a teleportrait to get us back home with the arcane conduit."

"Speaking of which, what's our next step?" I ask.

"Unfortunately, the spell isn't as accurate as I'd hoped," Zambrano says. "We're not very close to the demonic citadel."

"We'll need to make our way up there," Seraphex says, pointing with her beak up at the mountain in the background. "Olympus Mons, the tallest mountain in the solar system."

"It doesn't look *that* big," I say. "It's sort of like a really big hill, with a chunk taken out of it at the top." It doesn't look as big as Everest or K2 or any of the big mountains on Earth, with their sharp soaring peaks and glacial snowfields.

How are we on *Mars*? This is nuts. I quietly pull out my backup phone and snap a few photos. And then I pull out one of my back-up-backup phones and snap a few photos on that. You know, just in case. I may not have my videos of the eye of the hurricane, but Parth and Mei will probably find Mars even more cool.

"It's fourteen miles high," Seraphex answers. "Seventy-four thousand feet. Twenty-two thousand meters. Pick any measurement system you like. It's three times taller than Mount Everest."

"Oh," I say.

"But we can jump three times as high in the low gravity on Mars. So it's no big deal!" Zambrano quips.

"*Please* tell me we have some magical way to get up there?" I beg. "Not a week of walking or whatever. The food and water we brought won't last that long."

"Closer to a day of walking," Zambrano says. "But yes, I have a magical plan to get us up there. It would have been easier with Liao Ling here with us, but we'll have to make do."

"I'm glad she got away," I say. "How screwed are we out here without her help?"

"As long as we don't hit any heavy demon resistance, we should be fine," Seraphex says. "The conduit is usually guarded, but not heavily. The primary security system is magical. And you are invisible to the magical security alarm on it, being able to hide from both human and demonic magic."

I look down at my hands, which are still wearing the gauntlets that make me invisible to demons. The undetectability by magic comes naturally from the genetic changes that Susan made when she locked away her own magic.

We discussed this part of the plan when we were sketching out our strategy over the past days and months. My job will be to sneak past the demon guards and magic traps to grab the conduit. When we first came up with the idea, it seemed nice to be using my particular talents to steal from demons and not be breaking any human laws on Earth. Part of me wonders if, were Zambrano ever to be gone, I would be locked up for trespassing, theft, illegal border crossing, or any of my various other crimes.

Now that we're here on Mars, those more intellectual concerns are gone. Now I realize that I'm going to have to walk into a heavily guarded demon stronghold alone, and having left behind one of the two sorcerers who were supposed to be there to help me if trouble should arise.

"We must get the supplies out of the vessel before we depart," Zambrano says, gesturing back at the wreckage of the yacht. "In particular, there is a backpack that has a few powerful magical tools I need. We can leave the conventional weapons behind, I think. Better to travel light—you can't beat a demon with a machine gun."

I hear a skittering noise behind me and spin.

There's a creature that's crawled out from behind a rock. It's about three feet long and looks like a giant cockroach with horned antennae and gross mandibles coming out of its mouth. It's colored a dark rusty red, or perhaps the dust caked on its shell is behind the red color.

"Zambrano!" I shout, and he turns as well, grimacing.

"*End of my rope!*" Zambrano grunts and throws an arm out. What looks like a bright white magic lasso shoots out from his hands. But the red cockroach thing turns and bolts away, leaping behind a red rock outcropping. The lasso comes close but snaps tight and returns to Zambrano empty. The cockroach fully disappears into the rocks, leaving only a trail in the dust.

"Rodney crafted that spell more for strength than for speed and accuracy," Zambrano complains.

"And, due to Rodney Wint's focus on towing capacity over quick captures, that will be the end of the element of surprise," Seraphex gripes.

"What the hell *was* that?" I ask. "Is there actually life on Mars?"

"I've been to Texas, and even they don't make roaches that big," Zambrano cracks.

"It's a skittershell demon," Seraphex explains. "One of the lowest castes of our kind."

"I've never seen one before on Earth," Zambrano remarks.

"If you had the ability to magically move a demon across tens of millions of miles, would you waste that opportunity on a lowly little cockroach of a demon?" Seraphex explains. "They don't have any particular skills or value; they're cannon fodder in a demon army. It's usually the stronger and better-liked demons that make their way to Earth. It's been a long while since I thought about how many disgusting little ones there are in the horde."

"Fair enough," Zambrano says, nodding in agreement. "I certainly wouldn't want them on my planet."

"We should move quickly," Seraphex urges. "And get our gear and get on our way before the skittershell can alert its masters to our incursion. It must have sensed either the magic or the seismic activity when we made the transit from Earth."

We hurry into the broken shell of the yacht, and Zambrano uses a few forceful spells to push aside some of the collapsed metal so we can get our backpacks.

With our gear ready, we gather outside.

"How are we getting up the mountain?" I ask.

"We're going to fly," Zambrano says. "Or, more technically, we're going to shoot ourselves through the air. Except that it's primarily going to work because there's no air."

"I . . . don't know if I quite follow," I say.

"There's unfortunately no magic that allows swift and agile flight through the air. It normally gets very unstable, and there's no reaction mass to expel in an engine."

"Really?" I ask. "With all the things magic can do, it can't make you fly?"

Zambrano shrugs. "Think about how far human technology came before achieving powered flight. It wasn't until 1903. It's harder than you think! Theoretically, you could construct such a thing, and Leonardo da Vinci used magic to power his flying machine, but it's far too unstable for practical use. Magic users have never had the ability or inclination to build technological machines of that complexity. If one wants to fly, it's far easier to simply acquire a helicopter or airplane. They're basically free anyway."

"They're free? They cost millions of dollars . . . unless you steal them," I say, an annoying realization dawning on me as I say it. "Like all the boats, I assume? But what does that do for us now? There are no planes or helicopters to steal." I figured he was stealing them, because of course he was. It's nice to have actual confirmation.

"First off, I won them fair and square. In games of chance that I cheated at. In any event, we have two significant advantages here on Mars that we don't have on Earth," the sorcerer explains.

"Um, low gravity makes it easier to move quickly? To fly?" I guess.

"Something like that! And the incredibly thin atmosphere means none of that pesky air resistance that ruins my fun so frequently. If we use magic to blast ourselves into the air at a good angle, we will soar high and far, with low gravity and lack of atmosphere allowing us to fly great distances and accurately."

"And what happens when we get there?" I ask. "How do we slow down without splatting like pancakes?"

"I will decelerate without significant problems," Seraphex points out. "I am quite hardy."

"I will not," I complain. "Since I am not an invincible demon."

"Oh, we'll figure something out by the time we get there," Zambrano says.

"WHAT?!"

"I'm kidding," he says. "Get the fungus out of your backpack. I stuck it in the side pocket."

I look in my backpack, which to my surprise does have a hunk of fungus in one of the side pockets. It's a solid tan half circle of the kind you find hanging off the trunks of trees. It has a slit down the side that looks like it was made with a sharp knife or scalpel.

"Now reach inside the fungus," Zambrano says.

"Ugh, am I going to find something gross?" I complain. "It's going to be disgusting, isn't it?"

"I might suggest that it's your dirty little human fingers that are the gross part going into that delightful little combination of fungus and algae. It's a miracle of symbiosis. When was the last time you washed your hands?"

"It was. . . . We were having a battle, okay?" I protest. "Fine, here goes nothing."

I reach into the fungus and feel around. It's a bit spongy but not all that gross. Feeling around, I find a small, round pebble. I pull it out, turning it over in my hand. It's got a familiar look and feel.

"Is this the magic heavy pebble?" I say, putting the pieces together. In one of our early adventures, I used it in Chicago to break through numerous doors and some windows. It is fairly light when it's touching living matter—like when I'm holding it now in my hand—but without touching living matter, it becomes thousands of times heavier, easily breaking through various barriers.

"Precisely, our old friend the ponderous pebble," Zambrano says. "We'll use it as reaction mass to slow us down when we get near the top of the volcano. You hold on to it tight and hand it to me when I ask for it. *Carefully.* I will need one hand to stabilize us and the other to make us invisible with the illusion prism."

"Okay, sounds good," I agree. It's nice to have a job, but it's also nice to have an easy job. Hold on to the rock, hand it off when instructed. Piece of cake. "So it's called the ponderous pebble?"

Zambrano shrugs. "I made that up. I never used it before you were around; if I need to put some extra weight on things, I use magic. It has a ring to it though, doesn't it?"

"Sure, why not?" I agree. "Should we do this?"

"Yes, indeed!" Zambrano says, switching his backpack around backward to hang off his chest. "Get on my back, and I'll blast us off."

"You'll what?" I ask.

"I'll cast the spell that shoots us off the ground up into the air. We should get going before more demons show up."

I heave a deep sigh. "This is the most ridiculous possible way to do this, isn't it? Couldn't we have brought a Mars rover or a helicopter or something with us?"

"Do you have access to a vehicle that can climb or fly up the largest mountain in the solar system? It would take a quite specialized vehicle," Zambrano says, raising an eyebrow. "If you do, now is a rather late time to mention it."

"No, I don't," I admit.

"Precisely. And so, hop on!" he says with a shit-eating grin. "Let Uncle Zambrano give you a piggyback ride to the summit of the mountain."

"God. Damn. It." Reluctantly, I clamber onto Zambrano's back and help Seraphex up to lodge herself in between us.

First, Zambrano uses the illusion prism to make us invisible to our enemies. Luckily, once the effect is active, we can still see one another, but we appear mostly transparent.

With me still on his back, Zambrano turns, facing away from the mountain, and shouts an incantation.

"*Ad astra per magnas explosiones!*" he calls out, and we are jolted upward as the ground beneath us is blasted with white and blue force. As we rise, successive bolts of energy shoot out, exploding off the ground and rebounding to an invisible barrier around us. With each jolt we accelerate farther, the shield absorbing the energy of the push off the ground and making us go faster and faster. The spell directs the energy of the explosions in a lance of energy straight from the ground each time, impacting us and giving us head-spinning speed.

We are thrown into the Martian sky, twirling slightly before Zambrano mutters a small spell and flattens his right hand, stabilizing us. His left hand is holding the illusion prism, which is masking our travel through the sky. I can feel him as I hold on tightly, and if I glance down, I see his semitransparent body.

"I never could get that spell to work on Earth," Zambrano says with delight. "The gravity makes it so hard to get going at first. And then the air resistance caps your speed and range. With no air resistance, we've been able to get to a speed of around five hundred miles an hour."

"I do rather prefer teleportation, or at least flying first class," Seraphex complains. "The yacht was nice, with the sea breeze."

"Could you make a perpetual motion machine with this?" I ask, feeling the ponderous pebble, its weight light in my palm as the thin air rushes by us, howling.

"A what?" Zambrano shouts back.

"A perpetual motion machine. Or even use it to generate energy? Use its heavy mode to push down on a piston or lever or something and then touch it with something living while it lifts back up."

"Oh. Why would you want to do that?" He is using his hands to cast small stabilizing spells, keeping us upright and making minor adjustments to our flight. Below, the terrain moves by rapidly. My stomach turns slightly as I notice we're at our peak and starting to descend again. Even in low gravity, falling toward the ground does not feel good.

"Infinite free energy?" I suggest. "Power the world?" Ahead, the mountain is growing larger and larger, a massive plateau rising above the surrounding terrain.

"As the old demonic saying goes," Seraphex says, "'There's no such thing as a free lunch unless you can find someone who has lunch and kill him and take it.' There's a lot of power stored that went into the creation of the ponderous pebble. But it gets slightly weaker with frequent use. It would weaken over time as you expended kinetic energy from it."

"Oh. Damn," I say. "Too bad."

"Pebble!" Zambrano shouts, and I hand him the pebble, carefully transferring it with both hands to ensure it doesn't fall.

He holds the ponderous pebble in his right hand, and I can feel us grow less steady as he stops the stabilizing magic.

He opens his palm, pushing the pebble in front of us, but with almost no force so it's moving away very slowly despite how fast we are rushing through the sky over the ground.

"*Shove off!*" he shouts in a singsong voice and stabs two fingers forward. A pillar of spiky orange energy blasts at it.

The pebble accelerates slowly at first, then faster and faster. As it does, I can see on the ground below that our momentum is slowing down steadily. I'm no physics expert, but it seems Zambrano is pushing against the mass of the pebble to slow us down, which sends it at tremendous acceleration toward the ground.

Ahead of us, the pebble smashes into the mountainside, sending up a shower of rocks and dust. There's no sound, given the lack of atmosphere, but I'm very glad we are undershooting the area of the impact.

Our forward momentum has been slowed by pushing away from the pebble, and I feel a lurch as we start to drop. I grip tightly to Zambrano, ignoring his uncomfortable movements. This was his idea, and I'm not going to go tumbling off into the sky.

"*Schachtgleiten!*" Zambrano shouts as our forward movement has slowed relative to the ground. This new spell cuts down our falling momentum as well. I feel weightless as we slowly drift downward to the ground. I can't see the effects of the spell due to the illusion prism, but it is the same feeling I got in Chicago when he used a spell to slow my fall from the Willis Tower. He casts a few more small stabilizing spells, and we drift down slowly, with gravity greatly reduced even from its lowered Martian level. I'm grateful for that, with the sorcerer here to control our descent. When he used this spell to slow my fall outside the Willis Tower in Chicago, in order to keep myself from drifting out of the spell's column of effect, I was forced to use my clothes and some . . . less tasteful things as reaction mass to stay in the column.

We land smoothly and dust ourselves off. A few seconds after we've landed, there's a sudden but brief shaking of the earth and a rumbling beneath us.

"That was spectacular!" Zambrano brags. "It worked exactly as I planned."

"It was reckless and showboating," Seraphex says. "But it did work."

I flex my hands, which are sore and tingling from holding a death grip on Zambrano for so long. That was not exactly my definition of fun, but at least we didn't crash-land or something. "Great, so should we go grab the ponderous pebble?" I ask.

"Oh, it's embedded at least half a mile into the surface," Zambrano says breezily. "A small, indestructible and incredibly dense item like that, it would have ripped right through the rock. It may have even triggered some tectonic activity, which would explain the seismic shock after we landed."

"You mean it's gone?" I complain. "The ponderous pebble is gone already?"

"Cost of doing business," Zambrano answers airily.

"But we only just named it!" I say.

"We gave it a descriptive name, not like, Pierre or something," Zambrano says.

"It means 'rock' in French," Seraphex injects. "Poor Pierre the Ponderous Pebble, abandoned thousands of feet beneath the Martian surface."

"We could also have painted eyes and a smiling face on it, if we wanted, but we didn't do that either," Zambrano adds. "So losing it is no big deal."

"You two are not helping," I say in annoyance. "Now I miss the poor guy. What's our next step? Where is this demonic citadel where the arcane conduit is hidden?"

CHAPTER 12

I look out across the empty Martian landscape while Zambrano, his brow furrowed, does some small spells and consults with Seraphex to get their bearings.

Beneath the pale pink sky, I can distinctly see the curve of the horizon, with a range of volcanoes in the distance to my right and an endless expanse of reddish brown plains to my left. It is stunningly beautiful, stark, and utterly empty, and my sight of it is visibly sharp in a way that views from the tops of mountains on Earth are not. That must be from the lack of atmosphere to create haze and blurring. Even with the amber nexus radiating warmth, I can still feel a slight chill.

Looking up at the sky, I see a bright object in it, outshining all the stars. I've never been much good at locating planets and constellations, but I wonder if that might be the Earth.

For a moment, the fear and dread that I've been harboring for this whole trip melts away. Yes, I'm worried about how Rex is manipulating entire countries and stirring up disasters back on Earth. And I'm worried whether Parth, Liao Ling, and Mei are all safe with half our team off-planet and unable to help them. Not to mention Agent Crane, my parents, Susan . . .

But for a split second, that all fades away. And I'm proud to be here, fighting for humanity, standing on the highest peak on Mars, the largest mountain in the solar system.

"Are we the first humans to stand on this mountain?" I ask. "The first to get to its peak, even if we did use magic? But when Edmund

Hillary climbed Mount Everest for the first time he used oxygen, didn't he?"

"You're disregarding the many demons who have been on this mountain. You're also forgetting Sherpa Tenzing Norgay, who reached the peak of Everest at the same time," Seraphex notes dryly, "and still you are not even the first humans here. Merlin was here shortly before he died at the hands of Demon Duchess Typhoria."

"Goddamn old Merlin," Zambrano gripes. "Hogging all the glory for himself. Did he leave more of his traps behind as well?"

"I can't imagine he would have had time for that," Seraphex says. "After Merlin opened the arcane conduit gate, the demons came through and realized what had happened quite quickly. There was a brief battle, but as more and more demons came through, he had no chance. No mere human could stand long against a few major demons."

"He could have set up traps before he opened the portal though, correct?" Zambrano asks.

"Are you suggesting that before opening up the arcane conduit portal, Merlin spent time setting traps that were intended to catch intruders like us, thousands of years later, after a death that he must surely have known was almost inevitable?"

"I wouldn't put it past the old codger," Zambrano grumbles. "But the demonic citadel does seem like more of a challenge."

"We should move quickly, before my fellow demons realize what we are after," Seraphex says. "They are certainly aware of our presence. The landscape has changed over the centuries, but now that I have my bearings, I know the way."

We start off, walking with light low-gravity steps under the strange pinkish-orange sky.

Viewed from above, like in the maps we reviewed before making the trip, the mountain looks like a gigantic pancake with a dimple in the side, much flatter than most mountains on Earth. The ridged cliff at the outside, where we initially landed, is called the aureole, which also makes me think it looks kind of like a boob with an inverted nipple. Which isn't important, but you have to keep occupied somehow while bouncing across the mostly featureless Martian terrain. It's amazing how fast you can become acclimated to an environment and be bored and automatically check your phone. Unfortunately, my cell phone network does not have roaming service on Mars, and I don't have any podcasts downloaded, so I have to listen to the only thing I have access to, *The Zambrano and Seraphex Bickering Show.* Coming soon to your favorite streaming app.

After about half an hour of walking and bouncing along the landscape, we reach the edge of the caldera. Peering down over the rim, Seraphex points out the small flat platform that marks the entrance to the citadel. Luckily, this part we have planned for. Seraphex laid out detailed diagrams of the demonic citadel for us, which I've mostly memorized.

We use another *Schachtgleiten* spell to create a column of fall-slowing arcane energy for us to descend the cliff at the edge of the caldera. This time, with less adrenaline, I notice as we fall that the edges of it disappear above and below us, masked by Zambrano's use of the illusion prism.

After we land, we start walking and I clock Zambrano making small motions by the magical prism.

"Follow the plan, and this should all work," Seraphex says.

In between us, Zambrano has created an illusion of the figure of a giant demon rears up with fluttering batlike wings and a ridged, proud head and tusks coming out her mouth. She struts like a queen, though technically she is only a duchess.

I also look down at my hands and body and see nothing at all. The invisibility illusion is making them semitransparent, which at first makes me stumble as I try to walk on the uneven ground. Combined with the low gravity, it takes some time to get my footing and walk without tripping.

I do take one tumble, but with the lack of atmosphere to transmit sound, Zambrano, who is walking ahead of us, doesn't even seem to notice.

Seraphex, who had been riding on my shoulder, dusts herself off and gives me an annoyed look. Then she sees Zambrano obliviously continuing on and gives me a little wink.

"Thanks," I mouth and help her back up onto my shoulder. With the thin air, flying upward is more or less impossible for her.

"I shall graciously forgive your clumsiness," she says, "this time."

We continue along the way, moving down the rocky slope toward the citadel entrance.

"Is it possible that the security procedures have changed?" I ask after my brain and limbs have adjusted to the invisibility.

"There aren't serious security procedures here," Seraphex says. The demons are constantly at one another's throats, but they all know who is who. None of them has illusion magic to fool anyone else, and demons do not reproduce or die easily, so there is no real change beyond the shifting alliances and jockeying for power. And no one would dare question Typhoria, mistress of hurricanes."

"Let's hope they haven't changed that since Rex came back," I mutter.

"Worst case, I can handle a couple slitherfang demons," Zambrano says. "Wouldn't mind a little blasting, though it would probably attract unwanted attention, and we would need to rush while inside."

"Stop worrying; we can do this," Seraphex chides. "Now be quiet. I'll do the voice. They'll get suspicious if they hear anything else."

We walk around a few boulders, up a sloping pathway, and reach a platform with an unassuming entrance to a rocky cave. In front, a snakelike demon is waiting, standing stiffly at attention as it recognizes a much higher-ranking demon approaching.

I see Seraphex moving her mouth and hear the sounds of heavy footfalls. She is damn impressive with her vocal mimicry.

The guard demon has a long greenish snake body dusted in red Mars rock but with some scales showing through. Its head looks like a cobra's with glowing beady eyes and a hood flared out behind its neck.

"Duchessss Typhoria," the slitherfang demon hisses. There's something strange about the way that his voice hits my ears, as if it's coming from inside my head rather than from an external voice. "I wasss not told to expect you."

"So I defy expectations, Raskale," the haughty and cold voice of Duchess Typhoria says, issuing from Seraphex's little duck mouth. I can understand it, as well, in the same way. "Stand aside, servant."

I look down at the gauntlets and see there's a small gem that glows in sync as each of the demons speak to each other, in time with the sounds of their voices. It must be translating the demonic language they're speaking. That's a pretty cool bonus feature!

"Of coursssse, Your Graccce," the demon says, bowing and scraping. He hustles back to the door, performs an intricate tapping on a stone panel, and the large stone door slides open with a grinding that is audible even through Mars's thin air.

We pass by, and the creature eyes us as we do and then looks away, respectfully averting his gaze.

Moving along swiftly, we enter a long rough-hewn hallway with a surface of reddish rocks. It leads down at a gently sloping angle that takes us steadily deeper under the planet's surface.

"Something is off about him," Seraphex whispers once we're well away from the entryway.

"Why," I ask, "he gave us exactly what we wanted, didn't he? We needed the door opened and the alarm not raised. Isn't that good?"

"Exactly," Seraphex says. "Any low-level demon should be attempting to curry favor, or threaten us, or trick us. Not *calmly do his job.* That is very un-demon-like. Some are brutes, some are conniving, some are cruel. None are calmly professional."

"Perhaps the demonic culture has changed," Zambrano suggests. "You've been away for well over a hundred years. Perhaps they have modernized and have a Demonic Resources department. Team-building exercises. Vengeance Accounts Payable. That sort of thing."

"After fourteen centuries here, that type of total change seems unlikely, though I would welcome it." Seraphex sniffs. "We should make this quick. Let's get to the armory and grab the conduit."

"I'm switching the illusion to the fluffback demons," Zambrano announces quietly, making some adjustments to the illusion prism he's holding out. This is according to the plan, which calls for us to use the illusion of the powerful Duchess Typhoria to gain entrance easily, but then swap it for something less likely to attract attention inside—small scurrying creatures with horned heads and furry shoulders called fluffback demons. Demons can sense the presence of other demons, so we can't just be invisible, Seraphex will also have to mask her presence enough to impersonate a smaller demon.

I know, fluffback demons sound kind of cute, but trust me, the illusion of a small demon with a nasty pinched face and hunched furry shoulders is not one that anyone could love.

As we walk down the entry hallway, I notice Zambrano glancing around suspiciously.

"If you're looking for Merlin's traps, you won't find any," Seraphex says. "This entire citadel was built a hundred years after his death. There are low-level demon guards, but that's all. The citadel is the access point to the Torrid Red Wastes, the warm underground caverns where demons have taken shelter on Mars. The citadel itself is usually considered neutral territory unless there's a particularly nasty fight going on."

We pass through a series of chambers and corridors, somewhere between caves and actual architecture. They certainly don't have the precision and straight-edged construction of Merlin's Vault. They are lit by a ribbon of some sort of glowing reddish material that runs in a line down the center of the floor of each tunnel, splitting when the routes diverge.

We see a few demons scurrying by in the distance, and one large ironside demon comes directly down our corridor. We keep walking, and the illusory fluffback demon cowers and bows its head as it passes.

"Pathetic," the ironside sneers, shaking his head as we walk by. For a moment it slightly tenses its hand as if it's about to take a swipe at the smaller demon. But then it shrugs, probably deciding it's not even worth it, and it stalks off, its heavy footsteps vibrating the corridor.

We hurry deeper into the citadel, and at last reach a more neatly carved part of the structure. Along a passageway that slopes down, there's a massive door on the left-hand wall, a giant circle with a line splitting it down the middle. Carved around it are circular designs, swirling out to the edges.

"It's sealed like this," Seraphex explains, "so that lower-level demons can't have access to our weapons for their petty skirmishes. These doors will only open to the upper echelon of demonic powers. Dukes, duchesses, kings, and most importantly . . ."

"The demon queen," I finish for her.

"Very good; get on with it," Zambrano says. "Let's get in there, grab the conduit, and get out of here. This has all gone far too smoothly. I don't like it."

Seraphex walks up to the door. She stands there in front of it for a moment, her tiny body contrasting against the massive edifice of stone that she faces.

"In the name of Seraphex, the demon queen, open the armory to me!"

We wait.

There's a slight grinding sound, and my pulse quickens. Will it work?

But then the noise stops. The doors sit there, unmoving.

"Let me guess, that's never happened to you before?" Zambrano asks, earning himself a withering glance from the demon duck.

She steps closer to the door.

"*In nomine Seraphex, reginae daemonum, aperi mihi armamentarium!*" she declares, in what I recognize as Latin.

Again, the doors shake slightly, but not enough to open.

"*En tō onomati tēs Seraphex, tēs basilissēs tōn daimonōn, anoixon moi to hoplostasion!*" she tries.

I glance at Zambrano.

"Ancient Greek," he explains.

The door grinds.

Nothing happens.

Seraphex pecks angrily at the door, fluttering her wings against it in a rage.

She opens her beak, and screams, "*Ina* šum *Seraphex,* šarrat šēdī, *petē ana yâti bīt kakkē!*"

She stands back, and the door shifts slightly again but falls back into place and doesn't open to any meaningful degree.

"What language was that?" I ask.

"I don't speak it," Zambrano says, "but I believe that was Akkadian, the imperial language of Babylon. Seraphex, I didn't know that you spoke it either?"

"Spoke what?" Seraphex says. "English, Latin, and Greek all failed. I don't have any other ideas."

"You tried Akkadian too," I say, confused.

"I tried what?" Seraphex says. "I think I know what the problem is. But you're not going to like the solution."

"That is most peculiar," Zambrano says, eyeing the demon duck. "Do you genuinely not remember speaking in Akkadian?"

"Speaking in what? I don't know what language that is," she says, cocking her head to the side in confusion.

"Fascinating," Zambrano says. "Do you know of the ancient civilization of Babylon?"

"Is that from a video game?" Seraphex asks. "I never paid much attention to those. No opposable thumbs for the controller, and all."

"This is all very interesting, but we should focus on opening the door," I say. "If there's a way to do that?"

"Yes, let us focus on what matters," Seraphex says, shaking herself and ruffling her feathers for a moment as if shedding something. "The door will not open for me in this state."

"Have you been shut off from it?" Zambrano asks. "Did the demons reprogram it?"

"No," says with a shake of the head. "If they had, it would simply ignore me. The problem is that it will open for Seraphex, the demon queen. But it won't open for Seraphex, the duck. I'm too different from what it expects."

"I am *not* releasing the transmogrification spell," Zambrano says firmly. "Don't think I'm going to fall for that."

"You don't need to release it entirely," Seraphex says. "Only the smallest bit. Let a tiny amount of my demonic energy come out for a few seconds. Then you can return the spell fully."

Zambrano stares at her. "Is this a trick?"

"It is not a trick," Seraphex answers. "I am not lying to you. You know that."

The sorcerer looks over at me. "Bryce, we agreed you would be the moral conscience of the group. Is this a terrible idea?"

I open my mouth, then shut it. *I'm* the one who has to make the decision here?

"I don't know," I say. "We need more assurances at least. I guess?"

Zambrano nods.

"Seraphex, will you allow me to perform this spell, to let a small amount of your demonic nature be revealed? And do you know of any reason that I will not be able to reverse the effect, and put you back as you are, with the same restrictions and limitations, and no better ability to escape your form?" Zambrano glares at her, daring her to agree.

Seraphex nods. "I concur. I will let you perform the spell to completion, restoring me to my full duck form, with no changes. I will be equally as trapped after as before, in my every expectation."

Zambrano glances over to me again. "Well, what do you think?"

I sigh.

"I don't have a better alternative. Let's try it."

Zambrano nods grimly. He pulls his illusion prism out of his backpack. "The spell is ultimately derived from the power of illusions, though a thousand times more powerful. But this same artifact will work to store a small part of it."

Holding the prism out, he begins an incantation.

"*In using this transmogrification reversal spell crafted by Alix the Sorcerer, who is both beautiful and brilliant, I acknowledge that I am almost certainly making a mistake,*" Zambrano intones. At the mention of Alix, a wistful smile crosses his face. "*I am crafting the words of this spell in the lowly brutish language of English so that if some idiot like Zambrano or Rodney Wint uses it for a terrible reason, there is the greatest possible chance that someone nearby will hear and stop them. These final two sentences are intended to waste additional time, in order to give any saner individuals close by a chance to stop them, if they are indeed making a terrible mistake. It will be too late for anyone other than the spellcaster to stop the process, starting NOW.*"

As he finishes the words of the spell, ghostly tendrils of energy begin reaching from Seraphex, questing toward the prism.

"She did have a way with creating the incantations for spells, my Alix did," Zambrano says with a sad chuckle, blinking repeatedly.

Seraphex is bathed in a mix of light and darkness, swirling and growing, shooting shadows of spikes and claws on the walls. Crackling white magical energy flows across the empty space from Seraphex to the prism, while angry red energy swells up around her form as it grows.

I like the duck version a lot better. This Seraphex looks like she could tear me apart in a few seconds and wouldn't think twice about it.

"In the name of Seraphex, the demon queen, open the armory to me!" Seraphex says, and her voice comes out with thunderous undertones of harshness and violence, far beyond the normal vibrance.

Her head, still vaguely that of a duck but with ridges and horns rapidly growing out of it, turns to Zambrano.

It doesn't feel right, and I want my infuriating feathered friend back as soon as possible.

"You may stop it now," she says, her voice resonating with a dangerous fury.

"*I have made a terrible mistake. Alix was right as always; reverse the reversal!*" Zambrano says, and the white energy suddenly halts in midair and then flows back, wrapping around Seraphex and appearing to tighten like a python around its prey.

True to her word, she does not resist, standing calmly as the flickering shadow of her demonic form is bound and sinks back into her duck body, wrapped up by the white energy. I breathe a sigh of relief as the projections around the room disappear and her shape returns to normal.

In a moment, the magic around us fizzles out, and again we're just a sorcerer, his assistant, and a duck.

But while we were watching the glowing magic, the door has fully opened.

Ahead of us, the way to the armory is clear.

CHAPTER 13

We step forward into the armory. It's a long corridor with open-doored chambers on either side.

"I know we're here for the conduit, but can I *finally* get a cool magic weapon I can keep?" I ask. "Not that the gauntlets aren't great and all."

Zambrano looks at Seraphex. "You'll probably cut your own leg off, but it's your leg to cut off. What do you think, duck? Are there any good demonic armaments for young Bryce here?"

She has hopped ahead of us and is looking in each of the rooms. I stride forward, peeking in the first one. It's the size of a large moving truck, and on the wall are racks of weapons. Swords, axes, bows, clubs, a trident, and more.

"I promised to be your friend, Bryce," Seraphex says.

"Yes," I agree. "And don't forget it."

"Would a friend let a friend take an item of power that was haunted by demonic spirits and would, each time it was wielded, tear away at his soul and sanity?" she asks as we reach the next room, which is full of shields of varying designs.

"Ugh, no. No, she wouldn't do that," I admit.

"Oh, I'm sure Bryce could resist the temptation to turn to the dark side and become a murderous fiend," Zambrano says.

"The conduit is not like that," Seraphex explains. "It was created by humans. The rest of these items were forged by demons back in the glory days when we ran wild across the Earth. Once we were here on Mars, we reached an agreement to store them all here. Using them against one another was creating too much chaos, so we locked them all away to be saved for our eventual return to subjugate your planet."

"How charming," I say. "So none of them are safe? Not even a little one?"

We reach the end of the rooms, past one with a giant battering ram and another that is empty except for a single pen in an inkwell. We turn into the one on the left. It contains an assortment of fairly standard spears, but at the back of the rack is a staff that looks familiar.

It's a long twisted length of metal that looks sort of like three separate staffs braided together. I recognize it immediately—the other half of the arcane conduit. The piece on Earth was thrown into the sun and destroyed after the battle of Yellowstone, but this identical one is sitting here like none of that happened.

It is bound into the wall by what look like outcroppings of the stone itself, which are inscribed with demonic runes I can't decipher.

"Armory, yield the powers of this weapon to me," Seraphex says to the trapped staff.

"It doesn't recognize you, the same as before?" Zambrano asks.

"To release it, I will need to release a part of my demonic energy again," Seraphex says. "Just as before. You can stop the process at the same place, and I offer the same guarantees and assurances as I did then."

Zambrano grudgingly agrees, and they perform the spell again.

"*In using this transmogrification reversal spell crafted by Alix the Sorcerer, who is both beautiful and brilliant, I acknowledge that I am almost certainly making a mistake,*" Zambrano begins, and I can feel the nostalgia dripping from his voice accompanied by a sad smile.

He completes the spell and pulls a small part of the transmogrification spell back. Seraphex's duck figure is once again surrounded by shadows and magical energy.

"Armory, yield the powers of this weapon to me," she says again, and now the stone around the arcane conduit begins to glow and dissolve.

"This will take a minute," Seraphex says. "But you can undo the spell. Being half duck and half demon is not a pleasant experience."

"Does this feel like it's going too smoothly?" Zambrano complains as the energy of the spell rushes back into Seraphex, tightening on her and restoring her normal shape.

"Because none of your plans ever go smoothly?" Seraphex points out as she returns full to her duck feeling, the shadows and magical energy dispersing.

"My plans can go smoothly! Flawlessly. They are works of genius."

Seraphex looks over at me.

"How many of the plans you've been involved in have gone off as designed, without surprises, improvisation, or unexpected risks?"

"Um." I think about it for a minute. Poisonous frog, wrecked laser tag arena, battles with several massive demons, traps at the bottom of the ocean, multiple battles at sea . . . "I can't think of any, to be honest."

"But we always pull through, don't we?" Zambrano exclaims. "We work together and figure it out! As a team!"

"Bryce very often figures it out," Seraphex notes. "After your plan backfires or goes sideways."

In front of us, the stone holding the conduit in place is glowing brightly, as if molten, and has mostly receded.

"He's a very keen young man," Zambrano says. "He's made an excellent intern and assistant."

"Wait, I'm still an assistant?" I complain, though I don't care. The title is basically a joke anyway.

"Well, sure. What, are you jockeying for a promotion?"

I shrug. "I have helped save the world."

"Fine, you can be . . . I don't know, project manager?"

"Uh." Suddenly something catches inside me. Do I have any business *managing* anything? When I was Zambrano's intern, I jumped from crisis to crisis, trying to not get killed. Do I want to manage this madness? Have the responsibility and accountability of being *in charge* of something?

I stand silently, feeling panic clawing at my throat as my body freezes up.

"You bully me into offering you a promotion and then you back out of it?" Zambrano demands.

I take a deep breath. "No, no, I'll take it." It's a meaningless joke title anyway, right? Certainly any court system on Earth will hold me accountable for my actions no matter what the name of the fake job title the "dark sorcerer" gives me.

That thought started out helpful but did not end up making me feel any better.

"Does it come with a corner office?" I joke weakly.

"Yes, absolutely," Zambrano says. "That's the benefit. Done and done. Congratulations," he adds, vigorously shaking my hand.

"Wait, is there really a corner office?" I ask.

Zambrano grins. "Your room is already in the corner of the building. I'll have the birch butlers put a little plaque outside it that says 'Bryce Alexander, Project Manager.' Much more official than your old 'intern' hat. No parking space though. Not in New York City; don't be ridiculous!"

"But my room doesn't have any windows! Isn't a corner office supposed to have windows?"

Zambrano shrugs. "Too late, you agreed to it. The arcane conduit appears to be released from the stone." He steps forward and gingerly maneuvers it free.

The joking around has distracted me from my panic, but still, somehow the thought of being "manager" freaks me out. Could I manage a Samba Smoothies? A project at some big tech company? Sure! But now I'm the project manager of Project: Make Sure the Demon King Doesn't Kill Everyone. Yikes.

"We don't have all day," Seraphex says. "Bryce, it's time for your first duty as project manager. Use your gauntlets and pick up the arcane conduit. Slowly and carefully."

Cautiously, I step forward. I wrap my gauntlet-covered hands around the conduit and gently lift it up.

"Now walk it out of the room. There's a special protective spell that sets off alarms if any human or demon carries it outside this room."

Gingerly, I walk out of the room. It wouldn't surprise me one bit if the "alarm" included a jolt of electricity or a blast of acid or something.

But I walk clear of the room without incident.

"Okay, done," I say. "Wait, you brought me all the way to Mars just to pick something up and walk a few feet with it?"

"And what a splendid job you did of it too. You managed that project admirably," Zambrano says. "See, you're going to do great in your new role! Plus, now you also get to *carry it*," he adds with a smirk. "What career fulfillment!"

I guess my job description also includes carrying around anything that Zambrano doesn't feel like lugging. I grip the conduit in my gauntleted gloves, imagining I can feel the power resonating from it. Though, with my magical insensitivity, it feels like a big fancy hunk of metal. I didn't get an awesome enchanted demonic weapon, but these artifacts are supernaturally durable. So I guess I could bash a demon with this if I needed to.

"Hold on," Seraphex says, craning her neck to see into one of the other holding rooms as we pass by it.

"What?" Zambrano says. "We should get out of here before the demons realize what we're doing."

"You will want to see this," Seraphex says, flapping off my shoulder and hopping into one of the rooms. "I'm surprised this is here; it's usually out in the center of the Torrid Red Wastes, keeping things warm."

We step into the room, and Seraphex waddles to the far end. Sitting there on a low pedestal is a small globe of glass. Inside there's red power pulsing and swirling slowly. Its look reminds me of diagrams of the Earth's magma core underneath the mantle—pure superheated rock. As we get closer, I can feel heat radiating from it.

"Is this one cursed to corrupt and destroy us?" I ask.

"No, other than the fact that there's a giant demon hiding inside if you break it," Seraphex answers.

"It's incredibly powerful," Zambrano says, doing a few magic detection spells.

"Oh, and even better," she says as she approaches closely and squints at it, "the demon is our old friend Vulkatherak."

"Ah, yes, Volcanose," Zambrano says, recalling the nickname we gave for the giant lava demon we defeated many months ago. "He fled Earth for Mars, but it appears the demons here did not welcome him with open arms."

"Vulkatherak was planning to reinforce the prismatic prison, if he had gained the power of the demon legions, to keep the demon king from challenging him. After my former husband was released," Seraphex explains, "the demons on Mars probably joined forces to subdue and punish him this way. They are all looking to curry favor now that their king has returned. Vulkatherak couldn't run far enough away."

"What is the artifact called?" I ask.

"It's the heart of the volcano, a prison specifically designed for a lava demon," Seraphex explains. "They compressed his form to fit in the tiny sphere, and so all the energy that normally exists in him is super amplified. The demonic magic is desperately trying to restore him to his full form, and because of a quirk in his volcanic nature, that all comes out as heat. It's very scientific—heat increases exponentially as volume decreases."

"I was never that great in physics, but I'm not sure that's exactly how this sort of thing would work," I say.

"Demonic magic does work in peculiar ways, the same that mine does. But what can it be used for?" Zambrano asks.

"It's a power source," Seraphex explains. "Here on Mars, a lava demon usually is trapped in it, and they use it to release energy as heat. That's part of what keeps the Torrid Red Wastes so warm. But we could harness its energy to activate the arcane conduit," she says, nodding at the silver staff I'm holding. "At least for long enough to trap my former husband with our endless teleportation track. Unfortunately, it's nowhere near strong enough to hold him itself, even if he were the right type of demon for it."

"So what do we do with it?" I ask.

"Grab it and get out of here," Seraphex says.

Zambrano takes the small sphere, disappearing it into one of the interior pockets of his suit.

"Let's go," he says with a satisfied grin.

We reach the outer door to the armory, and as we pass outside it, it begins to close as if sensing the armory is now empty.

"This is perfect," Zambrano says. "We got our objective, and we got a big bonus as well. Now we sneak back to the yacht, and we are out of here, mission accomplished."

Personally, I never use that phrase, at least not prematurely. And this definitely turns out to be premature.

As we walk back up the corridor, a group of demons suddenly rounds the bend up ahead, purposefully marching toward us. In the lead is our fluffback friend from the main door, the cockroach-like skittershell demon we saw after we arrived, and a truly massive demon with enormous horns, spiked mandibles, and gigantic batwings that barely fit in this tunnel.

"It's the intruders I saw on the surface!" the small skittershell demon shouts.

"Assss I told you," the snake demon gloats to the large batwing demon. "Typhoria is on Earth, creating storms for our returned king. I knew she could not have returned so quickly."

"Oh, shit," Zambrano says. "So much for a smooth in and out."

"It was too good to hope for," Seraphex says, hopping up onto me and gripping my shoulder.

"*Suppressing fire!*" Zambrano calls out, shooting finger guns at the oncoming demons. Darts of violet and blue energy shoot out from his hands, swirling and splashing into the demons. They don't seem to do much damage but do push them back and distract them, continuing to shoot from the spot where he initiated the spell long after he's moved on.

"What do we do now?" I ask.

"Now? We run!" he shouts, turning and setting an impressive example of exactly what he suggests.

I'm light on my feet, though still awkwardly adjusting to the difference of gravity. Seraphex, with the lack of air rendering her unable to fly effectively, grips tightly to my shoulder with her feet and wings.

Zambrano, with his magically enhanced body, is hard to keep up with, but I've been running regularly, knowing that a situation like this was inevitable. I'm able to stay relatively close behind him.

"Can we circle around and get out?" Zambrano asks as both of us struggle to get a rhythm on the uneven floor with the unfamiliar physics.

"Take the next right and then another right," Seraphex suggests. "But they will likely have guards there."

"Worth a shot," Zambrano says and leads the way, pulling his illusion prism out once again. "Maybe we can fool them. Stay close."

But at the first right-hand turn, we round the corner and see another group of demons advancing, this time led by a tall and thin but muscular greenish demon with four arms and an extremely angular head.

It has glowing green eyes set in deep sockets that glare at us with piercing intensity. "Do not be fooled," she tells her entourage of skittershell demons. "They are directly ahead."

"No dice there," Zambrano says, backpedaling. "*Suppressing fire!*" he shouts again, pointing his fingers and sending tiny rockets of magical energy that blast the crowd of demons back.

"Your illusions won't work on the more powerful demons," Seraphex explains. "Especially not if they are looking for it, as they are now. They can sense the energy of both Zambrano and me, even if Bryce is invisible to them."

"Where do we go now?" I ask.

"They are driving us deeper into the tunnels, to the Torrid Red Wastes," Seraphex declares as we run down tunnels that lead downward, further down into the demonic complex.

"Is that as terrible as it sounds?" I ask.

"Now that you mention it, probably not," she says. "It's warm, but nothing you can't handle. And they are vast. If we can make it there, we should be able to at least evade them for some time."

We run through the confusing corridors, occasionally catching sight of demons down hallways, but Seraphex is able to guide us through the maze. Finally, the tunnels begin to widen.

"Slow down," Seraphex suggests. "Take this last bit quietly. Let's see if we can sneak past the entry point here."

We proceed more cautiously. Thankfully, with the poor noise conduction on Mars, our light human footfalls won't have alerted anyone. We turn the last corner, and Zambrano holds up a hand, signaling us to pause.

At the far end of this tunnel, where it narrows into an opening about the size of a small moving van, we can see a group of fluffback demons holding spears.

We stand there for a moment. The group is gathered at the cave entrance, looking around nervously. I get the sense that they were recently called up for this emergency guard duty and don't know what's going on.

Zambrano sticks out his tongue at them. He puts his hands up to his head and waggles his fingers.

"I'm pretty sure they can't see us," I say. They are chattering to each other but not focused on them at all.

Zambrano gives them the middle finger. "It's not about testing that. I have the regards of many different human cultures to deliver to them." He follows it up with a reverse peace sign, pushing his thumb between his index and middle fingers, giving a thumbs-up, and several other gestures, finishing by running the back of his fingers under his chin in an outward flicking motion.

"Are you quite finished?" Seraphex says. "We should sneak past these little cretins."

"I never get the proper chance for that sort of thing," Zambrano whispers as he begins to advance. "Move slowly; they can't hear you. I'll keep the illusion going."

We advance toward the fluffback demons. I can't help but try to place each footstep as quietly as possible, even though I know they likely won't be able to hear it. As we get closer, the real challenge becomes apparent. The demons are shifting around nervously, and they and their long spears are moving constantly.

Seraphex noiselessly hops off my shoulder and onto the ground and effortlessly scampers past the guards, her small size making it easy to slip by undetected.

Zambrano motions for me to hold back and goes first, concentrating fiercely as he controls the illusion prism with one hand, and he stealthily creeps forward. As he approaches, there's a large opening to the left-hand side, and he is able to press himself against the wall and pass through fairly easily.

Once he's through, he steps well back and motions for me to follow. I can see him focusing intensely as the illusion prism glows.

As I get closer, one of the fluffback demons walks over to the spot that Zambrano was occupying and leans against the wall, lazily letting his long spear out in front of him, blocking that area off from passage.

"These fluffback guards have very poor discipline," Seraphex whispers, her voice coming quietly through my earpiece. "If I could reveal myself in my full power, they would pay for their lax attention to security. There would be many lashings tonight and then even more guard duty to teach them the errors of their ways."

"Well, it's a good thing you're not still a demon queen," I say back in hushed tones. "For many reasons, not just that it helps us right now."

"I very much *am* still a demon queen, thank you," Seraphex retorts.

"Of course," I say. "Now let me do this."

I step forward gingerly, trying to watch all seven of the demons at once. They're crowded in the small opening here, but there still looks to be some space between two of them on the right. I move closer, but as soon as I do, one of them steps backward in frustration, gesturing angrily at another, and I can't see a way to cleanly make the move through.

"Be careful," Zambrano says. "You are invisible to them twice over, but they can still tear you apart if they get a hold of you."

"Even pathetic idiot demons like these can be fairly perceptive, if they put their minds to it," Seraphex explains.

I take a deep breath and move toward them again. But unfortunately, they are moving around again, and a spear held to the side blocks my path. Two more times I step up and am forced to pull back because one of them is pacing. Carrying this giant metal arcane conduit is not helping with my agility either.

I step back, grinding my teeth in frustration. I'm supposed to be able to help here, but now I'm only holding the team back. Why am I even here? They could already be fleeing into the Torrid Wasteland or whatever it's called by now and figuring out their next move, but it's too late.

The demons keep moving back and forth, and I'm so close that I can hear them talking to one another.

"The king returning is great news, but it does mean so much more work for us," one of them gripes.

"At least it brought some humans here. Maybe if we catch them, we'll get to eat one of them," the one leaning against the wall adds, licking his lips hungrily.

"Don't be such a sucker, Deverick, we'll never be the ones to catch them," another gripes. "And even if we did, the bigger boys would take them from us for interrogation or magic or whatever they do. Those other types don't understand how delicious a human body is. I'm not missing my one chance in thousands of years to eat one! The moment you see one, bite down and don't let go until you've got a mouthful."

"So if we catch them, we eat them immediately," the first one says. "Tell them that the human was trying to escape."

All of this discussion does not help me get up the courage to try sneaking past them again. They'll start eating me, probably before Zambrano could even do anything!

Grimacing, Zambrano circles his finger in a wrap-it-up motion. "We need to move," he whispers. "Just do it!"

I stand there, but I'm frozen looking at the demons walk back and forth, random and capricious. This is exactly what I've been worried about. It's my turn to do something helpful, but I can't figure out how to make it happen.

"He can't figure it out," Zambrano says. "It's taking more and more energy to keep the spell up. Do something, Seraphex."

"If I absolutely must," the duck grouses. She hops forward and approaches the fluffback demon lounging against the wall where Zambrano snuck by. Using her bill, she pokes at the demon's foot where it is holding his weight.

The demon slips and collapses in a heap, sending its spear soaring toward me. I dodge it easily,

"You're such a klutz!" one of the demons yells as the others gather around it, pointing and laughing.

I don't need to wait to be told—this is my chance. I stealthily creep forward, moving to the opposite side of the passage while the demons are distracted laughing at the one who fell down.

It only takes a few seconds, and then I'm well past them, their grating voices fading in the background.

Zambrano leads the way forward, and we emerge from the tunnel into a vast red cavern. Before I can even take in the scenery, I notice the heat. It's a sweltering, dry heat. Which normally helps, when it's a pleasant day in Arizona or New Mexico or something. But this is more like an intense and unpleasant sauna. Maybe if I had a wet towel and a hot tub waiting afterward, it would be nice, but I'm immediately sweating, which is particularly unpleasant under the gauntlets. But there's no way I'm taking them off.

There is a large main route that leads straight down to the floor of the cavern, but Seraphex points us down a path to the right along the cavern wall. Zambrano has relaxed, though he and I are both starting to sweat from the heat. He explains that maintaining the illusion is a lot easier when it only needs to block demons from seeing us at a distance.

The amber nexus around my neck adjusts quickly to the hot air, protecting me from the worst of it, though I can still feel the warmer temperature here. Once I get my breath back from the blast of hot air, I'm able to look out across the cavern and take stock of things. It is truly vast, with a ceiling arching up in a way that gives it the appearance of a sky made of hazy red rock. Whereas on the Martian surface everything is crystal clear and you can see for what feels like forever, down here there is dust in the air, giving things in the distance a hazy blur. The dust is greatly disturbed, in fact, swirling around in the air above us in angry clouds.

The floor of the cavern below is scarred, cratered, and wrecked far more than the surface above. There are deep trenches, pits, blast marks, and piles of rubble. And it extends seemingly forever out into the haze. The destruction is unparalleled, layer upon layer of it. It reminds me of those old Minecraft servers that have been around for like fifteen years and have seen generations of players come and go, leaving destruction heaped upon destruction for years on end. The name "Torrid Red Wastes" does make a lot of sense, now that I can see it. Here and there, I spot small groups of demons prowling, keeping guard, or in two cases fighting each other. Portions have seen so much violence that they are nothing but gravel and dust.

"What happened to this place?" I ask.

CHAPTER 14

Looking upward, I see the sky is lit not by the sun but by the glow of a host of small points of illumination, burning with red light on the ceiling and out across the surface of the wasteland.

"Well over a thousand years of immortal demons trapped here with nothing better to do than fight one another," Zambrano says. "Somehow I doubt they're doing demolition for a beautiful new luxury housing development."

"The demons keep a rough truce around the citadel," Seraphex explains, "to guard the armory and the exit from those that are banished to the surface for being too unruly. But here in the Torrid Red Wastes, they're allowed to relax and unwind."

"Relaxing and unwinding looks like this?" I ask, gesturing at the destruction.

"And that is what Earth will look like if Rex is able to have his way with it and bring all these demons home," Zambrano says. "A few demons is a disaster. All of them at once would be an apocalypse. It's no wonder humans spent three million years in the Stone Age, with demons roaming the Earth freely."

"Can he do that? Bring all of them back without both sides of the arcane conduit still existing?"

"He is likely able to bring them back one at a time. I believed it was just a handful of smaller demons, but we ran into Steve the ironclad demon, who had been transported, and if Rex was able to bring back Typhoria . . . our time may be running short. We need to trap him before he can assemble a great enough force. Even all the armies of Earth will struggle in the face of a proper demon legion. Without the arcane conduit, my former husband must be using human wizards to tap his own energy to bring demons back to Earth one by one. He's vastly more powerful than Vulkatherak was."

"Where are we going? We've got the arcane conduit," I say, hefting the twisted metal of the staff. "We need to get back to the ship so that we can get out of here."

"There's no way we could make it back through the citadel," Zambrano says. "By now they'll have it locked down tight with powerful demons guarding both ends."

"I have another route that we can take out, but it's risky," Seraphex says, "and will take a day of travel."

"Riskier than wandering into a fifteen-hundred-year-old continuous war zone full of bloodthirsty demons that have been missing humans to torment for that entire time?" I ask.

"Listening to you, one might be inclined to think you don't like my species very much," Seraphex says, pointing the direction to go as we take a small side path back up the cavern wall. "One could even suggest you're prejudiced against demonkind."

I gesture out to the fields of devastation, fairly confident that they make my point for me. "And in addition to that," I add, "you like this terrible heat. I assume you use demonic magic to keep it so warm in here? Or is it the constant destruction?"

"My apologies," Seraphex says with a total lack of sincerity. "Are you concerned demons might make your world warmer in an unnatural way? Because I may have to be the one to tell you that—"

"Yes, yes, I know, humans are also not good to the environment. But it's not like this!" I protest.

"Humans have been poor stewards of Earth," Zambrano points out as we trudge down the slope amid desolation and ruin. "We have also been damaging our environment."

"At least we have built things," I shoot back. "We had fifteen hundred years without demons, and we developed and invented and progressed tremendously. It looks like demons brawled with one another for that entire time."

"The great game of demonic court," Seraphex says, a note of wistfulness in her voice. "Unproductive, perhaps. But the pursuit of influence and prestige is the noblest and most satisfying there is, or so I thought."

"But now you've found—"

"Don't even start in on the healing power of friendship," Seraphex cuts me off. "Your justification for the existence of grubby little humans has turned my stomach enough for today."

Seraphex leads us down smaller and more remote paths, eventually going into a deep valley. We're forced to cut back and forth many times through the destruction of the rocky area and various obstacles.

Unfortunately, with all the demons actively searching for us, we can't make use of any faster sort of travel. So we have to uncomfortably bed down in a little hollow behind some rocks and make a night of it. I don't expect to sleep much, with only a lumpy backpack for a pillow. At least the amber nexus keeps me somewhat cool, and we have water and protein bars in our backpacks.

"How does it stay so warm down here?" I ask as I try to get comfortable on a pile of gravel. Whoever says camping was fun is clearly lacking in hardship in their life. Beds are awesome and shouldn't be taken for granted.

"Fire and lava demons, primarily, over the course of many years," Seraphex explains. "Similar to our old friend Vulkatherak. The natural rock is very insulating, so a small amount of heat has steadily built up over the centuries. Heat doesn't dissipate, causing it to get warmer and warmer. Demons like the heat, so they mostly stay in here."

After a night of fitful sleep, we get up and continue on our way, hiking deeper into the canyons at the edge of the Torrid Red Wastes. As we get closer to our destination, I notice there's less total destruction in this area. There are some intact boulders and fewer scorch marks and claw scratches.

"Are we farther away from the main demonic areas here?" I ask. "Do they stay more in the center of the cavern?"

"I suspect that it may be something worse than that. This is a very defensible area, up against a wall and with natural barriers around it," Zambrano says. "It would be a prize for any group that set up camp here."

"Your deductions are correct," Seraphex says. "There is a demon who lives here for those exact reasons. The other demons keep their distance. Eslarica is quite reclusive."

"And this is where we're going?" I ask. "To the home of the demon so dangerous that the other cantankerous demons won't fight her?"

"In addition to this nicely defensible territory, she was drawn to two other geographic advantages of note when she took up residence here," Seraphex says. "The first and well-known advantage is that the temperature in the cave is lower than the main part of the Torrid Red Wastes, which suits a grimfeather demon well. The second is a secret not known to most demons, but one can't hide these things from a queen. The cave that she lives in has a connection to the surface."

"So we sneak by her and get out of here?" Zambrano asks. "I can probably manage another strong illusion for a few minutes. I've had some time to rest since we've been hidden from view." He passes the illusion prism back and forth between his hands, stretching his fingers out.

"Unfortunately, that will not work," Seraphex says as we reach the wide mouth of a cave. "Eslarica is far too powerful to be fooled by Zambrano's illusions. She is likely already aware of our presence even from this distance."

As we step into the dark cave mouth, the demon duck is immediately proven correct. Once again. Which is pretty damn annoying, if you ask me. Which . . . no one seems to ever do.

"Serrraphex," a voice, hoarse and low, comes from deep within the cave. "It has been so many years. Welcome back to the Torrid Red Wastes, you old thorn in my side. You've gotten so much smaller though, and contained, haven't you? And . . . you've even taken a liking to your mortal companions, how charming. What a foolish promise to make, for such a silly human obsession."

"Yes, yes," Seraphex shoots back as she jumps off my shoulder and hops forward into the cave. "I'm trapped in this pitiful form, and even worse, I've sworn an oath of friendship to my humans. My friends. If you're going to mock me, let's have it."

"Oh, you make enough of a mockery of yourself," the gravelly and yet sultry voice that I conclude must be Eslarica's continues.

"And who is this that you have with you? The spell-slinging magician and his shadow. His ghost, if you will."

"I'm no magician," Zambrano almost shouts in annoyance. "I am a sorcerer, the last great spellcaster in existence. Well, one of the two."

"And I'm not a ghost," I add in protest since we seem to be doing that. "I'm very much alive."

"Oh, of courrrrse," Eslarica answers. "Zambrano and Liao Ling are the last two sorcerers who live and breathe, to the full extent of my knowledge. And young Bryce, you are indeed a living being. None of you are like the one whose awakening shakes the ground and stirs the winds."

"And who is that?" Zambrano demands. "Rex, with his hurricanes?"

"I am not your oracle," Eslarica states. "And beyond a few hints to tease you and amuse me, I only trade value for value. What have you come to barter with me?"

"We seek passage," Seraphex answers. "I know you have a secret route through your caves that goes to the surface. You need not give up any possessions or powers for us. I ask it as a favor for an old friend."

The demon duck has steadily continued into the dimly lit cave with Zambrano and me tentatively following. Zambrano has put away the illusion prism and is glancing around, hands at the ready to cast spells if things go south.

I am still wearing the gauntlets, though it seems Eslarica is able to perceive me in some way or at least deduce my presence.

"Old friend? Years with these humans truly has blemished your demonic nature. And what of my safety, my dear demon queen?" Eslarica counters. "Is that not worth my possessions and powers? If I assist you and your former husband wins this conflict and learns of it, my punishment will be swift and brutal. Kings do not take kindly to those who aid would-be usurpers, particularly former lovers."

"Very well," Seraphex says, coming to a stop as the tunnel opens up widely. Deeper into the cave, from the small amount of light that filters this far down, I can see the glimmer of two giant eyes set at far angles like those of a bird. "So we must negotiate."

"And what do you have to offer?" Eslarica answers, her dark eyes swiveling to regard each of us. "You have brought me that shiny little conduit. That is certainly a worthy bargaining chip, gleaming and attracting my gaze as it does."

"We can't trade that," Zambrano states flatly. "It's the entire reason we came here to Mars."

"A pity," the grimfeather demon says with a sigh. "But not surprising. You humans always want to keep the best trinkets for yourselves."

"I didn't bring much else to trade," Zambrano says, glaring at Seraphex. "I wasn't expecting to need to do this sort of negotiation. I have an illusion prism and a teleportrait, though we need both of those. And a water bottle and protein bars. Perhaps if someone had warned me . . ."

"What are those items?" Eslarica asks.

Zambrano explains the function and magic of the teleportrait and the illusion prism.

"Neither of those trinkets of common magical nature will be sufficient," Eslarica says. "Make me a proper offer."

"You better not try selling me again," I mutter.

"Never! I wouldn't be so unoriginal as to do that twice," Zambrano says dismissively. "Besides, you are my highly valued project manager. On the other hand, Great and Honorable Eslarica, would you like to trade our safe passage for this fine duck?" He gestures elaborately at Seraphex. "Look at the plumage on her! And such fine meat, though a bit tough. Almost invincibly tough, one might say."

"You're not trading me either," Seraphex snaps while Eslarica opens her beak and lets out a deep and gravelly laugh.

"Perhaps you could come with us?" Seraphex offers. "We could give you transportation to Earth when we return."

"You can't offer her that!" I protest. "We have enough demons on Earth already."

"We could make her give us certain promises to safeguard you fragile little humans," Seraphex says. "Eslarica is less immediately dangerous and hotheaded than most other demons."

"I will save you the effort of that tricky negotiation," Eslarica says. "I have no desire to leave my domain. I despised Mars when we were first exiled here, but it has become home. I have spent many centuries amassing my prizes," she adds, gesturing with one dimly lit wing to the glittering objects around the cave. "I will not abandon my treasure to be touched by the greasy hands of the miscreant demons who roam the Torrid Red Wastes."

Glancing around, the little that I can see in the low light looks more like junk and castoffs than treasure, but if it keeps this powerful demon here on Mars, I'm happy to call it whatever she wants.

"There are demons approaching, though they are doing so with caution," Eslarica declares. "But if they send a scout in here and find you, I will be forced to turn you over. Even I don't want to risk the wrath of Rexhalarkhart."

I look down at my hands and take a deep breath. I *finally* got a cool artifact to play with that's useful in our battles. But we need to get out of here.

"What about these?" I say, holding up the gauntlets. "They have magical power, and they will make a handsome addition to your treasury."

"Will they?" Eslarica asks. "Are they worth your lives?"

"Yes, they are," I answer. There's a pit growing in my stomach. These were a gift from Deirdre Moran and the druids, and I don't want to give them up.

"Come closer; look me in the eyes," the grimfeather demon croaks. "Explain."

I step forward, but in the darkness, I can't see anything and stumble as I try to walk, almost falling over. I pull out my phone and turn on the flashlight on the lowest possible setting.

The cave is suddenly lit up, the light shining off a pile of dull metal objects—rings, swords, armor, and coins—around its rocky interior. In the center of it is a massive creature, looking almost like a crow the size of an elephant but with twisted horns and ridges and dark black feathers and darker midnight eyes gleaming.

Eslarica opens her beak and croaks, surging forward toward me.

"I'm sorry, I'm sorry, I'll put it away!" I say, scrambling backward and tripping on the uneven ground, catching myself painfully on one hand.

"No!" Eslarica says. "What is that shining beacon in your hand? It glows and gleams, and it is glorious! Shine it upon my treasures."

My heart is beating faster, but part of it is excitement. I've lost plenty of phones in the past year; I can easily replace this one.

"I must *have* it," Eslarica says.

"Very good," Zambrano announces. "We will trade this mystical artifact of humanity's technological prowess in exchange for safe and secret passage to the surface."

"Oh, no," Eslarica says, her voice low and almost seductive. "I will have the glowing rectangle as well as the gauntlets. That is my price."

Zambrano looks over at me, raising an eyebrow.

"If you like the phone, how about two of them?" I suggest. "Instead of the gauntlets."

"Oh, now this is interesting. You have more of these devices. I delight in how they make my treasures shine!" She leans forward, eyes boring into me. "How many of them do you have, little bargainer? Enough to satisfy me?"

"How many do you require?" Seraphex counters.

"All of them," Eslarica demands.

Shrugging, I pull the second one out of my other pocket.

"More!" the grimfeather demon demands.

I pull my backpack around and give her the one that's in the outer pocket.

"MORE!" Eslarica rasps.

I dig deep into my backpack. There's another hidden at the bottom, under the food, clothes, and water. I've gotten paranoid, okay?

"All of them!" Eslarica says.

Sighing, I reach down and pull up my pant leg, where I've got one final phone strapped to my ankle.

"You know, I do pay for those," Zambrano says in annoyance. "They're not free. That iPad is connected to my personal bank account! I've spent centuries saving that money."

"That's all I have," I say. "If you want any of them, you'll make this deal with us."

"Is that all of them, Seraphex, in truth?" Eslarica purrs greedily, knowing that the demon duck will have to answer honestly even if I'm trying to trick her.

"It is every phone that Bryce has here on Mars, to the best of my knowledge."

"How frightfully specific," Eslarica says. "But is it every one of these 'phones' that you have the ability to give me, here and now."

"There is, as a matter of fact, one more that we could give you," Seraphex says. "But only if that will fully and finally seal our deal. Every phone that we have the ability to give you in this moment, in exchange for our safe and secret passage to the surface."

"I accept your terms," Eslarica agrees, sitting back with satisfaction. "All of your phones for safe and secret passage, to the best of my efforts."

"I'm not giving up my phone!" Zambrano hisses. "There are . . . private things on there. Passwords. Emails. Personal items!"

"I don't think she's going to mind if there's an embarrassing search history or some downloaded porn videos or whatever you have on there. Do you write bad fanfic or something?"

"I'm not giving my *nudes* to a demon!" Zambrano insists.

"I don't think she even knows how to use a phone," Seraphex says. "She enjoys the shiny lights."

"It's too big a risk. Those are my private collection! I only send them to very special people." Zambrano glares at me when I give him a look. "Only when they *ask* for them. I'm not an animal, Bryce."

"Look, just reset it," I say, gesturing for the phone. Grumbling, Zambrano unlocks his phone and lets me show him how to reset it, deleting everything.

We turn all of them on and turn the flashlights on as well, setting them up around the cave to shine on her hoard of metal items. I guess a demonic crow is not that different from a normal Earth crow, in wanting to gather all this junk.

I set them to low power and airplane mode, and very carefully don't mention anything about how batteries work, and the fact that these phones will all be dead within a day. Seraphex and Zambrano don't say anything either, so I assume that we're hoping we'll be halfway across the solar system before it becomes an issue and Eslarica comes after us looking for revenge.

"I trust that you will keep this transaction a private matter?" Eslarica says as we prepare to depart. "In exchange, I will rebuff the horde of demons that is assembling at my door. They will assume that I am harboring you, but they will surely have demons patrolling the surface as well. If they do attempt to follow you here, I will happily teach them a lesson in manners."

"We'll keep it quiet," I say. "Thanks for not letting them through."

"They have nothing left of value to trade for information or passage," Eslarica says, her beak opening in a sickening grin. "Over the many centuries, I have collected every piece of shiny treasure that's in the empty cavern and not stored in the armory."

"I will keep this secret," Seraphex agrees.

"And I as well," Zambrano adds.

Eslarica gives us a set of directions through the passages at the rear of her cave, which Seraphex seems to take in perfectly well but I could not follow. Like any modern person, I'm helpless without the maps on my phone. I am vaguely aware that there was a time before GPS and turn-by-turn directions, but I'm also aware of a time when people washed their clothes on rocks down by the river. Both ancient history, as far as I'm concerned.

With no phone flashlights, Zambrano uses his *Handlicht* spell to give us illumination as we go through a long, cramped tunnel that slopes gently upward. As we stumble our way through it, I trip and fall a few times, struggling with the combination of uneven surfaces, dancing light, and unfamiliar gravity. The lowered gravity helps reduce the damage of a few scrapes and bruises.

The tunnel is much straighter than the route we took inside the cavern, and luckily, it is taking us somewhat back in the direction we need to go. But it's still many hours of hiking. After a full day of twisting and winding passages, we finally see rays of daylight, and shortly thereafter we emerge from a tiny crack hidden between two boulders on the side of the mountain. I can see how this exit has remained concealed—you would need to climb down and risk getting trapped inside in order to find out if it goes anywhere.

We end up making camp overnight just inside the tunnel exit, figuring it's safer than going out onto the surface where we might be spotted from overhead.

"Another night of camping?" I complain.

"Don't you adore the outdoors? The mystery! The adventure!" Zambrano says.

"I love my bed. I miss my bed," I say. "This was supposed to be a quick in-and-out trip. I would have brought a tent or a sleeping pad or something if I'd known."

"Oh, you poor thing," Zambrano answers. "You're building character and saving the world."

I grumble, but there's not much to do but try to get some rest before we make our escape.

It takes me a while to fall asleep, which makes sense, given I'm bedding down in low gravity, and on a planet populated by hordes of demons, and this close to Zambrano's snoring. I did not realize this would be an extended camping trip!

I also can't help but worry about the rest of the crew back on Earth. We saw Liao Ling escape, which is good. But has Rex accelerated his plans with the governments? Triggered more natural disasters? Is Parth doing something stupidly courageous without me there to talk him out of it? And is Mei in danger? I suppose she puts herself in danger by working for these demons—though I guess the guy dodging demons on Mars doesn't have a leg to stand on there.

Even worse than all that, as I drift off to sleep, I start to wonder —are they all talking shit about us while we're not there to defend ourselves? Parth and I have been chatting online for a long time, he knows some embarrassing stories from my college days.

The next morning, we exit the cave and take a moment to get our bearings, though again I'm mostly lost. I can see that there's a gigantic volcano behind us, and I know we don't want to go back toward that, what with the army of demons and all.

But Seraphex and Zambrano are able to figure things out from the stars, though they do have a moment of confusion.

"What is that bright object in the southern sky?" Zambrano asks.

"That would be Deimos, Mars's smaller moon," Seraphex answers.

I look at it and recognize the bright light I saw during our arrival on the top of Olympus Mons.

"It's far brighter than it should be," he says.

"It was even brighter earlier," I add. "I thought it must be Earth."

Zambrano breathes deeply.

"What?" I ask.

"An object glowing brightly like that—I would have to guess it's some sort of stored energy being discharged. Technological, magical, it's hard to tell. But someone here on Mars is up to something. We should get moving."

He leads the way back toward the wreck of the yacht, which luckily is not too far from the tunnel exit. Zambrano has the illusion prism out again, which is lucky, because winged demons are circling in the sky.

"Bonepicker demons," Seraphex says, eyeing the figures hunting us in the air above. "We should stay on the surface and move quickly."

We bound quickly over the surface with Seraphex clinging tightly to my shoulder. As much as the hunting demons in the sky above, the caverns below, and probably the landscape around us as well scare me, it's kind of fun being able to soar through the air with each step.

After about an hour, we pause for a moment to pull our water bottles out, quickly hydrating before we continue.

As I stand still, I feel the earth shaking slightly. I look over to Zambrano, who has reached down and is pressing his hand against the ground with a concerned look on his face, casting what I recognize as one of his detection spells.

CHAPTER 15

Seraphex, is this normal?" Zambrano asks.

"Not for Martian geology or for demonic powers," Seraphex says. "We would be well served to teleport away from here as soon as we can."

"Let's keep moving, then," Zambrano agrees, shouldering his backpack.

We keep jogging along our path. I'm starting to get the hang of running in reduced gravity, though the nerves from it all are sapping the fun out of it.

Twenty minutes later I'm following behind Zambrano when he pulls up to halt and holds up his hand. "Something is here," he says.

"More demons?" I ask.

"No," he says, brow furrowed. "Powerful magic. Spellcasting. It's bleeding energy out. If you had magical sensitivity, you might feel it as well. Even your amateurish friend Parth would probably be able to see the force in the air as I do."

"I can also sense it," Seraphex says. "It's your pathetic little human magic. But, I must admit, quite a lot of it."

"What do we do?" I ask.

But before Zambrano can answer, the ground shakes intensely, much as it did when we first landed on Olympus Mons. I'd call it an earthquake, but I guess in this part of the solar system it would be more properly called a marsquake.

Whatever you want to call it, a hole bursts open in front of us, a giant crack in the Martian surface.

"Come here!" Zambrano calls, and I run to him as he raises a glowing orange energy shield around us. Seraphex leaps into the air and grabs tightly to my shoulder as a torrent of dirt and rocks rain down on us, but the shield easily deflects them. The debris settles, but Zambrano keeps the shield bubble up, glancing around with a grim expression on his face.

The air is filled with a haze of dust, but emerging from the cracked Martian ground ahead of us is a figure that clambers up and out. I can't see very clearly through the swirling air, but it appears to be roughly human-sized, someone wearing a tattered black cloak with a hood down over their face.

"So good that I have ensnared you, so-called sorcerer, before you escaped back to Earth," the figure calls out. "And that curious specimen you have with you as well."

I don't know if I'm the "curious specimen" or if Seraphex is, but either way I do not like it. And that voice is familiar. It has a breathy, raspy quality to it, but I feel like I've heard those strident tones before, somewhere recently.

"So-called sorcerer?" Zambrano sputters. "I am the last living sorcerer! Except for the one newly unfrozen one, but she doesn't count!"

The figure steps forward, and as the dust settles and the air clears, we can see him more clearly. Under the ragged hood of the cloak, bright bluish-white eyes stare out with a piercing gaze.

"You!" Seraphex practically squawks. "I know you to be dead! I have it directly from beings who cannot lie."

"He is dead," Zambrano states flatly. "Undead, at least. I've seen this before. Caravello, with her necromantic experiments. Only she never got it to properly work: the energy requirements were too high."

I realize with a start where I have heard the voice before. It felt far more human and noble at the time, but it was the voice that Seraphex used during the battle in the eye of the storm. To create a distraction, she used her vocal mimicry trick to fool Rex into thinking Merlin was there.

"Merlin," I croak. "Real actual Merlin?"

"A version of him," Seraphex says. "Something made from what he was."

"Zombie Merlin?" I ask. "Ghost Merlin?"

"Technically, I'd call him a lich, but I don't know that there's ever been a real one before," Zambrano says. "Caravello came the closest."

"Zombie Lich Merlin, got it," I say. "God damn."

"What are you, great sorcerer?" Zambrano calls out. "And what brings you here?"

"Buried, I was," the figure says, his voice a breathy whisper that somehow comes through perfectly clearly to my ears even with the low atmosphere. "But an entombment of stone has been broken. Dead, I was. But the shackles of death have been shattered. Drained of all energy. But a demon moon burns above, the power siphoned steadily over many centuries to bring me to unbreathing life."

"The quake when we arrived on Olympus," Zambrano growls. "That was you breaking out." He steps back into a guard stance, hands positioned for spellcasting. "Is this another of your traps?"

"The trap was set and baited, the energy of orbit stored in the demon moon over centuries," Merlin says. "Though I did not know what prey might wander into my snare. But this . . . this is better than any possible anticipation. At last, I shall have the answer to the question of my life."

"He's going to speak in nothing but poetry and riddles, isn't he?" I mutter under my breath, but the undead sorcerer hears me and responds.

"The riddle is not in my speech," he says, stepping toward us. He reaches up and pulls back the hood of the cloak. His face is a pale bluish white, mottled with cracks and scars, with some bits showing through to pure white bone underneath. "It is in reality. What *is* a demon? Where does it come from? And the great riddle of my life: Can they be defeated? Why have they been sapping the power of magic for so long?"

"And how will you determine that?" Zambrano asks. "What do you need from us?"

Zombie Lich Merlin stares at us, his glowing eyes twinkling in a very unsettling way. "You have created something new with spellcraft that we did not have in my time. It impresses, what you have done with the weakened magic of your late era."

As he advances, he waves a hand, and the orange shield around us flickers out. Zambrano growls and recasts it, but with another wave of the undead ancient sorcerer's hand, the shield disappears again.

"A demon, transformed," Merlin says, his voice breathy and menacing. "She is not the demon queen that she was. She is changed. Identity moved. The magic can recognize her in either state. Bound she is by the codes of demonkind. Because her pattern, in any form, is still unique."

"Yes," Zambrano says, backing up slowly. I can see the gears in his mind spinning, trying to think of what spell might work against this ancient power. "What of it? What do you want from her?"

"In the transition," Merlin says. "In between states—she is not quite a demon queen, not quite a demon bird. There, I can have her true nature. We can have the answers we seek."

"Don't let him do it," Seraphex says, and I can hear the fear in her voice. "It will not be good for me, or for you. If he alters me in that state, in between types, I don't know what will happen. I may cease to be myself."

"*I did start the fire!*" Zambrano declares, and twin gouts of fire fly out from his outstretched hands. Based on the trigger words, my guess is that this is a spell of his own creation.

Merlin holds up a single finger, and his mouth moves with words I can't hear. The two streams of flames converge on the finger and are sucked into it. His fingers glows brightly, neatly absorbing all the fire. A moment after the flames stop, the glow in the fingers winks out, and the spell is gone completely.

"*Eye of Jupiter!*" Zambrano shouts, casting the familiar gravity spell he used to pin me down all those months ago.

But Merlin shakes his head, and while he's pushed back a few inches, he claps his hands twice and speaks another inaudible incantation, then steps forward normally.

"Arcane energy I have stored, for one thousand and five hundred years, as I slumbered beneath the red rocks," Merlin intones, his voice now coming clearly to our ears again. "No magical spell's function can escape me no matter how recently you may have created it. Magic is magic, and I am its master."

Zambrano casts two more spells, sending roaring arcane energy at the ancient undead sorcerer, but each is dismissed just as easily.

"Very well," Zambrano says with a sigh. "You have bested me in this little duel. What do you want of us?"

The lich smiles, stretching a gruesome grin across his face.

"I have no need of your meager abilities—yet," Merlin says. "But I will have use of you after we interrogate Seraphex. Give me the enchanted glass item."

I can see from the tight clench of Zambrano's jaw that this insult is not appreciated. But the modern sorcerer says nothing.

"The spell you used in the armory is of a most clever construction, if a rather cringeworthy presentation," Merlin says. "Give me the glass device, that I may employ it."

Zambrano glares at him but produces the illusion prism and hands it over.

"I think this is a bad idea," Seraphex complains. "I do not like it."

She leaps off my shoulder and flaps her wings but falls to the ground despite beating them furiously, and she is unable to make much headway waddling on the ground before a simple spell from Merlin pulls her back and pins her on the dirt at his feet with a thump.

"Who knows, maybe he will do something good," Zambrano says with a tone that implies he doesn't think highly of that chance. "He was against demons, after all."

With the illusion prism held in a skeletal hand, Merlin begins a spell, once again his lips moving without me being able to hear the words. As far as I can tell, I only hear Merlin when he chooses for us to, with some sort of voice-casting magic.

Now that he's closer to us, I can catch some bits of sound, and I'm able to tell he's repeating the long-winded spell crafted by Alix that Zambrano used to bring out Seraphex's demonic nature in the armory.

Once again, white energy sparks from the illusion prism, wrenching a dark red force from within Seraphex. She is transfixed, and this time I see a roiling of the energy as she tries, without success, to resist the change. Rising up from her, I can see flickering shadows of her spiky and majestic demon self.

Merlin mutters various spells and moves his other hand, and the transmogrification spell pauses, the patterns swirling but with the white and red energies staying in balance. Above her duck body, the flickering representation of Seraphex's demon nature drifts in and out of focus.

Zambrano is staring daggers at the undead sorcerer using his illusion prism, and he's working his fingers as if he's eager to cast some spells. But he also keeps glancing at Seraphex, and I can read the curiosity on his face. His gaze meets my eyes for a second, and he gives an almost apologetic shrug as if to say *I know this undead sorcerer is dangerous, but I also want to see where he's headed with this.* I nod, reluctantly agreeing.

I hear Seraphex squawk in irritation, but she looks unable to move from her spot on the Martian rocks, where her body is lying pinned. Her duck head flops to the dusty ground, and I can see the half-visible demon above her become slightly clearer.

"*Deorc mægen unbunden,*" Merlin says, and the magical display in front of us vibrates like a puddle with a rock dropped in it and then settles back down to the same appearance.

"You are no longer in your demon body, or your transformed and bound home," Merlin says, his voice breathy, cold, and demanding. "I have freed you of the obligations and assertions of those forms."

"True," Seraphex's voice answers, mixed up and strangled by the magic, but still recognizably hers. "In this form, I am unbound from the past."

"You are able to answer any question?" Merlin asks.

"I am free to answer," Seraphex replies.

"Speak to me, then," Merlin demands. "What is the first element of the demonic code?"

"Being free to answer does not mean I am obligated," Seraphex's voice answers.

"*Deorc mægen beboden,*" Merlin intones, and the demonic form in the air again quivers as if struck. "*Dark magic,* I command you."

Seraphex pauses for several long seconds but then speaks. "The first element of the demonic code is that a demon cannot lie."

This one I've known for months; it was one of the first things I learned about demons like Seraphex. Merlin must know it as well, but I suspect that he's using it sort of like a polygraph, to test whether he's getting correct information and build up to whatever he's after.

"What is the second element of the demonic code?" Merlin asks.

"The second element of the demonic code is that a demon is bound by the terms of any pact they enter," Seraphex answers. The reluctance in her voice comes through clearly.

Again, this term I have known about for quite some time. But the third has always been a mystery, and Seraphex has refused to answer or entertain any sort of questions about it.

"What is the third element of the demonic code?" Merlin asks.

"I cannot say," Seraphex responds immediately, her voice coming through in a sort of trancelike state. "I do not understand why. I can feel the answer, but it is hidden from me. I do not like thinking of it. It is painful. You are unpleasant for making me try. Why must you be an unpleasant man?"

"The mind forges distractions, unfocusing from truth. *Deorc mægen ālȳsed*," Merlin incants. "You are released from the obligation to hide from knowledge under the demonic code, but from no other obligations. You may now contemplate your origins, but you remain bound by truth and promises."

Seraphex's voice screams, though the head of her duck body doesn't move at all. Still, the scream reverberates through the thin air around us. It pierces me, so painful to hear my friend cry out like that. I instinctively step forward, wanting to throw a punch at Merlin, but Zambrano puts out an arm, holding me back.

Finally, the scream ends, and Seraphex's voice returns. Now it is calm, dispassionate, and measured.

"The third element of the demonic code is this," Seraphex intones. "A demon may not ponder its own nature and origins, or the origin of the demonic code."

"You have been released from the third element of the code," Merlin says, greedy excitement dripping from his voice. "Now I will finally know, because you must answer. *What are you? What is a demon?*"

CHAPTER 16

Demons are the unconscious force of a million years of humanity's fearful expectations. We are the nightmares your longing called into existence." The shape of the demon has solidified further, and I can see the upper half of Seraphex's torso outlined clearly in shadow and swirling red energy.

"Be more specific," Merlin says with a wicked smile.

"Magic reacts to patterns," Seraphex says, her voice now perfectly calm and patient. "It can be created through careful training and synthesis, as when a sorcerer crafts a spell, training magic to recognize motions, words, or ingredients as triggers to act with arcane force. A skillful sorcerer can create a spell in a time as quickly as days, weeks, months, or years, using their mental expectations combined with careful mathematics and knowledge of powerful triggers."

Zambrano is watching with hawklike intensity but says nothing. I can see him glancing around, but it doesn't seem he has any better idea to get us out of this than I do. It makes me feel sick, seeing Seraphex torn open like this.

"That is the sorcerer's way of spellcraft, that conscious and rapid creation," Seraphex says. "But there is another type of spell that can be created. Slowly, bit by bit, from the expectations and repeated patterns of fear. Not over decades, or centuries, or even millennia. Demons were fashioned by the fears of an emerging human sentience. As you grew the ability to think, so you grew the ability to create magic unconsciously far before spellcraft was discovered. Demons were carved from the fear of what lurked outside the cheery light of billions of campfires across three million years. We haunted your age of stone, becoming more real over each iteration of a hundred thousand Paleolithic generations."

Time feels like it slows down as I take this revelation in. We humans created demons, by our own magical energy and expectations. We may have inadvertently caused our own destruction, without even realizing it.

Merlin's cracked pale lips turn upward into a sickening smile. "And so finally, we know what you are. Fear incarnate, a spell unknowingly cast by our ancestors."

"Is that all our imaginations created?" I ask, suddenly indignant, feeling defensive of us poor humans. "Our imagination isn't only darkness! Why did it create demons and other sorts of evil?"

"Oh, sad and ignorant human. There were good ones created as well," the shadow Seraphex says. "Spirits of forest and sky and brook. Laughing nymphs and dancing fairies. Playful river guides and protective mountain kings."

"And what happened to those kind beings?" Merlin asks.

Seraphex's shadowy upper half swivels, her eyes turning to transfix me with a burning glare.

"Before the demonic code, we were unstoppable. A million years of nightmares were capable of far greater violence than the idle wishes of daytime. Your spirits of hope and light? We killed them. By the time you learned to till the soil and harvest your crops, we had slain every one of them we could find."

"And where did the demonic codes come from?" Merlin demands, his gaunt and scarred face beaming with cruel desire.

"I do not recall," Seraphex's voice answers from the churning shadowy representation of her, halfway between forms.

"Who created them?"

"I do not recall," Seraphex repeats. "They came upon us, and the codes themselves forced us."

"What is their purpose?" Merlin asks.

"I do not recall," she says again.

"Is it to create a weakness in demons that humans could exploit?" Merlin suggests.

"I believe that is correct," Seraphex answers. "Once the codes were in place, clever humans could deal with us, trick us into making agreements, and know that they would be followed. It was especially bad, before we even knew what had been done to us. It allowed the blossoming of civilization, and led to our eventual banishment to Mars."

"We did use that against you," Merlin says, baring his teeth in an attempt at a smile. "Many demons promised to meet us at a particular location entering through the designated gate, and they were thus compelled to walk through the arcane conduit and come to Mars. Who created the demonic codes? Where did they come from?"

"I do not recall," Seraphex says.

"The creator of the codes, so very powerful and clever a being," Merlin muses. "Do you have any knowledge of the codes or the creator?"

"I do not recall," Seraphex replies.

Merlin turns to us. "Aren't you curious about this? Time stretches out endlessly with so many questions and so few true answers. Little sorcerer, haven't you wondered about these secrets for many years?"

"I have wondered," Zambrano says flatly. "But I would not choose to learn it like this."

"You don't have any questions you would like answered? Secrets that have sparked your curiosity?" The undead sorcerer tilts his head to one side, enjoying the moment and his power over us.

"Seraphex, do you know how we can defeat Merlin and stop this torture?" Zambrano asks.

"I do not," Seraphex answers.

"Your softness does you no credit," Merlin says with a sneer. Returning to Seraphex, he asks, "When did the demonic code take hold of you?"

"Time was reckoned differently back then," Seraphex says. "Years were given names, not numbers. After over millions of years of terrorizing our creators, we did not track the passage of them in years either, only in piles of skulls."

There's a new vibrating in the air, centering around Seraphex, as tension builds from this invasive spell.

"Give me the closest estimate you can," Merlin orders. "Roughly when in history? Where were you?"

"I was in China," Seraphex says as the vibration increases, causing small rocks to bounce around at our feet. "It was in the final centuries of the Xia dynasty."

"This magic quakes and shakes," Merlin says. "*I have made a terrible mistake. Alix was right as always. Reverse the reversal!*" His delivery of the incantation is rich with mockery and arrogance.

The white tendrils of magical force reverse their flow and tighten around the shadowy demonic form, wrapping it in glowing bonds and pushing it back into her duck body.

This time, however, after the magic has entirely dissipated, her little body lies still, like a corpse.

I kneel down, leaning in close. "Sera? Are you okay?" I ask. Somehow, despite everything that she just revealed about her demonic nature, I can't help but be concerned for her.

"Recovery will come to the demon queen in time," Merlin says, his breathy voice creeping me out as it comes from above me and close. "She is rendered helpless now. Your magic will return me to our home world, before the demonic hordes descend."

"You would like to come home with us?" Zambrano asks, and my stomach does a backflip. Earth has enough problems without an undead zombie Merlin.

"The energy gathered from the asteroid moon's gravity will sustain only so many hours," Merlin says. "In hibernation, it served. Active undeath requires continuous energy. I must feed on the living, and the two here on Mars are not nearly enough."

And that is so much worse.

"You would like to return to our world, to feed on the living?" Zambrano asks, incredulous.

"In my hibernation, I have been watching your fragile world from afar, as languages and customs come and go," Merlin says. "You have billions. A hundred thousand a day will barely be missed and will sustain me plentifully. Three times that are birthed with each rotation of the sun."

"One *hundred thousand*?" I exclaim. But Zambrano makes a shushing motion.

"Very well," he says. "We must make our way to the wreckage of our ship so that we can reverse the spell and all return home."

I can't believe Zambrano is just caving in like this. But if he won't fight, there's certainly nothing I can do.

Reluctantly, I pick up Seraphex's limp duck body. She's not breathing, and putting my hand on her heart, I can't detect a heartbeat. But on the other hand, did she ever have a heartbeat? Do demons normally have heartbeats? I don't know much about their physiology, let alone what they're like when transmogrified into waterfowl.

"Lead the way to your vessel, so-called sorcerer," Merlin says.

"As you command, mighty one," Zambrano answers, laying it on thick.

We can't teleport home a crazy undead ancient lich sorcerer or whatever and let him suck the life out of a hundred thousand people a day. Or maybe Zambrano has a secret plan?

As I stand, he pats me on the back comfortingly. I think I catch the faintest hint of a wink, but before I can tell for sure, he's turned and started walking toward the wreck of the yacht and hopefully our ticket off this rock. Ideally, without a mass murderer psychopathic undead sorcerer joining us.

Zambrano better have a secret plan, or I'm going to murder his pompous ass.

CHAPTER 17

I hold Seraphex's hopefully-just-unconscious body carefully in one arm and grasp the arcane conduit in the other as we move across the dusty red rocks, easily bounding down the side of the mountain. As we traverse the Martian landscape, I can see the bonepicker demons are still flying overhead, and instead of wide search patterns, they are now focused on us, following along closely. They do seem to be keeping their distance, however.

After ten minutes of walking, I glance to the right of our path and see a skittershell demon, fairly far off and moving with its cockroach-like gait. A few minutes later, I catch a glimpse of a slitherfang, peeking out at us from behind a rock.

"I see them. Merlin has the illusion prism, so we're not hidden any longer," Zambrano says quietly, dropping back to walk next to me while Merlin leads the way, seemingly confident enough in his magical superiority that he can ignore us. His motions are sickeningly jerky, as if he doesn't quite know how to use his body, but despite that, he is able to cover ground fairly quickly in the low gravity. "They must have a healthy fear of Merlin. I don't think they would be so timid if it were only the two of us."

"Well, that's nice," I say, frowning at the undead lunatic in front of us.

"We can't let him—" I start, but Zambrano cuts me off.

"He's too powerful. There's nothing we can do," Zambrano says. "Follow along and do what I say. Like a good intern."

"That's two promotions ago," I answer. "It's Mr. Project Manager to you."

"Tell it to HR," Zambrano shoots back. "But maybe you should try to be in an intern frame of mind."

I'm not sure quite what that means, but it's probably a hint for whatever he's planning. I try to remember anything particular about what I did as an intern. Mainly, it was being put in ludicrously dangerous situations, though that hasn't changed. I was also used frequently for my lack of being able to be detected by magical methods, due to my magical spark or whatever being locked away by Susan.

We continue walking along, the world eerily silent even as I see the bonepicker demons overhead and catch occasional glimpses of the other demons, who are still keeping pace with us.

"The reason the demons are based on natural elements, like animals or birds or rocks or stones . . ." I start. "Do you think that's because they're born out of millennia of human subconsciouses? We created them, so they reflect things that we fear."

"That does make sense," Zambrano muses. "And I wonder if that also dates when they appeared—the ironclad demons must only have appeared in the Iron Age. It would have created a huge amount of fear when groups with new unstoppable weapons arrived."

"So Steve is young compared to Volcanose or the rockhide demons?" I say. "It didn't seem to make him any smarter."

"That is true enough," Zambrano agrees.

I miss having Seraphex around to help clarify that sort of thing. Though I wonder if, with whatever changes happened due to Merlin's magic, she would be able to join our speculation and give us confirmation.

Another stretch of walking passes, and the demon sightings are growing more frequent. I worry if, when enough of them have gathered, they'll make a play. But before they can, we reach the wreck of the ship.

"Our escape: it must be taken with haste," Merlin says. "A gathering storm of demons approaches."

We step across the cracked and pulverized rocks where the teleportation arrival of the yacht wrecked the local landscape.

"I shall initiate the spell. Step onto the wreckage, both of you," Zambrano says. "You need to be in direct contact with the yacht in order to be taken back when the spell is reversed."

Merlin and I both advance onto the yacht, standing on its angled and cracked deck.

"Great sorcerer, did you notice the peculiar nature of the boy?" Zambrano says, gesturing at me.

"What do you mean, speaking of this nature?" Merlin asks, leering at Zambrano with suspicion in his eyes.

"He is invisible to magical detection," Zambrano says between incantations as he steps around the yacht, chanting spells and touching the glyphs carved on each part of the ship's structure. There's a buzzing that builds, a vibration I can feel through my shoes, coming from the wrecked part of the hull I'm standing on.

"What is this distraction?" Merlin asks. "On with the spell."

"As you wish," Zambrano says. "But it's a very unusual thing. With your great abilities, I'm sure you can detect it easily."

Pursing his cracked white lips, Merlin turns and regards me with his glowing white-blue eyes. I realize that this must be the "intern work" Zambrano had in mind. Being sacrificed to an incredibly dangerous being with far more power than me. That's just great.

The undead sorcerer whispers a few words and moves his hands, and his eyebrows rise in surprise.

"Indeed, he is a curious specimen," Merlin says. "Perhaps there is something to learn here, of the magic of the mind. Much has advanced in my time away."

He puts a hand out, fingers splayed, and I feel my body suddenly contract as a foreign force takes hold of it. As Merlin casts his spell, I see Zambrano continue going to various parts of the hull, resuming his touching of the glyphs to activate the teleportation.

He disappears below deck to complete the spell just as Merlin starts to clench his hand. Pain suddenly grips my body as he cocks his head to the side with a terrifyingly curious look on his face.

"How did you come to have the nature of this . . . this abomination?" Merlin asks.

"I think I'm great, thank you very much," I can't help but say as I feel my muscles clenching under the effect of whatever sort of magical probing Merlin is performing. Luckily, it doesn't make me fall over. Instead I freeze in place, and my grip on Seraphex's body grows tighter. I hope she's going to be okay—and I wish we had her here to help figure this situation out.

"A strange specimen, indeed," Merlin says.

"I'm glad I'm so fascinating to you all," I answer, though my voice is choked by the pain of an uncomfortable heat spreading through my body. "Why couldn't my aberration have been, like, being super tall or having a perfect jawline?"

"Impressive, the mental magic to steal your potential. Who performed this feat upon you?" Merlin demands.

"My mother," I answer, not sure if I should be telling him the truth, but it tumbles out.

"We all bear the scars of our ancestors' failures and mistakes, do we not?" Merlin says sadly. And for a moment, he's somehow almost relatable. Despite wanting to kill a hundred thousand people a day just to stay alive, or whatever sort of undead life it is that he has.

But before I can start to like him via some sort of Stockholm syndrome, Zambrano pops out from the hatch below deck.

He has a fierce grimace on his face, and he's holding a pair of machine guns, a gleaming AK-47 in each hand.

"If brilliant magic doesn't work, try stupid technology," he says as he squeezes the triggers on both weapons.

The report of the guns comes through the thin air to me, but it's just a tinny popping sound. But the muzzle flash is blindingly bright, and I can see as the bullets seem to cut right through through the magic defenses that pop up.

The bullets move faster than Merlin can react, and his wasted and skeletal body is flung into the air by the force of the two clips unloading on him simultaneously. His cloak flutters in the air as bullets push him farther away. As he falls back and his corpse-like form clatters onto the rocks, the magic holding me in place releases, and I collapse to my knees and the arcane conduit falls to the ground. As I struggle to my feet and grab the conduit staff, I see Merlin's body lying a few feet away from the yacht. Zambrano opens fire a second time, and the tinny popping sound continues as he unloads every round in the two weapons.

"Get that bastard farther away and destroy him," Zambrano says, handing me one of the guns and a rucksack full of spare clips. "I'll get the spell going and let you know when we're ready."

Trying to remember what Liao Ling taught me about the guns, I leave Seraphex and the arcane conduit staff on the yacht and fumble through reloading one of the weapons. Stepping up to the body on the ground, I see some slight bits of magical energy crackling around Merlin.

At point-blank range, I pull the trigger and let loose. Dust, rock, and bone explode into the air, and I close my eyes as I feel the force of the rounds kick into my body.

As soon as the clip is complete, I open my eyes again, staring through the debris to see the body, broken and shattered. Spinning the weapon around, I bring it down on him, using its metal weight to smash into the undead bastard's body.

"Trap this, you bastard," I say as I lay into him. It's nice to have someone to finally take out my anger on. And a would-be mass murderer is, you have to admit, a great choice for that. And I know what you're thinking, he saved humanity by defeating the demons and all that. But every instinct in me says that this necrotic monster is not the same guy whose noble voice I heard Seraphex imitate back on Earth. Sorcery drove him mad, and once he used necromancy to raise himself, he became a different person.

Plus, Liao Ling would probably say he was always kind of a bastard.

The ancient corpse, held together by pure magical energy, comes apart in a shower of dust as I tear into it.

"Bryce! Time to depart!" Zambrano calls out, and I reluctantly pull myself away from Merlin. As far as I can see, any trace of life or power is gone, and his body is now nothing but scraps of bone and ragged fabric on the ground. I do grab the illusion prism, which has survived the bullets with only a few small dings.

I kick Merlin's body one more time and sprint back to the yacht. I pick up the arcane conduit and Seraphex, holding them tightly as I scramble down inside the hull. Pulling my gauntlets off and putting them in my pack, I try to examine her body for injuries, but she looks physically intact, just unconscious.

A minute later, I poke my head back out, and around us I see demons emerging from the rocks and swooping down from above. In the forms of snakes, cockroaches, vultures, and one giant creature with massive horns, they charge the broken yacht. The demons' fear of Merlin kept them too distant, but now they are out for blood.

Before I can put the gauntlets back on, the vibrations are growing more powerful, and Zambrano pulls me down into the ship. I grab a doorframe and hold on as the sorcerer calls out the final words to the transportation spell. Pure white energy crackles in the air, and I feel the vessel shaking with violent force. I grip Seraphex's silent body close with one arm, desperately holding on to the arcane conduit with the other.

As magic swirls around us, I take one last glance at Merlin, wondering if I see some sort of sparks above his body. But before I can see any of it, the Martian landscape and sky disappear.

There is a roaring as we arrive at our destination, and I can feel the earth-shattering force around me as the yacht comes to rest, displacing the matter around it. I expect a flood of water, but none comes. Instead, air rushes into the yacht, and there's a burning sensation as natural air begins to rush into my lungs. My amber nexus seamlessly helps me to adapt, and after a moment of disorientation, I start to get my bearings. As I get back into normal breathing, I can hear and feel the ship cracking and shrieking as it settles in this new location. I hunker down while the metal shifts around me, and farther away there are loud crunches and bangs as the structure of the yacht is torn apart by the force of our teleporting entry.

Adjusting to the heavier gravity takes a moment, even after only a few days on the Martian surface. It's annoying, to be honest. Why shouldn't I be able to bounce around, light on my feet and able to easily leap high into the air? If you ask me, now that I know better, Earth gravity is dumb.

But despite having to lift my full-weight body up, I gather my demon duck and arcane conduit burdens and clamber up out of the ship. This landing didn't deform the ship much worse than it was already twisted, and it takes a few moments to climb up and out.

I have to push a piece of wreckage out of the way to get out. It's dusty and shattered, like an old piece of drywall or some other basic building material, and it has a broken bit of metal stud attached to it.

Above me I can see the sky through a hole that was probably cut by a part of the yacht that's jutting up and has punched a hole in the ceiling. In the large room around me, there are piles of wreckage and one wall that was bashed open as the far side of the yacht's hull collapsed and sent beams straight through it. Closer by, what looks like museum exhibits seem to have been smashed and battered by the ship's arrival.

We were supposed to reappear at the bottom of the ocean. Something has gone awry.

I glance down and see a large sign next to us, knocked from its pedestal to the ground. I can't make out most of it, but the headline says MARTIAN ROCK AND SOIL, RECOVERED FROM THE FLOOR OF THE JAVA SEA.

As the dust settles around me, I start to hear sounds other than creaking metal and concrete. Distantly, there are the noises of a bustling city. Closer, faintly, there's string music. I get a sick feeling in the pit of my stomach as I hold still for a moment and identify it.

It's Pachelbel's goddamn Canon.

CHAPTER 18

What is this outrage?" a familiar voice demands. "I had my servants recover the chunk of Martian rock hours after it was teleported to Earth, and chartered an incredibly expensive jet to have it flown here for my collection! And you have immediately both stolen my prize and wrecked my grand exhibition hall!"

I freeze, seeing the figure of Slickwad, the disgusting demon made of seaweed and eels, standing in the doorway to the large open room.

"You!" he says, pointing an accusing finger at me. "Delicious boy! Have you done this to me? After all the kindness and compliments I have heaped upon you, your lack of gratitude is disgusting. You could have been a fine and supple specimen in my collection, and instead you have brought destruction every time I lay eyes upon your comely form."

"I, uh. . . . It was an accident?" I try. "We had no idea you would recover the piece of Mars and install it in an exhibit."

"Ignorance is not an excuse, and it is very unattractive," Slickwad says, motioning with his hands to figures looming behind him. "You should work on that."

"I'll be sure to try being less ignorant," I say. "Right away."

Where is Zambrano? Did he somehow already bail on me?

"And a little makeup and some cologne wouldn't hurt either," Slickwad continues. "And consider a wardrobe refresh? But my extremely attractive advice is useless at this point. I can't tolerate your existence any further. This is the third time you have laid waste to a part of my menagerie. Ironclad, destroy!"

The two figures behind him turn out to be ironclad demons. Whether one of them is our old friend Steve is not something I'm able to guess. But it doesn't matter; they're going to pulverize me either way.

"Whoops! Time for an expeditious exit!" Zambrano's voice comes from behind me. I feel his hand on my neck, and glancing back I see the sorcerer's arm, fine suit tattered and covered in reddish Martian dust, holding the familiar teleportrait of the warehouse.

"I want to go to there," he says as the two massive ironclad demons begin mounting the twice-wrecked hull of the yacht and climbing toward us.

I hold tight onto Seraphex and the conduit, and with a *whoosh* we are transported back in front of the wall of teleportraits in the large laboratory room.

For a long moment, we both stand there, catching our breath.

"Merlin turned out to be somewhat of a dick in the end," Zambrano says. "And to think, I used to idolize the fellow."

"I always thought traps were kind of dumb," I agree.

"He was a great warrior for humanity once," Zambrano says, switching to defending his old hero. "What are a few infuriating traps in the face of saving the human race? As much as a pain in my ass as they've been."

"Fair enough," I say. "Sometimes we tolerate an annoying personality in the service of a greater good," I add with a meaningful pat on his shoulder.

He takes the arcane conduit from me and puts it on his lab bench while I gently place Seraphex's unmoving body on one of the comfortable armchairs. She's been beat up before, but I've never seen her unconscious like this. I figure she's a nearly invincible demon and will probably recover soon. But with magic, nothing is certain.

I turn and look over at Zambrano, who is shaking his head as he removes his ruined suit jacket. I'd feel bad for him, but he's the one who wore nice clothes to a safari on a wild planet. I guess at least he was well-dressed when he met one of his heroes.

"Merlin didn't, like, accidentally unlock my magic potential or something while he was doing that spell?" I ask. "Subtly alter me, whoopsie-daisy, now you're fixed by his immense spellcasting ability?"

Zambrano raises an eyebrow and waves a single finger in a complicated pattern, muttering words in what sound like Latin. "It's theoretically possible . . ." he grumbles, but then he shrugs. "Sorry, no such luck. Your magical nature is still locked away. Or maybe totally gone and was never there. Hard to say for sure."

"You know, it would be nice to know for sure!" I complain. "I should have asked Susan when I had the chance."

Zambrano shrugs. "Perhaps it's better for you not to have the ability to learn magic. If you were even to get it, you might discover that you're not very good at it."

"Screw you," I say.

We're interrupted by a weak coughing sound from the chair.

"Seraphex is back," the demon duck says with a weary raising of her head. "I am awake again."

"How are you?" I ask. "How was what he did to you?"

"I would rather not discuss the ordeal I have gone through," Seraphex answers with a pathetic little cough. Her voice sounds incredibly distant and tired. She did just have her demonic essence pulled out and abused by Merlin's powerful spells, so it's only fair to give her some time.

"But are you well?" Zambrano asks. "Are you injured or weakened?"

"I am willing and able to continue the battle against my former husband," Seraphex assures us. "The few powers I retain in this form are rapidly returning. Of course, you are welcome to return me to my full prowess if you'd like—"

"Don't be ridiculous," Zambrano interrupts.

"As you wish," Seraphex says.

As she stands and shakes off the first layer of Martian dust, I can see her vigor is already starting to return.

"Very good," Zambrano says. "Then I think we can declare that all another lively mission, fully accomplished? With a side bonus of pulverizing the undead lich version of possibly the greatest sorcerer who ever lived. A big win in The Gang Goes to Mars."

"We are not adopting a stupid team name," I say. "And if we did, it absolutely wouldn't be 'The Gang.' That's taken."

"Zambrano's Zealots?" the sorcerer suggests with a grin.

"That's even worse," I say.

"The Genius, the Quack, and the Invisible Boy Without a Soul?"

"No."

"Zambrano and the Squad of Insufferable Fools Holding Back His Genius?"

"Absolutely not."

"It's a good thing you're not an intern anymore," Zambrano says, "or I would have you working the photocopier for a month for this insubordination!"

"How many printouts of my butt do you want?" I shoot back. "Printer ink is more expensive than blood these days."

"Ugh, fine," Zambrano says. "I'm going to throw this suit away and take a bath. Let everyone else on The Anti-Demon All-Stars know we survived. Schedule a meeting or whatever."

"I don't hate that one, but we're still not doing it," I say.

He does change the group chat to that name, but none of the rest of us acknowledge it. We're not going to give him the satisfaction.

I do, however, check in quickly with everyone. An hour and a half later, Zambrano, Seraphex, and I have taken some time to get ourselves together, and with a few quick teleports, we soon have our team coming in from around the globe.

While the others are gathering, my phone buzzes, and I see it's a call from Mei. Thanks to Eslarica, I've had to order a new phone and get it all set up. I hope she's furiously raging at us in the dark now that the phones have likely all died.

"What's up?" I ask.

"What's up?!" she complains. "You destroyed my boss's menagerie. Again! I didn't hear he was having the Mars rocks moved to the menagerie until right before you pulled your little stunt. Is there any employment you can't ruin for me? I have a thousand contractors to call, and he is riding my ass to get this repaired as soon as possible. I definitely can't get away, he would notice."

"Sorry about that," I say.

"You're not really sorry," she chides me.

"I'm trying to be sympathetic," I say. "But Slickwad, is, well, he's gross as hell. And a liar and a cheat, and he's always hitting on me."

"Well, the retirement benefits are incredible, and I get four weeks of vacation every year. And the chimps serve lunch for the menagerie staff in the dining room for us every day. It's free and surprisingly delicious."

"Sorry to create extra work while we save the world!" I quip, and she laughs.

"All right, Bryce, you got me there," she says. "What can I do to help?"

"You're connected with the demonic networks. Is there anything you can do to gather information? Help figure out what their next move is?"

"Sure," Mei says. "I'll see what I can dig up."

A few minutes later we sit down, with Liao Ling and Parth joining Zambrano, Seraphex, and me.

"Sorry I couldn't stop them from picking up the Mars rocks," Parth says. "I stayed in the area, but the teleportation magic pulled the energy out of the storm, and Slickwad's ships moved in immediately. Lucky for us they didn't realize how the spell worked."

Zambrano can't help but smirk, and I can't help myself but grin.

"Serves him right," I say. "That stuff belongs at NASA or something anyway. Greedy seaweed bastard."

"But what happened on Mars?" Parth asks.

Zambrano tells the story, applying plenty of self-serving embellishments, but generally getting the details decently right.

"That bastard," Liao Ling says, shaking her head sadly. "He couldn't just go out a hero, could he? Had to leave one final awful trap for us—the trap of his power-hungry ass still existing."

"How long will it take him to regenerate?" Parth asks after we tell the final part of the story where we were able to jump the undead Merlin with a taste of modern technology. Zambrano made it sound like he looked incredibly awesome with his pair of machine guns, but to be fair, he did look pretty badass.

Zambrano shrugs. "A day? A year? Another thousand years? It's hard to say, honestly. I don't understand the magic behind necromancy, and don't want to. It's gross."

Seraphex nodes sagely. "It's a silly practice, this necromancy. Far better to be immortal by design, indeed."

We all glare at her, but she appears not to even notice.

Before we can go any further, my phone buzzes again, another response from a message I sent. This call is coming in from Agent Crane. I put her on speaker so everyone can hear.

"Agent Crane, I'm here with the rest of the crew. What's happening?" I say.

"We're called The Great Zambrano's Anti-Demon All-Stars," Zambrano says.

"We are not called that," I interrupt.

"Not a chance in hell," Liao Ling adds.

"Yeah, what if we have to fight something other than demons?" Parth adds. "How about The Generalized Evil Battlers?"

Shaking my head and laughing, I wave them all off. "Sorry, Agent Crane. Don't be fooled by the banter; we are very serious people, who are trying to stop a demon king. What's going on? How bad are things?"

"It's bad," Agent Crane says, her voice coming through the speakerphone without a trace of amusement. "A number of world governments have stopped sharing intelligence, while others have started passing us intelligence we know to be incorrect. I have been building evidence over the past few days to prove that was the case. We believe the heads of state or at least top officials from these countries have been compromised."

"Can't they fight him? Why are they all giving up!" Parth complains.

"He's demonstrated his power successfully," Agent Crane says.

I feel my stomach drop.

"He's personally invincible," she continues, "and has no home country or population to threaten retaliation to. In the past few days, there have been attacks on the homes and families of a number of government officials around the world, all with strong evidence of demonic involvement."

"Cowards," Liao Ling mutters. "Kings have more often than not kowtowed to powerful demons. . . . Some things never change."

"What's worse," Agent Crane continues, "is that I put together that report and filed it with my superiors this morning. It's got damning evidence, and is well sourced and corroborated. I marked it highest priority. I checked for comments a few minutes ago—and it was gone. Deleted entirely. No notes, no explanation. Someone with full administrator privileges removed it, all drafts of it, everything."

"Your United States government is compromised as well," Zambrano says. "This does not shock me."

"No government can be trusted," Liao Ling agrees. "Not in my time, not here in the far future. Humans are weak and pliable."

I glance at Seraphex, who is thankfully keeping her mouth shut and not drawing any attention to herself.

"That's fair," Agent Crane says. "Things have felt weird here for the past day or two. I'm going to keep talking to people and see what I can find out. I'll leave you to your planning."

"Thanks. Talk to you soon," I say before hanging up.

"What do we do, then?" Parth asks as soon as she's off the line. And I can feel everyone's eyes on me. I'm supposed to be holding this together.

Six months ago, I was mixing protein shakes and dreaming of learning magic. Now I'm supposed to coordinate the last hope for humanity? I guess what I really wanted to be was important. And I went out there and got it. And it feels . . . terrifying. Maybe quietly making smoothies and getting promoted up the corporate ladder wasn't such a bad idea.

"We have a plan," I say, trying to plow through my feelings. "We have the Caesar Special to weaken Rex and the severed half of the arcane conduit to trap him. All we need is to find him and trap him. None of this political stuff changes the strategy."

I look around the room and see the group nodding in agreement. Was that all it took to point out the plan? I'm starting to feel better myself, but then a message pops up on my phone. It's from Mei.

Did some digging, the text message reads. *Rex keeps my boss out of the loop, mostly, so all we know is that he has something big coming up. But I found a record of a purchase Rex made from the menagerie. Scales from the extinct southeast Indian naga called the "vajranaga," or diamond naga.*

CHAPTER 19

"What's a diamond naga, and why would Rex want its scales?"

"That bastard," Seraphex says. "My wretch of a former husband likely knows at least part of what we're planning."

"I was worried about this," Zambrano says. "We used the Caesar Special in San Diego at Larry's Lasers. It seemed likely that he would try to construct a defense against it. It's a simple enough spell, with a powerful ingredient like that. Even a mere wizard could put it together, and he surely has some of those nincompoops under his command at this point."

I reach up and massage my temples, feeling the futility of the situation starting to fill in.

"So the Caesar Special won't work?"

Zambrano, Liao Ling, and Seraphex chatter back and forth about arcane theory and enchantments for a few minutes, but even with my limited knowledge of spellcasting, I can tell from their tone that none of it is promising.

"I don't see a way past it," Zambrano finally concludes. "He knows the Caesar Special's form; he'll have made sure the enchantments protect from everything of that type. He's no idiot."

"I hate to say it, but I agree," Liao Ling adds.

"We'll come up with something," I say lamely as my phone starts buzzing again, this time indicating another call from Agent Crane.

I press the button to answer it.

"Agent Crane, we're all still here," I say. But there's no immediate response. Just some static and what sounds like a chair squeaking.

"Agent Crane?" I say.

"Did she butt dial us?" Parth suggests.

"Come in!" Agent Crane's voice says, distant and tinny.

Zambrano's hand shoots out, snakelike, and hits the mute button on my phone. "She is letting us hear a conversation in real time," he explains.

"She may be worried she will not be able to call us afterward," Seraphex says.

"Director Scott," we hear Agent Crane's voice, muffled, as if her phone is in her pocket. "I thought you were meeting with the arcane security team for the Geneva summit. What's going on? Who's outside?"

"I'm sorry to have to do it this way," a man's voice replies, a deep tone with a slight twang probably from the American south. "They wanted to come and arrest you, but I convinced them I had to at least tell you in person. You're relieved of your duties, effective immediately. I'm going to need your credentials, sidearm, and all your devices."

We hear a deep sigh. "I understand," Agent Crane says, resignation in her voice.

"After I remove your MSA clearances and access, the men outside will be arresting you for sharing classified information with the known state enemies Zambrano, Liao Ling, the demon Seraphex, and the traitor Bryce Alexander."

"Damn, I don't even get a mention?" Parth gripes.

"I had your approval!" Agent Crane objects. "Those conversations were all logged and reported per MSA regulations."

"There are no records of those alleged reports in our servers," Director Scott says. "Please don't lie about that. It endangers my reputation and only makes you look like more of a patsy for the traitors that you conspired with. Don't drag me into your treasonous behavior. You'll have your day in court eventually."

"They deleted all of it," Parth says, clenching his fists. "They're screwing her over!"

"And he's covering his own ass," Liao Ling adds with a sneer.

"None of this is necessary, Director," Agent Crane insists. "Why can't I continue to work my job? I was just on the phone now with

Bryce Alexander, Zambrano, and the rest of them. I'm the one they trust to share information with."

"You have been misinformed," Director Scott says. "The real threat was not Rexhalarkhart, the so-called demon king. That was misinformation spread by enemies of the state. The true danger comes from Zambrano and his cronies."

"They've saved the world multiple times!" Agent Crane protests.

"You clearly have been taken in by their act," Scott answers. "Which is why you can't be trusted with classified information or to act on behalf of the MSA."

"He's playing to an audience," Seraphex suggests. "Trying to prove his loyalty to whoever is listening in."

"You need me if you want to keep them cooperating," Agent Crane counters. "Things could turn around. Your current orders could be mistaken."

"The decision has been made at the highest levels," Director Scott says firmly. "Their presence on American soil cannot be tolerated any longer."

"Oh shit," I breathe. I meet the eyes of the other people at the table. Their faces are as grim as mine.

"You're making a mistake. I'm sorry this is all happening. I wish I could have prevented it. Here's my access card, my credentials, and my service weapon," she says, and we can hear items being deposited on a desk.

"My laptop is in the bag there; you can take that," Agent Crane's voice comes through, tightly controlled. "And I have my phone right here. I'll deactivate it," she finishes. And the line abruptly goes dead, presumably as she turns the phone off.

"Well played, Agent Crane," Zambrano says to the disconnected phone.

"Will they be able to tell that she was calling us?" Parth asks.

"Our government friend handled that brilliantly," Seraphex says. "She clearly stated she had been speaking with us. A difference of a minute or two from when she turned over her device. Unless someone looks very carefully at the time stamps, there will be no way to determine it. But it's a risk, certainly."

"That's good, at least. Hopefully she didn't put herself in danger." I can feel a weight settling on me as the seriousness of our situation sinks in. "But this is so bad."

"It is, indeed," Zambrano says. "A key weapon against Rex has been rendered useless. And the US government has been subverted by the demon king, without firing a shot."

I don't want to think about it. I want to go hide somewhere. We only just got back from three days camping on Mars, sleeping on bare rock and gravel. And now we have to deal with this.

"I suppose I always knew this day was coming," Zambrano says. "No national leadership's ego can cope with having me around for too long. It makes them look bad."

"They were co-opted by an evil demon," Liao Ling points out. "Not intimidated by you."

"One way or another, it always happens," Zambrano says with a shrug.

"How long do we have here?" I ask. "Before they make a move on us."

"Hard to say," Zambrano says.

"Your government friend took a big risk getting that information to us," Liao Ling says. "We should make use of the time."

At the same moment, we all start glancing around. Are the feds closing in? Will we be hit with a missile, will demons come crashing through the walls, or will MSA agents come rappelling in from helicopters?

While the rest of us are talking, Zambrano has already run to the stacks and is pulling key volumes off the shelf, piling them on the table. "I usually don't do a move like this on short notice!" he complains. "The mystical defenses would hold off most wizards or military attacks for a while."

"If Rex's demons are in the mix, that won't last for long," Seraphex says with an unusual note of sympathy in her voice.

"We need a secure place to relocate, where we can store my many artifacts," Zambrano says.

I look over at Liao Ling, raising a questioning eyebrow.

"You want to. . . . Ugh, really? You know, it's rude to invite yourself over to someone's home," Liao Ling says, exasperated.

"We need a place to go," I say. "Please."

"I hate houseguests. But fine. Only until this fight is over. We're not doing some shared base thing, okay?"

"Of course," I agree. "Just until we take down Rex. Then hopefully things will calm down, and we can come back."

Grumbling, Liao Ling pulls out the teleportrait to her personal lair in the South China Sea, which shows a pavilion surrounded by lush tropical foliage. Parth helps load up one of her arms full of books and grabs a full load of books for himself. Zambrano hands Parth the arcane conduit, which he holds under his chin. Liao Ling awkwardly puts her elbow in touch with his forearm, and the two disappear with a quiet *whoosh*. Meanwhile, Zambrano is running to his lab bench, pulling out key tools and artifacts.

I run to the front door, crack it open, and stick my head out. Through the chain-link fence, I can see that alongside the usual MSA security detail, three more unmarked sedans have pulled up. Far down the street, I can see a pair of vans approaching.

On the other side of the fence, I see Derek, who is standing alone, staring anxiously at the building. His hand is down on his sidearm. He sees me and raises his eyebrows in alarm.

"AMP," he mouths silently. Then loudly he calls out, "Bryce, we need to have a conversation with you. I have important information about the demonic threat."

"Can you come out and talk with us? Or let us come in? We have been authorized to share vital intelligence with you," a voice from farther back says, amplified by a megaphone.

"Uh, let me talk to Zambrano!" I bullshit. "I'll try to convince him to listen to us, okay?"

"That's good," Derek says loudly, rolling his eyes with exaggeration. "We need to work together to help our country and the world. Talk it over with him, we'll be here." Then silently and out of view of the other agents behind him, he mouths the word "demons."

"Great, I'll be back in a few minutes!" I lie and close the door.

I silently thank Derek for realizing what's going on. He's also taking a risk so that we can keep fighting even if their chain of command is compromised.

Inside the warehouse, Liao Ling and Parth have just come back from a teleportation, and Liao Ling is breathing heavily. I quickly move to them and help load them up with lab equipment and bags of supplies.

"They're going to use an AMP," I say. "Will that work through the mystical defenses?"

When the AMP was used against us at Larry's Lasers in Santa Cruz, it nearly got us and some civilians killed. It's a device that scrambles the magic in the area, making the underlying arcane math work differently. That makes connecting a teleportation spell between areas almost impossible.

"Unfortunately, yes, the protection magic won't shield us from the AMP. Other than keeping the smell of the explosives outside, I guess," Zambrano says. "And once the AMP is set off, they will have us trapped here and can hammer on the defenses until they crack."

"How long do we have?" Parth asks as he pulls down as many teleportraits from the wall as he can, creating a massive stack.

"There are vans driving up; we probably don't have long," I say. I grab the backpack I took to Mars, which is still sitting in the corner covered in Martian dust.

"I spent years assembling this collection!" Zambrano says. "So many priceless books and powerful enchanted items. We need at least ten or fifteen more trips to get the rest of the important items!"

"We can't risk it," I say. "What if the AMP goes off? We're trapped here, surrounded by enemies and likely demons. Maybe we could fight our way out or sneak out, but at what cost? Even if we could fight, we'd probably end up leveling the whole block."

Zambrano looks around the lab, shoulders slumping. There are massive shelves of books, drawers of ingredients and enchanted items, and many teleportraits still hanging on the wall.

"This is my life's work!" he insists. "I can't simply abandon it! We should stay and fight. Stand our ground. They have no right to do this."

"Bryce is correct," Seraphex says. "We should leave immediately and not come back. We have no chance if there is a significant force of demons on its way."

"If the government gets it, they won't destroy any of it. We'll steal them back, Z," Liao Ling says with a grim smile. "Traps may have been Merlin's specialty, but part of how he got into that was because theft and piracy were my things and he wanted to discourage me. Didn't work. I'll help you steal it all back, I promise."

"Thank you," Zambrano says, his brows knitting as he tries to control his emotions. "Very well. Let's make a tactical retreat." He grabs several more piles of books and shoves them into my arms. Even Seraphex is laden down with necklaces and pendants of various sorts. Zambrano shoves the Spyglass of Spinoza under one of my arms and piles even more books on top. My own magical gauntlets, luckily, are safely in my backpack. For himself, he runs over and grabs the big golden telescope that's been sitting in the corner, pointed at a blank brick wall the entire time I've been living here. Still no idea what it does.

"Everyone, link up," Liao Ling says, and we all crowd around her, making physical contact with her or one another. She never gave Zambrano a teleportrait to her lair, so we all have to go with her in one big group. She holds the teleportrait up awkwardly in one hand, though her arms are filled with books.

There's a sudden *whomp* sound, but Liao Ling is already speaking the words, "I want to go to there."

My nostrils twitch as the smell of ozone fills the air. What comes next feels like reality itself shaking and twisting. It's the same feeling as it was in San Diego—the arcane magical pulse, or AMP, that disrupts teleportation. Liao Ling yells, a cry of pain, but I can't make out what she's saying.

CHAPTER 20

My vision explodes in light, and my ears are filled with what sounds like a woman screaming. Is it Liao Ling, still? I think so.

The disorienting feeling of the AMP, like being drunk and high at the same time, somehow lasts for both an eternity and only a few seconds.

We emerge in the right location, luckily, the pavilion on Liao Ling's island, surrounded by tropical trees. But we do not come through smoothly at all.

Normally the teleportation process seamlessly adjusts momentum, height, and orientation without me even noticing it. However the spell is constructed, it fully accounts for the spin of the Earth and all the other relevant angles. This time, however, that does not hold. We appear completely sideways, nearly upside down.

My stomach lurches with the reentry to reality, and we all fall to the ground. I'm barely able to drop the items I'm carrying and throw my arms out. I catch myself on my elbows and knees, and the wind is nearly knocked out of me.

I'm lucky that the floor under this pavilion is packed soil and not stone, or I would probably be seriously injured. As it is, I'm cut and bruised in several places, but it only adds to the minor injuries already sustained from our Martian adventures.

It's nighttime, which makes sense since we're on the opposite side of the world. Luckily, it is a bright full moon, so I can see the tumbling bodies of my friends that are falling around me.

"Is everyone okay?" I ask as I stand and shake off the rough landing.

"I am fine," Zambrano says, brushing himself off. It looks like he landed with catlike reflexes and with no real harm.

"I'm good," Parth says. "Nothing serious."

Looking at him, it appears as though he has taken a tougher fall than I did, with blood flowing from cuts on both his elbows. But he's a maniac, so he's not going to let anything like a little physical damage stop him.

"I am well, thank you for your concern," Seraphex says. She, as always, is completely unharmed. She fluttered down, able to easily fly now that we're back in Earth's atmosphere. And she would have been fine even so, with her demonic toughness.

Liao Ling, on the other hand, doesn't answer. She's lying in a heap, eyes open and staring at the sky.

"Zambrano, look," I say, feeling a tightness gathering in my chest as I point at the fallen figure of Liao Ling on the ground. She's just lying there like a rag doll tossed aside in a video game.

He immediately leaps to her side, first checking her pulse and then laying a hand on her chest just below her throat and closing his eyes as he whispers a spell.

The rest of us wait for long moments as Zambrano works. Looking closely, I do see her rib cage is rising and falling slightly.

"I'm no expert in the healing arts," he says finally as he stands up, "but that should help her. I don't think she is badly injured. She simply spent all her energy keeping the teleportation as the arcane substrate shifted under her."

"The arcane substrate?" Parth asks.

"The mathematics of reality that underpin all physics and magic," Zambrano explains. "We got out before the AMP fully disrupted it. Liao Ling paid the price, but she'll be okay."

As if in response, Liao Ling rolls slightly, muttering something unintelligible.

Parth immediately starts tending to her, rolling up his jacket and putting it under her head and rearranging her splayed limbs to be in less awkward positions.

"Give me your backpack," he says. "It has a first aid kit, right?"

I hand it over, and he pulls out the medical supplies, carefully placing bandages on Liao Ling's minor wounds.

"Her mental function felt acceptable to me," Zambrano says. "She will be fine, but her body needs time to heal and reorganize itself. I believe the technical way to explain it would be . . . she has a hangover."

"That's good news," I say. "Hopefully she'll be okay."

"That teleportation. . . . I don't know if I could have done that," he says. "Changing the spell like that at the last minute, powering through the AMP disruption. I could feel just how intense and sudden it was. We could easily have been teleported into orbit, or to the middle of the Earth, or scattered in bits across the planet."

"She's more powerful than you, isn't she?" I ask. "With her old-school magic."

At first Zambrano just grunts. But then he nods slowly. "She has a tighter connection with magic. It listens to her. It's like it's familiar and comfortable with her in a way that I've never been able to achieve. Something has made magic shy away from us since the time of Merlin and Liao Ling. It's like an abused dog that can't quite trust again."

"That's really sad," I say.

"Is that why I can't cast fireballs yet?" Parth says from his spot by Liao Ling, where he's finishing up putting a Band-Aid on a small cut on her forehead.

"No, that's due to your hand motions; they need to be sharper and more clipped," Zambrano says. "I saw you practicing last week. Think less flow, more jagged. But you can blame it on magic if you want. And don't ever practice it inside again! Even if you're in Bryce's room. The birch butlers have enough to deal with without fire damage. Try it in my lab, and I will personally disembowel you."

"Sure, sure," Parth says. "More jagged, got it, Dr. Z."

"Ey! What are you doing here?" a gruff voice with a Chinese accent calls out.

It's one of the pirates from Liao Ling's ships, the one with a nasty scar where his left eye should be. How a pirate wouldn't realize you're supposed to cover it with an eyepatch for the vibes, I don't know. He advances, warily holding a machine gun with a wicked-looking bayonet gleaming in the tropical moonlight.

"Liao Ling brought us here," I explain. "She's . . . hungover. From magic, not alcohol."

As soon as he sees Parth, the man's wariness disappears as he rushes forward to check on her. "Captain!" he says as he kneels down. "Are you hurt?"

"That's Dao." Parth backs off to let the pirate examine his captain. "It means 'knife.' For the bayonet. Or for how he lost his eye, I couldn't quite figure that out."

"How did you let this happen to her?" Dao asks. "She is barely conscious."

"We almost got caught trying to escape New York City," I say. "The government was trying to capture us there. She cast the spell to teleport us, but it took a lot out of her."

Hearing that, Dao nods in appreciation. "She did good work, then. And thanks for taking care of her, young sir," he says to Parth. "These wounds are well dressed."

"We should leave her here in case she has injuries," Dao says. "I'll send one of the men to keep an eye on her and have food and water for when she wakes up. Come, I'll take you up to the villa."

He beckons, and we follow the grizzled Chinese pirate up a narrow path through the woods, higher on the island.

"I imagine you'll be staying on the island, if you were forced to flee the authorities in America?" Dao asks.

"Yes, if that's all right with you," I say. "We would appreciate it."

"Should be fine. We're down a few men who quit after that typhoon nonsense. Always good to see cowards and quitters go."

"How many pirates do you have here on this island?" I ask.

"Pirates?! We are not pirates! I am an honest businessman," the Dao retorts.

"Oh, sorry!" I say. "I guess I just assumed. . . . Sorry."

"I'm a proud, honest businessman and sailor," Dao says as we reach the crest of the hill and the back entrance to a massive villa with tan stucco walls and a terra-cotta tile roof. It's surrounded by dense trees and bushes from this side, but I can see the ocean through the brush. "One whose business happens to be waylaying the freighters of immoral governments and relieving them of their valuable goods at the point of my bayonet."

"Which immoral governments do you target?" Parth asks.

"All of them," Dao says. "Can you name a government in the world that isn't corrupt and immoral in one way or another?"

"He has a point," Zambrano chimes in.

"Certainly hard to argue against," Seraphex adds.

"Oh," I say. "So, is pirate not the appropriate term?"

"I prefer *privateer*," Dao suggests.

"A privateer needs to be authorized by a government," Zambrano points out.

"We are duly authorized by the government of Liao Ling Land to loot and plunder her many enemies of the state," Dao says proudly.

"Right," I say. "The enemies of so-called Liao Ling Land. Which is everyone? Anyone who has stuff you want?"

"Be glad it's not you," Dao says cheerfully. "Not today, at least!"

I want to question him further, but we are guests here, and he has a machine gun with a wickedly sharp-looking bayonet on it. So I follow along as we go in the rear entrance of the villa. He leads us up the narrow stairs of the back entrance and out onto the open balcony that makes up the main floor of the villa.

I don't know what I expected, exactly, but it wasn't this.

We're high above the water, looking out across an endless dark sea lit by the moon. There are also a few decorative lights that help to enhance the villa around us, but if I had something this spectacular, I would want it artistically lit to show it off as well.

The villa is built up above the cliffside, but also carved into the rocks of it, with stairways and balconies below. The massive main floor open balcony is flanked by two large buildings that rise up into the night sky. It looks like every room in the whole place has a seaside view.

In the bright moonlight, the jungle around us and the ocean crests far below are highlighted clearly, breathtakingly majestic.

"Wow," I say.

"Fantastic, isn't it?" Parth agrees.

"Pretty nice," Zambrano says, yawning. "If you go in for this sort of ostentatious tackiness."

"It's rather gorgeous," Seraphex says. "A materialistic being could speculate that I have clearly been the wisecracking demonic sidekick to the wrong sorcerer for the last few months."

"Maybe I should have traded you for our new friend Dao," Zambrano shoots back. "He seems competent, attentive, and respectful."

"You have paid me a compliment," Dao says, cocking his head to the side. "And yet I still feel insulted. Strange." He motions to a couple stocky men waiting near one of the doorways, who don't have the grizzled look of pirates and are wearing simpler attire that reminds me of resort attendants. "Let my men show you to your rooms. I'm sure you are very tired."

"How do you know we're tired?" Zambrano asks.

"I don't know, but I need you out of my way while I tend to my captain." Dao shrugs. "Also, you look like shit."

"Like shit?" Zambrano demands.

"Is that not the correct American colloquialism?" Dao asks. "My most humble and sincere apologies. "You looked 'pooped.' Is that the correct one? Or is the appropriate term you look like 'death warmed over'? Or you appear 'busted.' Is that the more modern slang? You must understand, I learned English from YouTube videos."

"We have been on three different sides of two planets, and we are exhausted," I interrupt before Zambrano, whose eyes are bulging out, can give a proper demonstration of the fireball technique he was telling Parth about. "Unless the world is literally about to explode, maybe we should get a little rest and give Liao Ling some time to recover, and then we can figure out what our next step is?"

The men show us to our rooms, which each have awesome balconies and all the amenities of a fancy resort hotel. I take a quick shower, crawl into one of the beds, and am out like a light.

The next morning, Liao Ling has slept off her hangover, and all of us gather back on the big balcony overlooking the ocean.

"Where did you get this place?" I ask, looking around in amazement once again at the incredible architecture. "You've only been back in action for a few months."

"This was my island before I was transported into the future to be here with you chuckleheads," Liao Ling says. "It was hidden away, wrapped in stealthy magic. It was undisturbed for many, many years."

"I always wondered if your island was a myth or real," Zambrano said. "Rodney Wint tried to find it on multiple occasions, but he came up empty. He asked me to help him, but Alix would have made fun of me if I'd made such an embarrassing failure. So I declined."

"Well, a couple decades ago a Chinese businessman and his hired gun wizards got lucky and stumbled right on it," Liao Ling says. "They found the entrance, and he used it as his personal getaway."

"And what happened when you arrived and found him here?" Zambrano asks.

"Liao Ling was not pleased," Dao says. "Not pleased at all."

"Gotta feed the fish in the aquarium," Liao Ling says with a nonchalant shrug.

"They have been well nourished these past few months," Dao says, nodding in appreciation.

"Wait, you've got an aquarium here?" Parth asks. "Where is it? How did I not see it when you brought me here before?"

I hadn't realized they'd been to the island together, but I suppose they have been working with each other regularly over the past week.

"Oh, it's down there," she says, gesturing to the ocean lapping at the rocks below.

"It's down on the cliff side? Is it built into the rock?" Zambrano says, peering over the railing down the jagged rocks.

"No, numbskull," Liao Ling says.

"She means the ocean," Seraphex says, enjoying the moment.

"The sharks," Dao says, grinning, his one eye twinkling with humor. "Down in our little shark tank."

"All of this banter is very amusing," Seraphex interrupts, "but we do have the business of saving your little human world to get to, don't we?"

"Yeah," I say. "Um, how the hell are we going to do that, again?"

CHAPTER 21

Rex has the diamond naga scales and is protected against the one magic weapon I was able to fashion that would even weaken him, the Caesar Special," Liao Ling says.

"I don't have any better spells," Zambrano says. "Nothing that powerful has been invented since your time. And all the stories say none of the artifact weapons does much against him."

"If I had the power to destroy my bastard former husband, believe me," Seraphex adds, "I would have done it many thousands of years ago. And in this form, there is essentially nothing I can do against him."

We look out at the ocean for a long moment, leaning on the balcony railing as we all rack our brains for an idea.

"I'm working on a new spell. The fireball, the jagged motion like—" Parth starts, but Liao Ling slaps his hand.

"If you must practice your fireballs, you can do it in the jungle," she says. "I don't want scorch marks on my tile."

"I was just kidding!" Parth objects. "Trying to lighten the mood!"

"Lighten the mood without making the gestures of a battle spell, if you would be so kind," Zambrano says, shaking his head in annoyance but also in a bit of amusement.

"Casting the fireball is impressive, but you need to do things in the proper order," Liao Ling admonishes. "I showed you the Shanghai Sudden Shield while these bozos were on Mars—keep practicing that. You've got to keep your motions smooth, not choppy like those European spells."

"Hey, I'm working on it!" Parth protests.

"I'll run you through it again later. That pronunciation is going to take some work," Liao Ling says. "Now, does anyone have any ideas for how we don't lose to Rex now that the Caesar Special won't work? A Shanghai Sudden Shield is great, but it won't do a thing to stop a demon king's claws."

We all stare at one another in silence, no one offering any helpful suggestions.

I'm supposed to be the one getting everyone to work together. With no magic or special abilities, what else do I have to offer? Even Parth is just a few hand adjustments away from being able to cast a fireball.

"Bunkering up is always an option," Zambrano says. "We're already in a magically hidden location. What if we work on gathering supplies and strengthening the magical defenses and try to ride it out?"

"I thought we were over the whole 'run and hide' thing?" I say, annoyed. "Didn't we deal with that already?"

"I'm merely attempting to enumerate our various options," Zambrano says petulantly. "Make sure we consider them."

"Okay," I admit. "I don't like that option, but that's not a bad plan. Before we give up, let's think through *everything* we *could* do."

Below us, the morning sun is shining on a vast and empty ocean, endless waves stretching from horizon to horizon. It's gorgeous, and impressive. Also, I realize that after this conversation I am definitely going to need to ask Liao Ling for some sunscreen. The tropical rays are beating down the heat of a thousand suns. Well, the heat of a single sun, but that's enough for the sensitive skin of a mere human.

"Good plan," Liao Ling says. "What options do we have?"

"Charge into battle with him, knowing the odds are stacked against us but hoping for the best?" Parth suggests. "Bravery first, planning later?"

"That is, technically, an option," Seraphex says. "Even better, it's achievable with the resources that we have at our advantage. Marvelous work."

"Easy," I say. "Sometimes you need to get the bad ideas out first. Or a bad idea will lead to a good one."

"How does the old phrase go?" Seraphex says. "'There are no bad ideas in brainstorming, only bad people.' Is that it?"

"I suspect you're thinking of 'There are no stupid questions, only stupid people,' but whatever," I say. "What are our other options? Could we negotiate with Rex? Offer some sort of truce to buy us time?"

"We have no leverage against him. Nothing to offer him that he wants, other than our surrender or our deaths," Seraphex says.

"What else?" I say. "Run away somewhere? Find allies?"

"I can't think of any allies who would possess any weapons that would harm him," Zambrano says. "Druids, wizards, world governments—they're all in the same position we are. Rex has more raw horsepower; no one can go toe-to-toe with a demon king."

"Could we construct some sort of new spell to neutralize him?" I ask.

"In theory, anything is possible," Liao Ling says. "But the Caesar Special took years of magical research and luck in finding a particular weakness. And none of us have any ideas of what sort of other weaknesses a powerful demon might have."

"And for research, we only have a fraction of my library," Zambrano says. "Your government is even now probably breaking past the mystical defenses and tromping their dirty boots through my workshop."

"Now you know how I feel having all of you here," Liao Ling says, though she's smiling as she says it. She's not serious, or at least, only a little bit serious.

We all pause, thinking it over as the sound of waves far below filters up, a dull but pleasant roar. It would be nice to visit this place at a time when the world wasn't ending.

"If you want to beat someone at something," Liao Ling says, "You need an edge. Like at the gambling table. Or, as I've discovered in these past few months, in your stock markets. A little knowledge goes a long way. You only need to know one thing no one else does. Then press that advantage to the hilt, twist it, and take your victory."

"My favorite knowledge advantage," Dao says, having walked up to us with a tray of food that he sets on a nearby table, "is the knowledge that I have a knife and can draw it and stab you all in one motion before you can react. It makes card and dice games so much less stressful, knowing that. I used to hate them."

"You just murder the other gamblers?" Parth asks. "And take their money?"

Dao shrugs. "Sometimes I win at the gambling part. No need for knives then." he says and turns and walks back into the villa.

"What edge could we possibly have against him?" Seraphex asks, her tone more depressed than usual. "He's the highest power level being in the solar system, as far as I know, in direct conflict at least. Even if I were in my full demonic form, I couldn't match his strength for more than a few minutes. Information is my favorite form of power, but he seems to know our next move before we even get there. We only barely escaped him in the typhoon. And he's chased us from our home."

"Well," I ask, "what do we know that he doesn't know? Anything?"

"I can't think of anything," Seraphex says.

I pause, breath catching in my throat. "You can't think of it! Brilliant!"

"What are you on about?" Zambrano asks, brow furrowed in annoyance.

"The one piece of information we have that Rex doesn't have is the one thing he not only doesn't know but *isn't even capable of thinking about*."

"Oh," Zambrano says. "Oh! Yes, that is an interesting idea."

"The knowledge of the nature of demons," Liao Ling says. "Clever. He won't see it coming because he literally can't think about it due to the third law of the demonic code."

"Brilliant!" Parth says.

"How does knowing where he comes from help us?" Zambrano asks, still not totally on board. "We learned about history thousands of years ago. That's a far cry from a weapon that will weaken Rex while we trap him in the arcane conduit."

"The question I would ask," I say, scrunching up my face as I think about it, "is how was the demonic code applied? How was it created? Who created it? It happened at a specific time. How, and by whom? It's a long shot, but there could be something there."

"When was it created?" I ask. "During some Chinese ruler's reign?"

"Seraphex?" Zambrano asks. But the duck is staring off into the distance.

Finally, she turns to us and cocks her head to the side as if replaying the conversation in her mind.

"Yes, I was in China at the time. It was at the end of the Xia dynasty," Seraphex finally says. "But I don't think it happened there; no one in China at the time had that level of power. It could have been anywhere else in the world."

"So around 1800 to 1600 BCE, then," Liao Ling says.

"There was a lot happening in the world around then," Parth says, looking at information that he's pulled up on his phone. "Major civilizations in the Indus valley, Egypt, Mesopotamia, Minoan culture, the Norte Chico in Peru. Any of those?"

"I don't know. Is there anyone else who was alive at that time that we can ask?" Liao Ling suggests. "That was almost two thousand years before my time period."

"We can't ask any demons," Parth points out. "As much fun as it would be to capture and interrogate one. They won't be able to remember anything."

I look over to Zambrano. "You're the most knowledgeable about who and what is still around at this point. Any ideas?"

"I'm not sure. And there was nothing in my library about it. But . . ." He scratches his chin as he thinks it through. "I do think I might know of one being who could be able to shed some light on it. He's got a temper though."

I groan. "I'm assuming we're going to have to ask for help from someone who hates you because you were a total dick to them a long time ago and they haven't forgiven you because you never even tried to apologize?"

Zambrano glances around, biting his lip. "Well, yes. Yes, that is a mostly correct assumption. Is that a problem?"

"It's certainly telling about your moral character," I say, "but we've always handled it in the past."

"Is it someone you slept with, again?" Seraphex asks.

Zambrano brightens. "No! No, it is not. Nothing like that."

"Small victories," Seraphex mutters.

"I'm not an idiot; I'm not going to get my private bits burned off," Zambrano adds.

"I retract my statement," Seraphex says. "I strongly recommend you date this individual."

"Why is it only a mostly correct assumption?" I ask. "We should know as much as possible before getting into this situation with some ancient being who is probably quite powerful?"

"Well, you said you were worried I had been a dick to this being a long time ago," Zambrano says. "It, ah . . . wasn't very long ago."

I rub my forehead, feeling a headache coming on. "Who was it, and what did you do?"

"Remember that phoenix egg we stole from Slickwad back when we were fighting Demon Duke Volcanose?" Zambrano asks.

"Yeah," I say. "We let it hatch in Saskatchewan to draw Volcanose away from his headquarters. Because phoenix is a delicacy for demons, or something."

"Correct," Zambrano says. "And it mostly worked, though Volcanose did come back while we were making our escape."

"Right," I say. And then I realize the effect that Zambrano's plan must have had on the phoenix himself. "Damn it. Didn't you say at the time that it was the last known phoenix egg? And you risked it like that?"

"It seemed like a good idea at the time!" Zambrano says.

CHAPTER 22

Before we head out, I give Mei a quick call to check in.

"How are you doing?" I ask. "Are you safe?"

"As safe as I can be, risking everything to try to help a ragtag group of antiheroes save humanity," she says. "But I'm okay. I heard the MSA raided your spot in New York. Are you okay?"

"We're getting by," I say. "About to follow up on a lead that might help take Rex out."

"That's good," Mei says. "Rex's plans are accelerating. I'm not supposed to know, but I have access to logistics data from supplies that are going around to different demons and demon-aligned wizards. Everything is leading up to an event happening at roughly the same time—the date of some big summit in Geneva. They haven't requisitioned anything beyond that."

"More time pressure," I say with a chuckle. "Just what I was hoping for."

"I hope you find something good on your trip," Mei says. "Don't tell me the details if I don't need to know them. I can't reveal what I don't know."

I want to tell her everything, the secret origin of demons, the mysterious origin of the codes, the phoenix in Canada— But she's right. If I tell her, it puts all of us at greater risk.

"Yeah, that's probably for the best," I agree. "Time to be in secret agent mode. I don't want to put you at any additional risk."

"Thanks," Mei says. "I have to admit, I'm curious. You'll have to fill me in on all the details later on, okay?"

"Absolutely," I say. "It's a lot though!"

"I'm counting on it," Mei says. "I would love to spend some time with someone who's not a demon or an evil wizard who works for demons. You stay safe out there, okay? Let me know if there's anything else I can do to help. You've got this."

I'll admit that her encouragement makes my heart feel a little something, but there's no time for that now. It's a big change from when we first surprised her in the demon duke's office months ago and she tried to call in rockhide demons to flatten me.

"Appreciate it," I say. "Good luck."

A few hours later, we've got everything ready to start our journey, including inconspicuous clothes, hats, and sunglasses. There are cameras everywhere these days, and who knows which state actors are sharing surveillance with Rex?

Luckily, Zambrano does have a teleportrait for Winnipeg. From there we get a car to take us to Saskatoon and hire a local guy with a pickup truck to take us up into the Cypress Hills. Eventually we get as close as we can on a road, and we leave the confused local behind, telling him we'll be fine and don't need a ride back. He watches in concern as we hop the fence and start hiking in what to him must seem like a random direction without a trail or anything.

Parth comes with us, but Liao Ling stays behind to guard her island, with the assignment to try to figure out where Rex is hiding and keep tabs on his latest moves in case we're able to find something we can use against the demon king.

While I have a bunch of food and hiking supplies in my backpack, Parth is carrying a heavy pack Zambrano shoved on him right before we left, with a warning not to open it until he tells him to. If it were me, I would have asked about what sort of magical explosive or living creature with tentacles is waiting inside, ready to run amok, but Parth takes it without comment. I'm not sure if he's less experienced with Zambrano's antics or just more chill than I am.

I guess my main purpose in coming along is to make sure Zambrano doesn't say anything too stupid. And Seraphex might be helpful, but mostly I want her so we can keep an eye on her. I've been worried about her since whatever Merlin did to her on Mars—something about her mannerisms has been off, like she's thinking extra hard about everything she says, and she's looking off into the distance sometimes, like she's lost or mulling things over. I wonder if demons can get PTSD? I would probably be pretty messed up if someone ripped my soul out of my body, asked a bunch of uncomfortable questions that pried into the very nature of my existence, and then shoved my soul back in.

"Are you sure we shouldn't send me in alone to negotiate with him?" I ask as we start the hike. "Or teleport Liao Ling in to do it once we find him?"

"No, he's too clever for that," Zambrano says. "He keeps tabs on events all over the world. He surely knows Liao Ling is back and that we're working together. I hate to do it, but I'm going to have to apologize in person for us to have any chance of getting his help. Anything else will only piss him off."

"We'll get to see some real fireworks though, right, Professor Z?" Parth asks.

"Yes, we will certainly see some big flames," Zambrano says. "He claims he's dying and being reborn over and over again, when in truth it's a garden variety transmogrification with a perceptual state change. He's a braggart and a peacock, if you ask me."

"I can think of at least one other person I've been around lately who fits that definition," Seraphex says.

"Oh, Liao Ling isn't that bad," Zambrano says obliviously.

Parth and I meet eyes and stifle our laughter as we reach the bottom of one slope and start up the next.

Our visit to the Cypress Hills is yet another experience that would be lovely if we weren't here trying to stop the demon king from taking over the world. The fall air is crisp, and we're walking through rolling hills with trees, grasses, rock outcroppings, and a nice view at the top of each hill. On a lazy afternoon with a few friends and some drinks in a backpack, this would be a nice hike. Instead we're moving quickly, catching little cuts on brush, and all I have in my backpack is protein bars and water. I need to start keeping bags of trail mix on hand, the kind with M&M's in it that feels like healthy hiking food but is basically candy. At this point, I feel like I deserve it.

"If this phoenix is so knowledgeable, why haven't we asked for his help before?" I ask.

"Well . . . he's pretty pissed at me. You'll see," Zambrano says.

"You did feed him to a demon," Seraphex says from her usual perch on my shoulder. "I hope you've got a good apology ready."

"Yes, because you know I am so great at those," Zambrano says with a chuckle.

"I've dealt with worse," I say with a shrug. "I'm sure you can handle this."

"Ugh, damn it," he says as we crest a hill. "Am I growing and changing or something? I promised myself I would never do that."

Pausing for a moment, Zambrano casts a quick spell, nods, and points to another hilltop in the distance.

"We're getting close," he says. "It should be over there."

"Over there" turns out to be easy to see but is a big hill that requires another forty-five minutes of walking.

"How does it feel, having another sorcerer back in the world?" I ask as we cross a stream running in the gully between the hills. "Since the others have all been gone for so long?"

"It is nice," Zambrano says with a heavy sigh. "As annoying as she can be at times. But so are the rest of you, so I can deal with that. But of course I'm worried."

"Worried that she'll go mad?" I ask. "That you'll have to kill her?"

Zambrano shrugs. "She's much younger than I am in terms of her body's age. She was only around sixty when she was trapped in the prismatic prison with Rex."

"She's a child by sorcerer standards," I say with a chuckle.

"It must be annoying that she has more raw power than you," Seraphex adds, and Zambrano waves his hand dismissively.

"Yes, yes, because my huge ego can't take it. You caught me," he replies. "The truth is, you don't survive as long as I have in the arcane arts without getting over the fact that in any given topic, someone out there likely is better than you at it. You get to the heights of power by acknowledging their skill and learning what you can from it. That was the beauty of the Sorcerers' Circle. Alix and Caravello put it together initially, but we all benefited from it."

"It is sad that it's gone," I say.

"That is the stark truth. I often think about the things that could have been if we had only been able to stay alive. Caravello's mathematical brilliance. Zuzanna's ability to heal broken minds. Alix's power to transform the physical world. Oluijimi's dreams for medical and biological magic," Zambrano says wistfully. "His dream for a magic that built and grew, rather than destroyed. All lost to climactic battles or creeping insanity. We could have been so much more."

"Do you want those things?" I ask. "Do you truly care about them?"

Zambrano shrugs. "Okay, sure, I'm the guy who likes to solve his problems with fireballs. I don't want to do those things. I don't want to spend my days carefully tending a garden." He stops for a moment, catching his breath as we hike up a steep slope of the hill. "But I want the type of people who do want them to exist. To do them. Because I can't. Olujimi was a healer, a grower, a creator. If he was a tree, growing and bearing fruit, I'm simply . . . a gun. Or a hatchet. A tool to destroy, not to tend a growing garden."

"Could you be though? Could you build, like Olujimi wanted to?"

Zambrano laughs sadly. "Fireballs are more fun. I've never had the appetite or focus to learn those things. That's part of how magic works. If you don't *need* to learn it—if you're not driven and genuinely curious—you're not going to learn the most powerful spells."

We reach the top of the hill, and Zambrano casts his locator spell one more time. He points to a tree, which stands alone at the top of a hill. It's far and away the largest tree in the area and might be the largest we've passed by today.

We hike up to it, and Zambrano grins, slapping the big tree. It's a giant evergreen, stretching way up into the sky above us. The sky has turned from bright and cheery to a deep blue, with the last rays of the setting sun outlining the tree as evening descends.

"Wow, this thing is big!" Parth exclaims. "I can barely get my arms halfway around it!"

"The Ol' Immortal Barbeque always likes to pick the biggest tree around. Like this fine specimen of ponderosa pine," Zambrano says.

"Wait, is he in there?" I ask. "Should we back away? Can he hear us?"

"Oh, Ash can hear us all right. Never stops listening, this thing, especially in egg form. Hears all sorts of things, in the egg dream or whatever he calls it."

"How do we wake Ash up?" Parth asks, knocking on the trunk the same way Zambrano did, which makes my heart skip a beat but doesn't seem to do any harm.

"Don't worry," Zambrano says, seeing my alarm. "Hit this big pine as hard as you want, it won't do anything."

"Is it inside there?" I ask, curious despite myself. "In egg form?"

Zambrano points to a small hole about five feet up on the trunk, with scorch marks around it. "When he's transforming by choice, he drills in there, like some sort of blowtorch woodpecker. And then he dives in and transforms into an egg on the inside. Usually he gets warmer and warmer over time as he expends magical energy, and the heat builds up inside so intense that it triggers the regeneration, and the whole thing goes up in smoke."

"Awesome," Parth says.

"How long does the process take?" I ask.

"Oh, usually years. With a big tree like this, probably decades or even a century or more," Zambrano says.

"Do we have a method to kick-start the process?" I ask.

"Is it a way that will make him even angrier at you than he already is?" Seraphex adds.

"Is this method what I'm thinking that it is?" Parth finishes the interrogation.

"We do have a method, it absolutely will infuriate him, and I suspect the method is exactly what Parth is thinking of," Zambrano says. "I'll simply shoot a. . . . Hmm, now that I think of it, young Parth, this might be a good chance for you to work on those skills you've been practicing."

"Hell yeah," Parth says.

"Come, I'll show you how to get the movements right," Zambrano says and takes Parth aside. They're immediately consumed with working on the finer points of spellcraft, with Parth sending little spurts of sparks and tiny candle-sized flames out every time he tries the spell.

Seraphex hops down onto the ground, and we stand back and watch as Zambrano, clearly enjoying himself, shows Parth how to master the precise techniques of a fireball spell. The look of intense concentration on Parth's features as he tries to follow the movements and make the sounds is pretty funny.

"*Pyrobolus!*" Parth says as a sad little spark comes out of his hand.

"They're wasting time," Seraphex says. "Zambrano could have done this by now with his own power. He is procrastinating because he doesn't want to face Ash."

I shrug, watching the two working on their technique. "I know we're in a hurry, but this has already taken a full day. I feel like they need this. And having Parth able to cast a powerful spell may be useful."

"You're probably right about that," Seraphex says. "I've rarely seen Zambrano so happy. Other than perhaps when he's taunting you."

"I'm supposed to be feeling something right now," I muse, watching the two of them. That yearning, that burning desire to learn magic. It led me to risk so much.

"Do you want to be doing that? Learning how to cast spells? Using magic?" Seraphex asks.

She's right to ask. The whole reason I came to Zambrano in the first place was because I wanted to learn magic, to become his apprentice. And when Seraphex was on the verge of passing through the arcane conduit portal and regaining her powers, she offered to help me regain the ability to learn magic. But I refused because it would also mean letting her return to her full reign of demonic terror.

"A few months ago, I would have been furious. So jealous of Parth. But at this point, I don't feel anything," I say. "I don't know that I *want* to spend my life studying obscure magical techniques. Maybe that's just my way of coping with not being able to do it. But I think I'm over that. It's not what the world needs from me."

"And what do you think the world needs from you?" Seraphex asks.

Parth hoots in celebration as he sends a small ball of flame at the tree. It barely singes the bark, but I smile as I see him succeeding. Zambrano is also grinning, proud of his work. He's a good teacher when he's in the right mood.

"Organizing all of you. Convincing two cantankerous sorcerers to cooperate, keeping one of them from doing something horrible to you, coming up with plans, avoiding death, and even coordinating with the government when they haven't been co-opted by a demon king. That's what I need to be doing, not learning to cast a few half-assed spells. Unfortunately, I keep freezing up when I'm supposed to be leading."

"Is that what you think?" Seraphex asks, cocking her head at me.

"Yeah, usually it's Zambrano who comes up with the big magical plan, or you or Liao Ling. I'm sometimes able to point out some flaws, which is nice I guess."

"When has one of Zambrano's plans gone smoothly?" Seraphex asks. "In all the time we've been together? Has one of them ever happened according to the play he drew up?"

"Well . . ." I take a long moment, thinking about it. "This one hasn't gone belly-up yet?"

"Every single plan the old coot makes goes to shit. And I'm unfortunately obligated to state that I'm also part of that. You've bailed us out, improvised a fix, or come up with a connection to make it work. And you don't have any magic powers."

"*Pyrobolus*," Parth shouts back at the tree. He's been able to get the incantation and motions down, and is able to shoot a larger fireball at the tree, take a break, and then send another significant one at it. I can see the bark starting to char and burn.

"That's true, I guess," I say. "I've done all right for being just some guy."

"You are," she says, eyeing me thoughtfully, "far more than 'just some guy.' You are the glue that holds this whole operation together and have often been the ingredient that makes it possible for us to save the world."

"You really think so?" I ask.

"I am incapable of lying," Seraphex says with a peal of regal laughter. "Bryce, we have been over that point *so many* times."

Now that Parth has the spell down, Zambrano joins in, sending a massively powerful fireball right at the tree trunk. The back is burned away, and there are flames starting to lick at the wood itself as thin smoke begins rising.

"Thanks," I say, leaning down and patting her little duck head. She takes this physical touch with grace and stoicism. Honestly, it's rather awkward, and I probably won't try again. "I guess that makes not being able to learn magic a lot less of a big deal—if I don't need it to do the job I have to do."

I smile at Parth, pumping his fist after shouting out "*Pyrobolus*" once more and sending another fireball at the tree, where it explodes in sparks.

"That's good," Seraphex says. "Because what I offered you back in Yellowstone was factually correct but not the whole story."

"You couldn't have unlocked my magic potential?"

"Oh, with my demonic powers and some help from compliant wizards, I could have gotten the job done," Seraphex says. "You would have gained the ability to do magic, unlocked and reset. But it would have also completely scrambled your brain. No memories, no history, no built-up personality. You would have been a blank slate, learning to speak the same way Liao Ling did, only without retaining anything of what makes you, you."

"God *damn* it, you nasty little duck," I say. "You are a piece of work, you know that?"

But like the jealousy of Parth, my anger at Seraphex doesn't have any weight behind it. That was back when we were getting to know each other. And before she agreed to be my friend, which altered her.

"You did something a little bit like that, didn't you?" I say. "Made a choice to change yourself."

"I didn't lose my memories," Seraphex says, "but I did start a process of change when I made that promise. When I made that friendship agreement, the demonic code forced me to alter some significant parts of my nature. It was a sacrifice. But I do hate my former husband that much."

"Aaaaand you did it because you like us, deep down, right?" I say. "You've grown to love and appreciate us?"

"I have no comment on that matter at this time," Seraphex says haughtily but with good humor. I guess that's what I'll have to take.

Zambrano shouts as he and Parth simultaneously send fireballs at the giant ponderosa pine. The whole trunk glows orange with heat, and suddenly giant clouds of acrid black smoke are pouring out of the tree, roiling up into the air.

"It's happening!" Zambrano calls as they back away from the tree.

I back away as well, and Seraphex leaps up, flapping her wings. "He doesn't like demons. I'm going to circle around and see the scenery," she says, and with a few beats of her wings disappears into the dusk.

Smoke pours forth, and the sound of cracking and sizzling wood fills the air.

And then, all at once, the entire tree bursts into flames.

CHAPTER 23

Fire roars into the late evening sky, and we all step back as a wave of heat rushes over us. Flames erupt up the trunk, race across the branches, and wash over the needles, which explode in a symphony of sparks. A bright halo of flame engulfs the massive pine, and in moments the entire tree is glowing red, like the brightest log in a long-burning campfire.

The heat batters us back a bit farther and then stabilizes.

"It's incredible," Parth says.

He's right. The flames are majestic, lighting up the landscape, a blazing beacon of pure energy.

Before long, the skeleton of branches, leaves, and trunk begins to crumble into ash. First the leaves and branches fall, and then chunks of the trunk begin falling off. For a moment I'm worried they're going to start a fire in the grass and foliage of the hilltop, but the blaze was so furiously hot that it burned up every bit of fuel. As pieces fall down, they fall apart into nothing but charred ashes.

As the trunk comes apart and sheds blackened dust, a figure emerges from inside it, a bird that looks to be made of pure fire, burning brightly. His face and beak blaze with energy, and his plumage is row upon row of resplendent gleaming feathers, shimmering like molten metal.

Hunks of blackened wood fall off the top of the tree, and the tree fire burns itself out, leaving behind only a smoky ruined stump. Perched on it is the world's last known phoenix.

"Mighty phoenix!" Parth says loudly, stepping forward toward the bird even though the heat is still quite intense. "Creature of majesty and beauty, will you aid us in our time of need?"

Ignoring Parth completely, the phoenix turns and fixes a burning gaze on the sorcerer.

"What the absolute shit, Zambrano?" the phoenix says with a vaguely European accent I can't place. Probably because it's an immortal being that has existed throughout a wide variety of cultures across time immemorial, I guess. But I would also guess, somewhere in western Europe. "You damn trash wizard, always putting me in danger for your own schemes."

"Learn to read the vibe," Zambrano mutters to Parth, shaking his head. Turning to Ash, he raises his hand in a shrug.

"I rescued you from that awful demon's menagerie—that should be worth something, shouldn't it?" the sorcerer says. "Besides, you still owe me."

"I liked it in there!" Ash retorts. "It was a nice clear case. I was safe, it was climate controlled, and time was slowed down for me. Everything in the world happens in such a hurry. Perceiving your entire world is a lot more tolerable when it goes by quickly. And then you came along to 'rescue' me, and leave me right where a lava demon can fly up from Chicago, pop my egg with his disgusting lava breath, and eat me."

"Yeah, I am sorry about that," Zambrano says somewhat sheepishly. I can tell he does feel at least a little bit bad about it. It's always nice to see the signs of humanity in there!

"And then I transitioned back into egg form, so the ugly bastard stuffed me in another tree, and he ate me up again. He did it three times, which is insanely unnatural. Worse than you waking me up just now, which for the record I am also not happy about."

I'm finally able to place the voice. He sounds like one of those pretentious German DJs. You know, the kind who make you feel bad about never having been to Berlin, since you need to experience the techno scene there to truly understand techno. Even though you really don't like techno, don't need to understand techno, and can't afford to go to Berlin even though it would probably be great. You know, that kind of guy. We've all met that kind of guy, right? Just me? Fine. But you get it.

"I'm sorry about Zambrano," I say. "He's a dick, we're all aware of that. But we do need your help. So more demons don't overrun this world. And try to eat you."

Ash turns on me, fiery plumage swirling in the night. "I'm not a warrior, I'm not here to fight your battles for you. In a few minutes, I'm going to go back into my egg form, and if you heat it up again immediately, I will burn the ever-loving shit out of you assholes."

"We don't need you to fight," I protest. "We need information."

"That's what everyone always wants," Ash says. "But they never like it when they get it, do they? Oh no, they get exactly what they want and then get all pissed. I don't like knowing it all either, okay?"

"Do you know everything?" I ask. "Everything that happens in the world?"

"No, not like you're thinking," Ash says. "It ends up being largely rumors and hearsay. I try to avoid telling it to you mortals. It only makes you angry, because it's bits and fragments of information. And then when you humans find out something you don't like, or you go and do something stupid with it, you blame me! I prefer to rest in the shell state and watch the show."

"But you'll help us?" I ask. "It's important. You will suffer just as much as we will if demons take over this planet. But you know that already, don't you?"

The phoenix huffs, sparks flying out of its nostrils.

"I do know that. I know how bad things are. With this demon who thinks he's a king, not to mention the other asshole, the magic lich halfway across the solar system. But I'm not going to help you because you're rude and manipulative. And I'm not going to assist the garbage-tier mage over there, who thinks that because he dredged me up from the wreck of the *Titanic* that one time, he can come bother me for free information any time he damn well pleases. Or use me as a diversion for his breaking-and-entering scheme. And you were the one who stole me? Did you think I had forgotten?"

I sigh. I guess from his perspective, I was complicit in getting him eaten multiple times. There goes Zambrano, once again implicating me in something horrible as part of one of his schemes.

He turns, body still glowing brightly, to Parth. "But you showed the proper admiration and respect. So I'll help you out. What do you need, kid?"

"Um. Thanks," Parth says. "I mean, thanks, oh great and powerful phoenix. We have come to request your counsel, to know of your vast visions in the egg dream."

"It's okay," the phoenix says. "Tell me what you need. My time in this form, out here in your cold world, is very limited because you woke me up so soon."

"You don't already know what we want?" Parth asks, genuine curiosity in his voice.

"I see bits and pieces of the world in the egg dream. I'm not omniscient, I can't listen in on every one of your boring conversations. What specifically are you after?"

I notice that while Ash is still burning brightly, he has already dimmed a little bit from the blazing intensity of his initial appearance.

"We need to know what happened a long time ago," Parth says. "Specifically around the end of the Xia dynasty, roughly 1800 to 1600 BCE. The creation of the demonic code that restricts demons from lying and binds them to verbal contracts."

"You came all this way and hatched me just for a history lesson?" Ash says. "You cut my rejuvenation process short because you were curious about what happened three thousand years ago? It couldn't wait?"

"We are trying to defeat the most powerful demon in existence. Someone previously was able to bind his power, and that of every other demon," Zambrano interjects. "We want to know what that was. Who did it. And how, if possible."

"Yes," I say finally. "Yes, that's exactly right. We are desperate for any way to beat the Demon King. It's a logical lead for us to follow."

Ash glowers at me.

"We're trying to save the world," I say. "Which, I would remind you, includes you."

Sparks fly off Ash has he grimaces at me. "So you commit a war crime against me and then expect me to forgive you and help you?"

"Demons should be a common enemy, shouldn't they?" Zambrano points out.

"They did destroy around half my kind," Ash admits grudgingly. "Without enough fuel, eventually the rejuvenation process fails, the spark dies, and the egg won't form."

"Who killed the other half?" I ask, and Zambrano shoots me a warning glance.

"Greedy human wizards," Ash says, looking at Zambrano with a piercing gaze. "Overly ambitious, egotistical, each thinking that what they did was vitally important and the best for everyone."

"I do apologize for that. All of that did happen before my time, you must remember," Zambrano says. "We also . . . brought you a gift," the sorcerer adds. "Mr. Parth, the backpack?"

"Well, why didn't you *say* that!" Ash says.

I can see Zambrano's tactic here. Don't offer everything right up front, let Ash get his anger out first, and only then make an offering.

Parth steps up into the heat and opens the backpack. What he pulls out is just chunks of wood, rectangles of roughly the same shape and size.

"What is it?" I whisper.

"Exotic woods of all types from all over the world," Zambrano whispers back. "As soon as we decided to come here, I made a quick trip to a furniture maker in Rotterdam who stocks all sorts of exotic lumber."

While we discuss, Ash has directed Parth to set out the lumber in a little pile, like you might do for a campfire. As soon as he's finished and backs away from the pile, the phoenix swoops down, perching comfortably. As his claws grip the top piece of wood, something in a rich burgundy hue, it starts to smoke and ignite.

As the pile of wood underneath it ignites, the gleaming bird shakes out its feathers like a dog shaking off water after swimming in a pond, sending a shower of sparks across the hillside.

"Okay, that's much better," Ash says. "This will buy me a few more minutes. And the particular combination of this timber is quite pleasing. So, despite my continuing fury at your actions, I will indulge a little history lesson while I consume this fine fuel. What was it that you wanted to know again?"

"The history of the demonic code. Who created it? And how?" Parth says.

"It would be . . . around the closing centuries of the Xia dynasty, you said. There's so much that's passed in the dream," the phoenix says. "Let me cast myself back there. Sift through the shadowy fields of memory."

He closes his eyes and sits lost in thought as the flames flicker around him. As the blaze grows, I can see he's settling deeper into the makeshift campfire, happily basking in the heat.

At last, eyes closed and voice distant as if in a trance, Ash speaks. "There is so much. Where could it be? A hundred billion of your tiny little lives are stored in my mind. Many millions, in that time alone, around the Earth."

Suddenly, like lightning, something strikes me. I turn to Zambrano.

"What was that language that Seraphex spoke in the demonic armory on Mars?" I say. "She didn't even realize she spoke it. Could it be related?"

Zambrano looks at me, mouth dropping open.

"Ancient Akkadian. The language of Babylon," he says. "Not much of magical history is known from that time period. But there was at least one sorcerer active during that era.

"Oh yes!" Parth says. "There was something about that in my arcane history class."

Zambrano turns back to Ash.

"Hammurabi. Could it have been him?"

"Ah, yes," the phoenix says, still deep in a trance. "The creator of the Law Code Stele and the rules inscribed upon it."

"Hammurabi's laws, inscribed on his stele," Zambrano explains. "A fascinating historical artifact, but how does it connect to demons?"

"The words on the stones themselves explain his laws for men, Hammurabi's code. But that is in some ways a distraction, a careful cover, in order to keep the stones safe. The true power of the stele is deeply imbued into the stone. That is the magic of the demonic codes."

"Hammurabi created the demonic codes?" Parth asks. "And they are tethered to his stele? To the stone of his code?"

"It was a most brilliant piece of magic," Ash continues. "Had any other limitations been put on demons, the creatures would have eventually figured out how to overcome them. They are clever, nearly indestructible, and will always find a loophole eventually. No prison can hold a demon forever. But this magic, while it only bound demonkind's actions in some small ways, also bound them from being curious about its origin. A combination that, over the course of history, weakened them enough to allow the rise of man and eventually their exile to a rocky wasteland across the solar system."

"What else?" Zambrano insists. "What more do you know of it? How can we use it to defeat the demon king?"

"Defeat him? Hardly," Ash says. "There is no easy solution there. The magic of the code is long since set. The stone itself is an artifact of immense power, but well guarded against any sort of meddling, by humans or demons."

"Is the stele in danger? Is it a vulnerability for us, for humanity?" I say. I hate to bring up worst-case scenarios, but we need to know the risks. "Could it be destroyed and we lose the demonic code?"

"Hammurabi's spell was vast and complex. The stele itself is as an artifact, nearly but not entirely indestructible. More importantly, it has the third element of the code on its side. A demon cannot contemplate it. Any time a demon gazes upon it directly, it will be struck with amnesia and confusion until it looks away. So it is protected. But sorcery in the time of Hammurabi was much stronger than either of you living sorcerers possess. You cannot modify it or control it. It has no power to defeat the demon king."

I instinctively look for Seraphex to see her reaction, but she's flown off somewhere. I wonder if she'll even be able to understand any of this when we tell it to her, given the restrictions of the demonic code.

The wood piled underneath the phoenix has nearly burned down, converted in just a few minutes into a pile of embers.

"Damn it," Zambrano says.

Parth shakes his head, deflated.

"It's a tool," I say. "It's an artifact that can short-circuit his brain for a brief time. Maybe that's all we need."

"He'll still be an indestructible and impossibly strong demon," Zambrano gripes. "We have to physically get hold of him and wrestle him through the arcane conduit portal in order for the plan to trap him in the endless loop to work."

"A confused and stupid demon king is an easier target than a clever and determined one," Parth points out.

"It's *something*," I say.

"Something," Zambrano mutters. "A scrap of hope, perhaps."

"Is there anything else you can tell us?" Parth asks the phoenix, who is starting to move back and forth, aggressively settling into the coals around him as if trying to absorb every bit of heat.

"That is all that I can recall," Ash says. "And my fuel and fire are fading."

He closes his eyes, relaxes, and opens his mouth. Instead of speech, music comes out of it, a lilting birdsong that starts low and slow and then swells. It pauses periodically, and Ash stays perfectly still, eyes still closed, waiting in silence. And then he starts again, letting the song lift its way through the air. As it goes on, what was first a gorgeous melody takes on a mournful, aching tone.

"It's his mating call," Zambrano says. "The only problem is there are no other phoenixes out there to answer it. The second-to-last phoenix was lost in the 1300s in Persia. Like fire, they can be reborn over and over again. But if they're deprived of fuel for long enough, the ember goes cold and that is the end of it."

"That's very sad, to be the last of his kind like that. Remind you of someone else?" I say, patting Zambrano on the shoulder.

"Yes, it does," Zambrano admits. "We lonely few."

"At least Liao Ling is back," Parth points out.

"That's nice, sure." Zambrano says. "But don't worry, I'm not going to try to 'mate' with Liao Ling," Zambrano says. "I don't want to wake up with a knife between my shoulder blades."

"Hot," Parth whispers.

Zambrano and I both roll our eyes.

"You know, I can hear you, assholes," Ash says as he comes to the end of the song. "Inside of the egg or out of it."

"Thank you for your help, oh great, wise, and beneficent bird of flame," Parth says.

"Oh, shut your dumbass mouth," the bird says. "None of you humans fool me. It's time for me to find a new tree."

"We could take you back to Slickwardinaeous's menagerie," Zambrano offers.

"All right, you caught me, I didn't like it *that* much," Ash says. "Good luck stopping the demon king." He lifts up, flapping his wings and sending waves of sparks and soot sailing through the air. "I don't want to be a demon brunch again anytime soon."

He circles us once and then with a mighty flap of his wings, begins moving rapidly. With each beat of the phoenix's glittering red and orange wings, he accelerates further until he's a dot of light streaking away from us into the evening sky. A trail of sparks falls down in his wake and then disappears into the deep blue gloom gathering around us.

CHAPTER 24

W ell, that was depressing," Zambrano says as we gather our things and prepare to return. Neither Parth nor I have any reply to that. I still feel like Ash gave us something to work with, but it's not much. A few moments of confusion and disorientation for Rex, perhaps.

It's weird not to be able to teleport back to the warehouse, which has become my home over the past many months. Luckily, we convinced Liao Ling to give us a spare teleportrait back to her island lair.

So Zambrano shoots up a magical flare to signal for Seraphex to return, and as soon as she lands on my shoulder, we use a teleportrait to return to the mysterious hidden island in the South China Sea. In an instant, dusk turns to a bright, sunny morning. We take a few minutes to clean up and get ourselves together, then send a message to Liao Ling to let her know we're back.

Luckily, as remote as this island is, she's got a satellite hookup with Wi-Fi, so we're able to stay connected to current events. It's extremely helpful for important research, which does not mostly constitute doomscrolling that alternates between relevant but incredibly depressing news and funny videos that I've missed while we've been so busy.

The state of the world out there is scary. Word has gotten out that something is going on, though no one quite knows what it is. World leaders are acting erratically, and a couple have died in mysterious accidents. There have been disasters, border disputes, market crashes, and nations are at one another's throats.

I pull out my phone and stare at it for a long moment. Should I call my parents? They're probably fine—they live in a quiet suburb, and Rex doesn't seem interested in targeting random civilians. But what if the compromised government decides to use them as leverage against me? What if I contact them and put them in more danger by drawing attention to them? My finger hovers over the button to dial my mom.

Maybe it's better if they stay completely out of this. And the last thing I want is to drag them into the magical chaos that's become my life. There's also Susan. I hope she's staying hidden successfully. At least she knows what's going on and has experience with this sort of thing. And then there's my extended family, my college friends . . .

There's no time to evacuate everyone who could potentially be used as a hostage against us. I turn the phone off and slip it back into my pocket. We need to beat Rex as soon as possible. For my parents and for everyone else.

A bit later, we're sitting on the big balcony again, looking out across the water. The sky above is overcast with dark clouds billowing. There's another typhoon brewing, heading to wreak havoc, this time in the Philippines. At the same time, a massive hurricane is building on the other side of the world, ready to wreck the Caribbean and the American south.

"Typhoria's work," Seraphex says, inclining her head at the depressing sky overhead. "My former husband is using the demons that he has to further destabilize the balance of power."

Zambrano, Seraphex, Parth, and I have sat down at tables in what is now our makeshift headquarters. Zambrano hasn't been allowed to spread out, but Liao Ling did give him a large room farther down the cliff where he's stored the books and artifacts we were able to save from the warehouse.

With a *whoosh*, Liao Ling pops into existence. After handing off to Dao a jacket that has a large stain of blood on it that I don't want an explanation for—and she doesn't offer an explanation for—she sits at the table with us.

We give her a quick rundown of our trip, including the small but possibly helpful information about the Law Code Stele of Hammurabi.

"That's something," Liao Ling says. "But not much. Even if we can get him to the stele, or the stele to him, a few moments of fuzzy brain won't make him helpless. He'll still be a ridiculously powerful brute of a species that shouldn't exist."

I glance at Seraphex, who looks displeased but refrains from saying anything.

"Are you able to understand all this, Sera?" I ask. "Aren't you blocked from hearing it?"

"When Merlin released me of the third element of the demonic code, he made a permanent change," Seraphex says, scrunching up her duck face as she thinks about it. "Unfortunately, I don't seem to be able to lie or go back on my promises, however. It would be such fun to be able to get in a few fibs here and there. Those infuriating first two elements of the code are intact."

"That is for the best," Zambrano says dryly.

"How are things in the rest of the world?" I ask. "What did you find out while we were gone?" My thoughts then drift to Mei, who's surrounded by deadly demons but somehow nonchalantly passing us intel while pretending to help them. I'll have to check in with her as soon as I can.

"It's bad out there," Liao Ling says. "Not only all the things that you see on the news. We thought Rex was co-opting governments in order to take control of them. To rule the world. But it's worse than that. He's been playing them against each other, building up two different sides. Offering them threats, bribes, whatever."

"What is he trying to get them to do then?" Parth asks. "Why would you want to have leverage over governments if not to control them?"

"Rex has no desire to rule the world of humans," Seraphex says. "He will want destruction. Reset."

"The demon is, sadly, correct," Liao Ling says. "Rex has been building up two grand coalitions, alliances of alliances, frightening each nation into joining one side or the other. Some think that under his influence, they will be protected. Others want to fight him. But I think he's been encouraging both sides, not trying to build his own power."

"Okay, but how is that different from normal politics?" I say. "Nations form and break alliances all the time."

"Each side worries the other is planning to strike first. But there are forces in most nations trying to stop things from exploding into war. They're gathering at a summit in Geneva to try to work things out."

"That sounds good," Parth says. "Maybe they can sign a treaty or something? Rex can't force us to fight one another. Everyone knows a major war would be suicidal for everyone."

"That is the hope," Liao Ling says. "If we don't have a means to defeat Rex right now, maybe we could help the peace summit go successfully. Buy us some more time before the bombs start falling."

"He won't let the peace summit succeed," Seraphex says, her voice low and defeated. "This is not the first time he's done this. The assassination of Theban tyrants, Cyaxares's butchering of the Scythian leaders, the massacre at Baoping Pass. He'll either convince someone to take action, or more likely intervene himself, and kill everyone there. As soon as that happens, he'll stage an attack on one side and blame it on the other. And then in a matter of hours, it's total war. Governments decapitated, industries destroyed. Rex will rule over the rubble of humanity's foiled dreams, fulfilling his goal of reversing your technological progress."

"Merlin and I stopped him before," Liao Ling says, voice full of resolve. "We'll do it again."

"But how?" Seraphex asks.

"You tell me how, you monstrosity," Liao Ling shoots back, clenching one fist and raising another to cast a spell.

"Hold on," I say, motioning for Liao Ling to stop. While she gives me a healthy dose of side-eye, she does refrain from attempting to blast Seraphex to bits. "We're all on the same team here."

"Are we?" Liao Ling asks.

"Yes," Zambrano says. "We all want to stop Rex. Let's focus on that."

"Thank you, Zambrano," I say, desperately still trying to hold everyone together. It feels like that time I hosted a party with both my college friends and my high school friends, and they did not mix together well. But worse, obviously, because the only stakes then were an awkward night. Whereas now we have the prospect of demonic attack *and* a fresh world war.

"You will have my full cooperation in whatever plan you devise to defeat my former husband," Seraphex says. "There, you have a demon's binding promise."

"Whatever," Liao Ling says with a sigh.

"We can use the stele to get the drop on him," I say. "He won't have a way to predict that and stay one step ahead of us because he's incapable of thinking of it. Where is the stele, anyway?"

"It's in the Louvre museum," Parth says, the article open on his phone. "Rex won't be that far away if he's going when the summit starts in Geneva tomorrow."

At that, Zambrano's face darkens, and he shakes his head slightly, staring into the distance.

"If we move it, that might give Rex a chance to start to figure out that it confuses him and notice that we're setting a trap," Seraphex suggests. "We should lure him there under some other pretense and make our move when he arrives."

"How do we know it will be him and not Steve or some other group of demons we don't want to tangle with?" Liao Ling asks. She has an edge to her tone, but she's at least contributing to the discussion.

"Greed," Seraphex says. "If he believes we're there after an artifact of immense power that can defeat him, he'll have to come there himself—he can't afford one of the other demons getting a hold of it."

"Mei can probably help with that," I suggest. "Plant information among the demons that gets back to Rex. Cause the big bad demon to make a detour to Paris. Jump him when he busts in to try to stop us."

I glance at Zambrano, who appears to be listening but distracted, a faraway look on his face.

"Which means that what we still need is a way to physically move Rex into the arcane conduit portal itself," Seraphex says.

"Both of your powers combined?" Parth asks, gesturing at Liao Ling and Zambrano. "You were able to hold him back out on the ocean?"

"Water is different," Seraphex says. "His body isn't adapted for it. On solid ground, we'll have a much tougher time. And in the end he's incredibly strong. A couple of sorcerers won't be able to stand against him."

We sit there for about twenty minutes, throwing out various ideas. We might be able to move the stele, or bring in modern weapons, or find some sort of artifacts, but none of it will help. The portal has to be stationary, so it comes down to forcing Rex through it without knowing how or exactly when he'll arrive. Zambrano tosses out a couple thoughts but still seems distracted.

"None of this gets us even to a fifty-fifty shot of success," Liao Ling complains. "And that's if everything goes according to plan, which we know for sure it won't. I don't want to gamble on those numbers."

"We need to manhandle the most powerful force in the solar system," Parth says with a sigh. "What can possibly compete against that, even for a minute?"

We sit quietly for a couple minutes, watching the clouds roll over the dark and brooding ocean.

Is this it? We just freeze, out of useful plans, and the world ends. Or we go in with some wild long-shot scheme that's surely going to fall apart the moment it begins? The conference in Geneva is happening tomorrow.

Parth takes a long look at Seraphex, opens his mouth, then closes it.

With a start, I realize what he's thinking. I give him a meaningful look and put a hand up to signal for him to pause.

This is a good idea. An idea that might work. But we have to present it right, or the opportunity will be lost. I take a deep breath.

"I think we have a tool that will work. A way to give us a fighting chance of getting Rex into the portal no matter what sort of attack he makes. Combine that with two sorcerers, and I think we can pull it off."

"Okay, great," Zambrano says, raising an eyebrow at me. "Let's have it."

"You're not going to like it, either of you," I say, pointing at the sorcerers. "I need you to promise me you'll give it a fair shake. And impartially judge it as best you can, putting aside personal feelings."

"Very well," Zambrano agrees.

"Fine," Liao Ling says, eyeing me suspiciously.

"Okay, great. So, the thing is, we need to fight the most powerful being in the solar system," I say.

"Yes, we know that," Zambrano says. "What of it?"

"So we need the second most powerful being in the solar system on our side."

"What do you mean?" Zambrano asks, but Liao Ling immediately gets it.

"Oh, hell no," she says. "He means Seraphex. He wants you to return the demon queen to her original form."

I glance at Seraphex, who is watching calmly and curiously. I might have expected a bigger reaction from her, but she's playing it cool.

"I see," Zambrano says slowly. "There's a reason Alix wrote the spell the way she did. It's a very clear reminder. That spell was crafted at great expense. Both in time and resources, and in what we lost, personally."

"How is the spell a reminder?" Parth, who hasn't heard Alix's lengthy incantation yet, asks.

"She made the words of the incantation a warning against using the spell, to try to get the user to stop, or someone nearby to intervene," Zambrano explains. "We played at the edge of this dangerous precipice already, and Merlin did the same. There's a reason neither of us took the spell to completion. A demon queen is incredibly dangerous."

"I know," I say. "I wouldn't ask if it wasn't tremendously important. We have to save the world."

"It does sound awesome," Parth adds. "The two most powerful demons of all time, battling it out. King versus queen, husband versus wife, the epic showdown."

"Ex-husband," Seraphex notes.

"How exactly are you and the demon king exes?" Parth asks. "Is there, like, a demonic divorce court?"

"It could be said that marriage is a matter of the heart and mind," Seraphex answers. "The government of India issued your parents a marriage license—but if the Indian government disappeared tomorrow, would your parents cease being married?"

"Huh," Parth says. "I guess not."

"Don't be distracted by her clever words," Liao Ling interjects. "She is tricking us somehow. She will find a loophole."

Zambrano looks over at the demon, sitting in the form of a duck and somehow still looking regal.

"I would require certain assurances if we were to even consider this plan," he says.

"If you release the transmogrification, I promise that after my former husband is contained, I will allow you to return me to my form, Zambrano." Seraphex says this with great seriousness.

"She's free of the third element of the demonic code," Liao Ling says suspiciously. "Who knows what her promises are worth?"

"Merlin only released her from the third element," I point out.

"It's true," Zambrano agrees. "I heard it as well. Merlin specifically undid that element of the code, and only that one."

"Even in undeath," Liao Ling says, "Merlin isn't stupid enough to release a demon queen from the bonds that control it. Which is exactly why we shouldn't follow this plan."

"What do you think, Mr. Parth?" Zambrano asks. "Should we risk it?"

Parth looks torn. I can tell he doesn't like going against Liao Ling, but he also doesn't seem like the type to back down.

"I don't mind the risk," Parth says. "And I wonder if it's the only shot we have. That said, we all have to be on board. If Liao Ling isn't in, we'll fail for sure. We need to all agree."

"Thanks," Liao Ling says.

"Though I'll happily fight him myself if needed," Parth adds.

"Just because you can cast a mediocre fireball," Zambrano says, "does not mean you're ready for a demon king."

"If we can maybe find another one of those magic swords?" Parth suggests. "Or another rocket launcher? Can it be my turn with the rocket launcher this time?"

I look over at Seraphex, who has been quietly watching us talk.

"What do you think, Sera?" I ask. "You're the one who's going to be doing this."

"I think that it should be your decision, not mine," Seraphex says. "I doubt you will trust my opinion either way. I believe that returning me to my full form and powers gives us the best chance of success at capturing and trapping my former husband. As to whether that is a choice you want to make—I leave it in your hands."

"Fair enough," I say.

"I don't like this idea. I have avoided it for over a century. But I told you I would outsource my moral judgments to you, Bryce," Zambrano says. "I don't like it. I can hear all the sorcerers of the

Circle over my shoulder, screaming that it's a terrible idea. But if you think it's the best way, then I'll accept it."

There's a long moment of silence.

Finally, Liao Ling sighs.

"She killed my brother," the ancient sorcerer says. "I know she's changed to some extent. But a demon is a demon. Still . . . I am far from the world and time I call home. And while I like it here, I won't pretend that I understand it all. Bryce, I trust you. If you think this is our best shot, it's your call. I'll support you as best I can."

I sit there, blinking. "Um, wait, I didn't ask to be in charge. I'm not the leader."

"Everyone else here is crazy," Zambrano says with a shrug. "I'm not about to call you the leader. But when it comes to a big move like this—let's say that you're the representative of humanity here. The voice for the common folks."

I sigh. "Okay, then." I look at Seraphex, who's sitting calmly, waiting for my decision along with everyone else.

Everything in me wants to freeze up, or crawl away, or tell them they need to decide on it. But I have to make this call. If I'm all of humanity, I sure as hell wouldn't want these three magically-endowed psychos making big choices for us. Or Parth, for that matter, with his willingness to risk everything at the drop of a hat.

I look over at Seraphex. She's weird, and dangerous, and has tried to tempt me into mistakes before. But since then, she's become a real friend. And she's helped and supported us through deadly situations, one after another. She definitely bailed me out when I was trapped in the nose of a sea serpent. And she guided us safely through Mars when she easily could have turned us over and joined the demons there.

"I think we have to risk it," I say. "Unless a better plan comes along in the meantime. And if Rex blows up that summit in Geneva, all hell will break loose. We have to act now."

As the words hang in the air, I see everyone nodding in agreement. Did I just make that decision? The smoothie guy from New Jersey is somehow in charge of whether or not a demon queen is potentially unleashed in the world. Is humanity screwed?

Maybe, but we're going to at least go down fighting.

"Fine," Liao Ling says. "Anyway, if we already have one super-powered demon about to trigger a world war and rule over the rubble, how much worse could having two around be?"

"Vastly, vastly worse," Zambrano says unhelpfully. "But this plan may be worth the risk. Now that we've agreed to do it, I have to say . . . it sounds fun."

"Demon royalty battle royale!" Parth says, grinning. "Let's go!"

CHAPTER 25

We spend the next couple hours hammering out the key elements of the plan. Knowing we can't expect any cooperation from the various governments, we have to get creative. And ultimately, hope that the timing of it all lines up and we can improvise when it doesn't.

Once the broad outlines of the strategy are set, we go into prep mode. Zambrano and Liao Ling work on the magical preparations, making sure the arcane conduit is good to go, and powering it with the trapped form of Volcanose that we stole from the demonic armory on Mars. Liao Ling makes a quick trip to teleportrait Parth to Paris, where he is casing out how we can enter and exit the museum, and sending back reams of videos and pictures of the floor plan and the exhibit hall where the stele of Hammurabi is currently displayed.

Meanwhile, I'm on the phone with Mei, and then Zambrano teleportraits me to Istanbul, where I get in a cab to deliver a package.

I pick an inconspicuous little kabob shop near the docks for us to meet up at, and get a table. I'm wearing a baseball cap and sun-glasses, once again trying to avoid cameras and witnesses. The place is brightly lit; I guess I should have picked somewhere dimmer, but this is what I got off Google Maps. There are TVs playing different soccer games all over the place.

"Ugh, this place sucks," Mei says as she slides into the chair across from me. "Couldn't you have picked someplace with lower lighting?"

"Sorry," I say, "that would have kept us more anonymous, yeah."

"Oh, no," she says, "this is fine. No one would believe I would come to a place like this. I just can't enjoy a drink under fluorescent light with TVs everywhere."

"I do think TVs should be illegal in nice bars," I agree. "They put so much work into incredible decor, and then BAM, there's a TV blasting away. I didn't make plans to visit a bar with twenty-dollar cocktails to see the Knicks game."

"Or a thrilling Turkmenistan versus Kyrgyzstan match," Mei says, gesturing to the TV closest to us. "With a score of nil to nil after thirty-five minutes, how thrilling?"

"I'm guessing we shouldn't stay to witness the game's gripping conclusion," I say, handing her a package under the table.

"No," she says as the waiter comes over and she orders two Turkish beers for us. "We should drink these as fast as possible and get out of here. What am I doing with this thing you just handed me?"

"It's a fake logbook from an artifact trader who doesn't exist," I say. "Slip it in with some new acquisitions where Slickwad will find it. It has notes that Zambrano bought a stone with a special incantation carved on it. Make sure Slickwad sells that information to Rex. Seraphex is sure he'll connect it to the *Winged Victory of Samothrace*, which is in the Louvre. The incantation is made-up bullshit that makes it sound like the *Winged Victory* has the power to destroy any demon."

"Does it?" Mei asks. "Does the *Winged Victory* have the capacity to destroy Rex?"

"It sures *sounds* like it does, doesn't it?" I answer.

"It does," Mei admits, downing a healthy dose of her beer and making a sour face.

"Look, we're headed to the Louvre," I say. I try some of the beer as well. It's okay, but I've never been a big beer guy. "We need to get Rex to come there, one way or another. I don't want to say more than that. Just in case."

"In case trying to help you gets me captured and have lie detection magic and truth serum potions used on me by security mages?" Mei says. "And then magically healed and dropped on the street, likely with mild to moderate PTSD?"

"And how do you know that?" I ask, raising an eyebrow.

"I've handled calendar appointments for the interrogations a couple times," Mei answers with a sigh. "Look, at this point I'm not qualified for any other career, okay? Morgan Stanley is not going to hire me with 'demonic aide' on my résumé."

"I mean, employee of the dark sorcerer is not going to go over any better with HR recruiters," I say with a chuckle. "I doubt even the smoothie shop would take me. We're kind of screwed."

We toast with our beers, though Mei only takes a sip of hers. "This stuff is gross. I need a proper cosmo or a negroni or something. It doesn't matter, I guess. You should get out of here, and I need to get back."

"You're right," I say, draining my beer. It definitely looks weird if neither of us finish.

I order a car, and we chat as I watch its approach on the app.

"Is there anything else I can do to help?" she asks.

Stop working for demons as soon as possible, is what I want to say. I'm sure she doesn't want my opinion on her life choices, but I feel like I have to say something anyway.

"Well, look, when this is all over . . ." I start, then trail off.

"Fine, I'll get a proper drink with you," Mei says before I can finish. "I'm tired of spending all my time with demons and the sort of people who would work with demons. But I don't do anything below the belt on the first date, you got it?"

"Um, I was actually going to suggest you stop working for demons," I say. "It's super dangerous and also wildly unethical."

I instantly realize how dumb that sounds. Especially when I would totally want to go on a date with her, demon employers or no demon employers. I work for a guy called a dark sorcerer and monitored by all the world's governments in case he goes insane, which is a very real possibility if not inevitability. And my other friend is a duck. A demon duck.

Mei doesn't slap me. But she sure looks like she could. And would. Honestly, I'm not sure why she doesn't.

"I'd love to have a drink with you though," I say. "It would be great to hang out when the world isn't ending. Though Zambrano will never let me hear the end of it."

Mei glares at me.

"I should have said 'Yes, that sounds great' and left it at that, huh?"

"Yes, Bryce, that would have been a better decision," Mei says.

My phone buzzes as the car arrives, pulling up next to the curb.

"On the off chance the civilized world doesn't end, maybe we can try this conversation again?"

"Sure," she says with a laugh and shake of her head. "That will definitely put me in a more receptive mood. I'll consider it."

"I'd better get back to the sorcerers before they blow themselves up," I say. "And figure out how I'm going to convince Zambrano to teleportrait me out here for a date. And I guess I'll research bars in Istanbul."

"Just survive, okay?" Mei says, giving me a hug before I turn to get into the car to return to the spot where Zambrano can teleport in and grab me.

"Someplace classy! No bars with TVs in them! And no Turkish beer!" she shouts as I reach to close the car door.

This all feels like a mistake. An awkward mistake. Hey, at least I'm not trying to date an ancient sorcerer like Parth is.

Maybe I'll die trying to save the world and won't have to figure out what was going on back there.

CHAPTER 26

Back on Liao Ling's island, we all try to get a night's sleep, though that's a challenge. Luckily, I'm exhausted from the last few days, so despite my nerves and the million thoughts competing for attention in my head, I'm able to get some rest.

After a quick breakfast and gathering our final supplies, we're taking a teleportrait into Paris, appearing in a little alley that somehow still has a view down a romantic-looking boulevard. Zambrano, Seraphex, Liao Ling, Parth, and I appear with a quiet *whoosh* in the center of an apartment that is filled with antique furniture.

While it isn't dusty or anything, it doesn't look like it's been lived in at all, just cleaned regularly. Based on the sloping ceilings and the beautiful windows with a view of the Parisian streets, historic buildings, and skyline, I'm guessing this room is at the top of one of the buildings in one of the older districts. Morning in the South China Sea is late night in Paris, so the view out the windows is a nighttime cityscape with lights dotting the buildings.

Zambrano leads us out the door, down four flights of stairs. We exit into an empty street, though down the block I can see a square where a couple late-night cafés are open with a few tables of patrons sharing bottles of wine.

I've never been to Paris before, and I have to admit it's striking. The lights, the wide streets, the classic architecture—I can see why it's so famous, from the first few blocks.

We've swapped in new disguises, though Zambrano still insists on wearing a suit. In fact, it seemed like he spent even more time than usual picking it out and getting it set. But with hats, sunglasses, and scarves, we shouldn't be too recognizable by either cameras or the police.

I catch a glimpse of myself in the reflection of a shop window.

"You know," I say, "this scarf is great for hiding my identity, but it also seems like a dashing affectation, perfect for the fashionable Parisian streets. Should it be my new thing?"

"No," Seraphex says, even though she's hidden in the top of my backpack.

"Absolutely not," Zambrano adds.

"You look like the worst sort of tourist," Liao Ling continues.

"I think it looks nice," Parth says.

While we spend another minute joking about our outfits, Zambrano walks along, scowling at everything.

"What's up, Mr. Z?" Parth asks. "You look down."

"Are you worried about our plan?" I ask. "If you think it's not going to work, we need to make that call now. I can still text Mei not to plant the fake evidence. Or is it that you don't want to have to play the bad guy again?"

"I was enjoying the fact that some of the nimrods on your social media apps were starting to like me," Zambrano says. He's very controversial, but since the battle of Yellowstone he's had a solid fan base. "But it's not that," he continues. "This is a harebrained scheme, but if I'm being honest, that's kind of 'my thing,' so I can't complain."

"Then what is it?" I ask, worry increasing as I see his brow furrowed as he glances around.

He doesn't answer as we cross the street and pass by a small bar with a small group of patrons inside, laughing and bullshitting with one another as the bartender closes up.

"This would be easier if it was a busy day," Zambrano says with a heavy sigh. "This was our time, wandering the streets late at night, visiting our various haunts, checking in with our friends. Causing no small amount of trouble."

"You haven't come back often," Seraphex says, her voice muffled.

"I go to the apartment once a year to update the teleportrait," Zambrano admits. "Other than that, I haven't been to Paris in a hundred years. I thought it would have changed more. Just some more cars and cell phones," he says, motioning to a somewhat drunk man strolling by, his nose buried in his phone.

"I guess Paris is still Paris," I say. "They don't update the architecture, at least in this part of town."

"It's the eternal city, or so they say," Parth says.

"They don't say that; that's Rome," Zambrano replies.

"Oh right!" Parth answers with a grin. "It's the city of brotherly love."

"That's Philadelphia," I correct him. "Paris is just called the city of love."

"It was, for me, for a time," Zambrano says a wistful note in his voice. "The apartment we arrived in was where we lived on and off for most of the 1800s into the early 1900s."

"You and Alix," I guess.

"Yes," Zambrano answers. "We were together for hundreds of years. But those times in Paris were the best of them. We'd finally figured out how to tolerate each other, mostly. Only took three centuries. And I loved it here."

"I thought you hated French people," I point out.

"Eh," he says with a shrug. "They grow on you. It was a good time. After the first fifty years of practicing the accent, things got better. But now . . . they remind me of all that I've lost."

We get to a bridge and cross over the river, and I think that I catch a glimpse of Notre Dame in the distance. Or maybe it's one of the other big churches, it's hard to tell. I'm starting to wonder why we didn't take a car, but I guess Zambrano wanted to have this moment.

"I skipped a thousand years, but I feel like you're more out of your own time than I am," Liao Ling says. "I like it here in the future. I can wear pants anywhere in the world and no one bats an eye."

"I'm hundreds of years older, in lived years," Zambrano says with a shrug. "You can repair the parts all you want, but the mileage adds up."

We walk in silence for a few minutes, finally reaching the Louvre. We stand across the street from the massive building, with the famous giant glass pyramid entrance out front in the courtyard.

It's perfectly still here, silent other than the occasional distant shout, honk of a car, or wail of a siren from over the river.

"I'm tired," Zambrano says.

"Once more unto the breach?" I say. "For old times' sake?"

"What do they teach in schools these days?" Zambrano asks. "That's Shakespeare, from the stuck-up assholes from the other side of the channel. We're in Paris. It would be '*Aux armes, citoyens!*' or maybe '*Aux barricades!*' Alix and I were revolutionaries here, you know. Before the guillotine became the solution to every problem and then the whole Napoleon nonsense happened. They thought I was a villain by the end then too."

"We need you to be the villain again," I say.

Zambrano laughs. "Yes, Bryce, you do. You wanted to work for the dark sorcerer. The governments all think I'm one. So let's give them the show they want."

"Why don't people understand you're fighting for them?" Parth asks. "You show up every time there's danger!"

"And everywhere I show up, there is destruction, casualties, and unhappy property owners," Zambrano says. "I don't have a PR agency or government press conferences to make my case."

"You also regularly disregard laws, steal valuable artifacts, and intentionally antagonize international magical authorities," I point out.

"I'm not going to apologize for being fun," Zambrano answers with a shrug.

As a group, we walk up to the Louvre museum entrance. I unzip the top of the backpack, and Seraphex sticks her head out, watching from over my shoulder. Parth and I slap on fake handcuffs, so that we can play the part of hostages.

As we approach, a group of guards at the door at the base of the Pyramid de Louvre start shouting things in French. Zambrano shouts a phrase back that I can't understand, but I do catch a couple of swear words. And from my limited experience with Spanish, I catch a few words and get the general sense that he's saying something about their mothers. They do not seem amused.

The guards pull out their weapons, a couple of them with pistols and a few more military fellows with machine guns.

"*Méiyǒu huǒ de chái,*" Liao Ling intones, waving her left hand in a snuffing motion and pointing at each of their weapons. She explained this spell to me yesterday; it translates as "no fuel for the fire" and cuts out the oxygen around the gunpowder in the guns.

As we approach, the guards continue to yell and pull the triggers of their guns, but nothing happens except for some clicking sounds. They scream into their radios in French, backing up in panic.

"*Blue bubble bouncer, bubble bounce this bothersome bore*," Zambrano says, snapping first with his right hand, then his left, and then his right again. He does this several times, and for each, a blue bubble of force wraps around the guards and carries them over in the direction of the river. I hope the French guard school includes swimming lessons.

Finally, a single security guard is left. As we approach, he clicks his handgun helplessly, then finally in desperation throws it at Zambrano.

"*Deja de moverte!*" Zambrano says, jabbing his splayed fingers at it, and the pistol stops in midair. With a second motion, it drops.

The guard, panicked, backs up against the glass door to the giant pyramid.

"You can't come in here!" the guard says in heavily accented English.

"I can go wherever I like," Zambrano says. "Get out your phone."

"My phone?" the guard says, confused.

"Pull out your phone and record a video," Liao Ling says, grinning.

"Yes, mademoiselle," the frightened man says, pulling his phone out of his pocket and putting it on record.

"I am the Dark Sorcerer Zambrano," the sorcerer says straight into the phone's camera. "My friends and I are going into this museum, and we will be inside for a some time." He glances around, backing up and also playing to the many security cameras visible around the entrance door. "We have two hostages." He gestures to Parth and me. "And we are also holding everything in this museum hostage. You will evacuate all personnel from the entire museum immediately, for their own safety. If you try to enter or interfere in any way, we will destroy your museum, and also blow up the blocks around it."

"You should also evacuate those too," Liao Ling says, "In case we explode the whole place. Also, by the way, I'm Liao Ling. Pleased to meet you, French government or the world, whoever sees this video. You all will get to know me soon enough. Keep your distance, or we'll kill you."

"It would be so fun to be able to lie," Seraphex whispers in my ear. "I'd love to be able to do it again someday."

"Don't test us," Zambrano says. "We are two powerful and ancient dark sorcerers, and if you cause trouble, we will obliterate you."

"We're privateering your national heritage," Liao Ling says. "A boarding party of sorts. And we'll sink it if you try anything."

"Unless you leave us alone," Zambrano adds. "Which is the best way to not have your precious *Mona Lisa* or *Venus de Milo* blasted into bits. Don't be stupid."

"Now get out of here," Liao Ling says, pushing the guard away and giving him a kick on the butt as he scrambles to escape, clutching his phone to his chest.

"Parth, do you want to do the honors?" Zambrano asks, gesturing to the closed glass door that stands between us and the museum.

"Aren't I intended to be a hostage?" Parth hisses.

"I'll make it look like I made you do it," Liao Ling says, pointing her fingers threateningly at him. "Mostly we want to confuse and delay them and attract as much attention as possible to get Rex here quickly."

"And get civilians away to safety," I add.

"Sure, whatever, that too," Liao Ling answers with a shrug.

"*Bala-kṣepa*," Parth says, and despite his handcuffs, two green balls of energy shoot out from his hands, smashing the glass doors open.

Carefully stepping over the broken glass, we cross into the pyramid and then descend the stairs to enter into the museum itself.

CHAPTER 27

Alarms blare, but we ignore them. As soon as we're inside, Liao Ling and Parth peel off, heading to the roof to spot the approach of Rex. Liao Ling has her demon detection, while I've reluctantly given Parth the Spyglass of Spinoza, which I've come to think of as mine. But I feel like I need to stick with Zambrano and Seraphex to make sure things go smoothly. I toss off the fake handcuffs, knowing my gauntlets of invisibility are ready in my backpack and I have a surprise ready for Rex if I can get close enough to him. I wish we'd had time to steal another rocket launcher, but Seraphex is convinced it won't work as well a second time. And the gauntlets also wouldn't hide it. Their powers are limited to a person and clothes, not a massive metal weapon.

Once again, we're all hooked up with our headsets and radios to keep in touch. I still think Seraphex looks adorable in hers, but I keep my mouth shut. The great thing about planning to break into and take over a public museum is that most of it is a matter of public record, and there are floor plans and maps easily available online. So getting to where we need to go is not a problem.

"Room 227 of the Richelieu wing," I say, pointing the way from the map I've been studying for the past day. "On the ground floor."

There are several closed security doors between us and the stele of Hammurabi, but with a wave of his hand and a few words, Zambrano sends them careening off their hinges and clattering on the floor.

The look on his face is intense, as if he's enjoying each inanimate piece of architecture he gets to destroy.

My phone buzzes, and I pull it out and glance down at it.

Rex took the bait as soon as he heard that you broke into the Louvre, he just left Geneva at a dead run, the text from Mei says.

I report this to the team.

"My guys will monitor it," Liao Ling says, referring to her pirates, a few of whom are in Paris nearby while others are in a helicopter over the French countryside to give us advance warning when Rex is approaching.

As we near Room 227, a side door opens, and a crowd pours out of it. More security guards, led by an older man in a suit. Zambrano practically growls in annoyance as they stand in the way to the final door to the room.

"I am Marcel Fournier, chef de sécurité de nuit," the man says, standing at the head of the security team. The other men look nervous, but Marcel does not betray any fear. I can see by the way they glance at him, how his courage is keeping them together. "You are trespassing on property of the government of France. Monsieur Dark Sorcerer, we will not allow you to steal our art and artifacts."

"We're not here to steal anything," I say.

"But there will be massive property damage," Seraphex adds unhelpfully.

"Stand aside," Zambrano demands, flexing the fingers of his right hand. "I'm not supposed to hurt you. But I will."

"I will not stand aside," Marcel answers. "These artifacts are in my care. This museum and its contents belong to France. You do not belong here."

Before I can do anything, Zambrano throws his hands out as if throwing a ball at the men.

"*Eye of Jupiter!*" he shouts, and Marcel and his guards are pushed back, slammed into the walls. A couple of them are military types carrying weapons, but the gravity spell pins them so thoroughly that they can't even move their arms or aim their weapons. It looks like an extreme version of those carnival rides that spin you around so fast the centrifugal force flattens you against the walls.

"I belonged here. We belonged here," Zambrano roars. "For a beautiful century. And we wanted to help, to make it better. We went to the barricades, we joined your countrymen, though our agreements with the Circle meant we would not use our magic to political ends. For a beautiful moment, she was so inspired. She saw an incredible future."

"Who are you speaking of?" Marcel manages to croak out, holding himself up and staring down Zambrano despite the weight of arcane gravity on him.

"Alix," Zambrano says. "My love. My light. My partner. She believed in your revolution, so I joined her. But everything you tried to do to make the world better turned to shit." He stabs his hands forward, and the security team groans and squirms as the increased gravity crushes them. "Heads rolling, mass executions, endless backstabbing, the reign of terror. You killed a king and replaced him with an emperor. You betrayed every one of your principles. And you betrayed Alix. It broke her. That was the day I lost her. When she lost her belief in humanity. If she had had that, she never would have turned to demonic magic, never let its power break and corrupt her. All because YOU FAILED HER!"

"Zambrano," I say quietly, slowly moving close to him. I glance at the security cameras in every corner of this room. We have a chance to complete this plan if we're allowed to do it alone. If Zambrano doesn't back down, it will be terrible not just for the life lost, but for the reaction it will provoke. We can't fight both Rex and the French military at the same time. Our plan relies on them keeping their distance and thinking they can negotiate with us.

"It was men like him," the sorcerer insists, staring directly at Marcel, fury blazing in his eyes. "Men who believed in their institutions, followed their little rules, played their little parts. They brought disaster. To their country. To Alix. To me."

"It wasn't them," I say quietly, placing a hand on his shoulder. "The French Revolution was over two centuries ago. None of these men had anything to do with it."

Through my hand, I can feel the intensity of Zambrano's breathing.

"There's a reason I haven't come back here," he says, his voice a low rasp. "And I'm here to help them. To save them. I should simply kill them all. Crush them."

"They don't know that," I say quietly. "They're trying to protect their art and artifacts."

"They completely failed. They won their freedom and pissed it away," Zambrano says. "And it cost me Alix."

"They didn't get it right then," Seraphex says, gentler than usual. "They figured things out eventually, at least by their standards."

"It took four more republics to get there," Zambrano growls. "I'm not an idiot. I followed the history." He's still angry, but I can feel his bloodlust has cooled.

I did not follow all the history as closely as Zambrano, but I do have the general gist of it. Many missteps, some wars, revolutions, but eventually they became a democracy with elections and human rights and all of it.

"We're here to do a job," I say, reaching in and gently pushing Zambrano's hands down. As I do, the spell cuts off, and Marcel and his security team drop to the floor, noisily catching their breath. "These people didn't commit any crime."

"Other than being French," Zambrano grumbles.

I can't help but laugh. "We're all guilty of something," I mutter. But you have to respect Marcel Fournier standing up, dusting himself off, and facing us again.

"Mr. Fournier," I say. "We aren't here to hurt you or steal your art. In fact, we may be able to work together."

"What are you talking about?" Marcel asks.

"A demon is coming here," I say, forgetting our cover story. "Surely you've seen how things are falling apart in the world. Wars, disasters, and more. It's all caused by this demon, Rex. And he's going to come here to try to kill us."

Zambrano opens his mouth to say something, but I wave him off. He's not going to be able to help here.

"Why do you bring your battles here?" Marcel complains.

"This is where the stele of Hammurabi is, and it weighs several tons, and we don't have time to move it or a place to take it," I say. "The die is cast. The demon is on his way. I'm sure your government is aware a demon is running full tilt through the countryside from Geneva, making a beeline for Paris. We have to fight him here, and we need you and everyone else out of the way of it."

Marcel glances over to one of the military guards with a gun. The man presses his finger to an earpiece, speaks under his breath, and gives him a sharp nod.

"Even if I believe you, what would you have us do? Let the museum be wrecked in a battle?"

"Liao Ling, how long do we have?" I ask, speaking into my own radio earpiece.

"Just over two hours," she says.

"You have time. You need to get as many pieces away and to safety as you can."

"That's impossible!" Marcel complains. "So many artifacts, they must each be handled carefully, moved precisely . . ."

"You must have procedures for fires," I suggest. "And various other disasters. You have two hours. Better get started. Begin with the ones that are most valuable and closest to this room," I suggest. "We'll do our best to minimize damage, but there are no guarantees."

Marcel opens and closes his mouth several times, then gives a heavy sigh.

He turns and motions and starts barking orders in French. At his direction, one of the guards opens the door to the room we need access to, rolling his eyes and pointing at the ones that we blasted down on our way in.

We enter the main room, where the massive stele of Hammurabi dominates the center of the chamber.

CHAPTER 28

The stele is a huge edifice of black rock, standing twice as tall as me. I step up and look at it, admiring the incomprehensible writing chiseled into it.

"The third element of the demonic code has been deactivated for me, but looking at that thing is still unsettling," Seraphex says.

The security guards scurry around the room, gathering as many items as they can carry, in some instances breaking open cases to grab them. They're going to have a long two hours of moving things to safety.

Alarms have been blaring this whole time, but Marcel speaks into a radio, and the blaring shuts off.

"Are you okay?" I say, stopping Zambrano once we're inside Room 227 and the door is closed.

He's breathing heavily and still has a wild look in his eyes.

"I was going to blow up and kill all those guards," he says, looking down at his hands in confusion, "because of something that happened well over a hundred years ago."

"You didn't; that's what matters," I say. "We worked it out. They will try to save the most important artifacts."

Zambrano sighs. Completely out of his usual character, he gives me a hug. Then immediately steps away nonchalantly, like it didn't happen. "You pulled me back. You saved them. And me."

Seraphex is still sitting on my shoulder but remains uncharacteristically quiet.

"I'm here for you, buddy," I say. "But you made the choice yourself."

"That's nice to hear, but . . . this isn't going to get easier. This deterioration may keep coming."

"Look," I say, "if you get out of hand, I'll just murder you, drop your body in the East River, and take the warehouse for myself. It's a sweet pad. Now, let's focus. We've got a job to do here."

Zambrano chuckles. "You always know what to say. I hope the government doesn't wreck all our stuff."

"Those government thugs better not take my favorite pillow," I say. "I brought that from home a couple months ago. Do you need a hand with the conduit?"

I've successfully gotten him back to normal, or at least what passes for normal for a somewhat insane centuries-old sorcerer, and together we're able to get the conduit set up on the ground, with clamps set on the museum's polished limestone floor, holding it up in the right spot. The long bright staff gleams in the dimness of the museum's nighttime low light. I saw the other end of the arcane conduit activated in Yellowstone, with a massive array of pylons harnessing volcanic energy to power it. Luckily, we have a simpler solution. Zambrano also adds an extra piece onto one end, the compressed sphere of Volcanose, the heart of the volcano that we stole on Mars.

"It's nice not to have to set up all that gear Volcanose had in Yellowstone. Thanks, you old bastard," Zambrano says, eyeing Volcanose's spherical prison with a satisfied smile.

"Police and military have arrived," Liao Ling says over the radio. "But they seem to be setting up barricades around the museum, not rushing in. If they start coming in, I'll put on a light show to make them think twice."

"Keep them out of this wing," I say. "But if they want to help with removing the key art and artifacts, that's okay. The security team is already doing it."

"Why are we bothering to save a museum?" Parth asks over the radio. "It's a bunch of art and old stuff. The fate of the whole world is at stake! Museums are boring; it's all standing around."

"Museums are boring, I admit that," I say, "I still think we shouldn't let the great art of human history be destroyed by a demon."

"What are you talking about?" Zambrano says from across the room where he's setting up the arcane conduit. "Museums are full of ancient knowledge, art, and artifacts! Just because your modern peasant brains are too burned out by social media to appreciate them, doesn't mean they're bad."

"Thanks for your opinions, gentlemen, but let's stay on topic. I'll put the fear of sorcery into these government types, and see if they feel like cooperating," Liao Ling says. "I'll tell them that if they go near your room, you're going to blow it up."

"Whatever it takes," I say. "We only have to stall and confuse them until Rex gets here."

"Governments move slowly," Zambrano says. "They're not going to stage a full-scale assault of their own museum against two sorcerers on a rapid timetable. They'll be gathering mages and wizards, consulting with committees, and will try to negotiate first."

The process of getting the arcane conduit set up is nerve-racking. Zambrano has me help, holding the clamps and the conduit in place while he tests and does different spells. The heat of the heart of the volcano, no longer dulled and controlled by the amber nexus that I had on Mars, is fairly intense close up, and I'm soon sweating.

As we work, the security guards around us carry various installations out of the room. They are moving quickly, and I hope they're getting all the most important stuff. I'm guessing Rex will be even less gentle than we were when he arrives.

Finally, the conduit is set up. With a hum and a crackle, it projects a red rectangle of energy upward, its interwoven hues shifting, moving, and sparkling. It's about six feet wide and twenty feet tall. Large enough to accommodate Rex, but we're going to have to stuff him in sideways.

When the portal was connected to Mars, I could see demons massing through it. But now the portal is a uniform shimmering blue-gray field. A magical gateway to nowhere. Exactly what Rex deserves.

"He is approaching," Liao Ling says. "My guys can see him. The police and military don't look like they're about to make moves. I'll cast a couple long-distance attack spells at him to get him fired up, and then Parth and I are coming down there to join you. Hopefully, he charges in immediately so we can spring the trap."

"Mr. Fournier," I say, flagging down the head of security who is directing operations in the next room. "I suggest you take your last load of art and get everyone out of this building. I'm very sorry, but it is about to become a war zone."

The older Frenchman gives me a dirty look. "You Americans think you can barge into anything and tell us what to do."

"Within a few minutes there are going to be not one but two giant demons fighting in this exhibit hall. I don't want to be here, but I have to be. You and your staff don't need to be here. I'm sorry for the damage that's about to be done here, but let's try to minimize the loss of life."

Marcel Fournier grumbles about Americans, magic users, and young people, and then switches into French and continues saying what I assume are very rude things. But he calls his security team, and at least the ones in this area appear to grab their final artifacts and head for the exits.

A moment later, Liao Ling and Parth arrive, breathing heavily from running downstairs.

"He is coming," Liao Ling says.

"And he is *pissed*," Parth adds. "That spell with the lion was awesome; you should have seen it."

"Oh, you know that one?" Zambrano says. "It's very popular with security mages these days."

"Know it?" Liao Ling says, cocking her head to the side. "I created it!"

"So badass," Parth says under his breath.

I roll my eyes, but Liao Ling smiles at the praise.

"You're absolutely sure I should do this?" Zambrano says to me, motioning toward Seraphex, who is standing in a large open part of the room, waiting expectantly.

"That's the decision we made," I say. "And it's too late to back out now, I think. The plan is in motion, and Rex will be here soon."

"Very well," Zambrano says. "I'm trusting you on this." He steps forward, and pulls out his illusion prism. "*In using this transmogrification reversal spell crafted by Alix the Sorcerer, who is both beautiful and brilliant, I acknowledge that I am almost certainly making a mistake,*" he says. "*I am crafting the words of this spell in the lowly brutish language of English so that if some idiot like Zambrano or Rodney Wint uses it for a terrible reason, there is the greatest possible chance that someone nearby will hear and stop them. These final two sentences are intended to waste additional time, in order to give any saner individuals close by a chance to stop them, if they are indeed making a terrible mistake."*

We all glance at one another, and no one says anything.

"It will be too late for anyone other than the spellcaster to stop the process," Zambrano finishes, *"starting NOW."*

White tendrils of magic stretch out from the prism toward Seraphex. Once again, she glows with swirling light and dark, and shadows rear up around her. Powerful white arcane force courses from the prism to her, and this time it doesn't stop. It increases more and more—a river of energy shooting back and forth.

With a thunderclap and a roar of magical force, Seraphex's form suddenly grows, twisting in the energy as the transmogrification takes hold.

A moment later, the magical light and energy evaporates, leaving her standing in the room, her duck form entirely gone.

She is sleek, gleaming, with a dark iridescent sheen to every surface. She does not have the cape she wore in the illusions that Zambrano once showed me, but she stands immensely tall, towering over the rest of us. She has some small horns and spikes around her body, but otherwise is mostly human shaped, though she doesn't have hair but instead a molded, regal-looking crown.

She looks definitively inhuman, with her holographic dark skin and claws on both hands and feet, but I have to admit that something in me notices she still has an aggressively feminine body shape. I don't find it attractive, but part of me worries that Parth will, with his death-wish approach to life and risk.

She flexes her newly real muscles and claws, and trumpets a sound of pure joy. The small radio receiver that she had strapped to her duck head has fallen to the floor beside her.

"This is what I am!" she roars. "Now at least you see me in my true form, the majesty and power and beauty."

"You're still going to help us though, right?" I say. "We had an agreement."

Seraphex looks down at me, tilting her head to the side as if regarding me for the first time. "Yes, small human, I will assist you in defeating the demon king, as my duck form agreed." Her voice is recognizable, but with a depth and resonance it has never had before.

"I'm sorry, Alix," Zambrano mutters. "Let's hope Bryce is right and you were wrong."

Before we can discuss further, we hear the sound of gunfire and screams outside the museum, followed by the boom of what sounds like artillery. A few moments later, the entire building shakes on its foundation.

The door down the hall is still open from when I went to tell Marcel Fournier to leave, and at the far end of it, there's the aftermath of an explosion. The floor is strewn with bricks, limestone, mortar, and plaster. While we came in the front entrance, only breaking through some doors, it seems Rex has decided to take more of a Kool-Aid Man approach to visiting the Louvre.

The terrifying demon tears through the wall, then turns to face down the hall at us. To my right, Zambrano has an illusion prism out, and I glance over and can see that the stele of Hammurabi and the arcane conduit portal are both hidden. That may not hold out as he gets closer, but for the moment it is blocking Rex from the effects of the stele. I just hope that, when the time comes, the effect will be strong enough.

"There you are again, you traitorous trollop," Rex's deep voice booms down the hallway. He steps forward, not running but steadily approaching. Even a demon king seems to be wise enough to approach warily. "Is this truly you, in your full harlot reality, or another vile illusion?"

"I am here," Seraphex answers, her voice a mocking purr. "In every bit of my glory and majesty. All that you could have had but foolishly threw away."

"Perhaps if you had remained properly loyal and obedient, as a good queen should, and not a wanton strumpet, things would have been different," Rex answers, getting closer with each powerful step and making my pulse beat faster and faster. "What a tragic end your lascivious nature led us to."

"Perhaps if you had properly satisfied your queen, indeed, we would not have fallen apart," Seraphex answers.

"Gross," Zambrano and I say at the same time.

But Seraphex's plan appears to be working, if it is an intentional plan. Rex is advancing straight at her, eyes burning in fury, ignoring the silly little humans around her. He shoots one of his darts of red energy at her, probably to check if she is an illusion. It bounces harmlessly off her dark prismatic body in a shower of red sparks, and she stands her ground, glaring at her former husband.

For our part, we are backing away into the corners of the room while Seraphex is standing right in front of the invisible stele. Zambrano and I go to one side, while Liao Ling and Parth head to the other. I've got my gauntlets on, so I also should be invisible to Rex, even more so than the trap we've set. I've also pulled the industrial-grade megaphone out of my backpack, the final little piece of the plan I grabbed during our prep time.

As Rex approaches, a new voice crackles over our radio.

"Bad news," Dao says. I can hear the beating of the wings of a helicopter in the background as his voice comes through. "There are more demons coming. Looks like big metal guys and one that has a bunch of storm clouds around her. They must have followed along after the king one came from Geneva. We'll hold them off as long as we can."

"How will you do that?" I ask, trying to imagine a few modern-day pirates fighting off demons.

The earth shakes as the sound of a loud explosion comes from the street outside.

"We acquired a few Eurocopter Tiger attack helicopters from the military base outside Paris," Dao says. "We were able to negotiate renting them at a *very* discounted day rate." The voice transmission shuts off, and we hear the sound of distant gunfire.

"Please don't destroy all of Paris," Zambrano says, both annoyance and respect in his voice. "But thank you. Let's get this over with and make our escape—machine guns and missiles won't hold off demons for long. Especially if Typhoria is there."

Before any of us can reply, Rex is stalking into our room. He's so tall that he bashes right through the top of the doorway, sending showers of plaster across the room. But he doesn't break his stride. He moves forward, standing face-to-face with Seraphex.

"You bitch," he says.

"You sad, sad creature," she answers. "If only you hadn't tried to control me, my husband, this could all have turned out differently. Do you think the sorcerers would have been able to defeat us had we been together? Our division destroyed us and doomed our kind to over a millennia of imprisonment."

"It may not be too late," Rex says. "You could assume your old role. I am your husband and king. You are my wife and queen. Together we can conquer this work, reduce it to rubble, and enjoy an eternity of tormenting the few humans who remain. Never again make the mistake of letting them achieve technology, society, or culture."

"It was enjoyable though, wasn't it, watching their little developments over the centuries?" Seraphex says. "Even if it cost us."

My stomach drops. Seeing the demon queen standing there, eight feet tall and gleaming in the light, it's hard to imagine her on our side. What if there's some loophole? But she did say moments ago after her transformation that she would help us.

Still, I am suddenly desperately worried. What if she has done all this to betray us and I made the most boneheaded decision in human history? What if this ex-duck is about to get back together with her demon ex-husband?

Seraphex and Rexhalarkhart, demon king and queen, glare at each other.

Then Seraphex laughs. "Would you apologize to me?" She is backing up slowly, and Rex is following her, closer and closer to the stele of Hammurabi.

Rex looks at her gravely. "I said I would never, that last night we were together. And so I am bound."

"You are bound by so many words you cannot take back," the demon queen replies. "And I believe they are evidence of your true feelings. And so now you must be removed."

My confidence is growing, though I don't like the fact that Seraphex felt like she needed to have a whole conversation and feel him out. But toxic exes have a way of unbalancing us all. Following our plan, I use the invisibility granted by my gauntlets to stealthily creep up behind Rex.

"Even back in your true form, you forsaken hellcat, we both know you are no match for my strength."

Seraphex laughs. "Perhaps that is so. But I have allies. And tricks. Now, little sorcerer," she bellows.

Zambrano shoots an annoyed glance at the demon queen, but he passes his hand over the magical prism in a precise motion, and the illusion drops.

"What is . . ." The demon king's voice trails off. Rex stares at the stele, his motion suddenly frozen. His eyes, unblinking, are fixed on it but also looking past and through the massive black stone edifice.

"*End of my rope,*" Liao Ling and Zambrano shout at the same time. White lances of energy shoot out from their hands, coming at Rex from either side. The white arcane energy wraps around each of his wrists. Zambrano uses the connection to pull at him from one side, while Liao Ling is using the same spell to yank him from the other side.

As they hold his arms, Seraphex leaps forward, grabbing him in a vicious embrace. She tries to pull him, and he stumbles forward for a moment before roaring in anger. He pulls back against both the spells and Seraphex, taking a full step away from the stele and the arcane conduit's portal.

I put up the megaphone, sneaking in as close as I dare. Battling with Rex, Seraphex grunts and growls, and they both howl in pain as their claws strike each other.

"The third element of the demonic code," I say, my voice amplified by the maximum power of the megaphone, "is that a demon may not ponder its own nature and origins, or the origin of the demonic code."

Rex freezes again, shaking his head as if trying to physically rid himself of the thoughts in his brain.

"The third element of the demonic code," I repeat, stepping closer and aiming the megaphone right at his giant horned head, "is that a demon may not ponder its own nature and origins, or the origin of the demonic code."

Rex slumps, his movements becoming less coordinated. Seraphex hauls at him mightily, and the twin sorcerers use their magic, running to the open portal and pulling the demon king toward it. One of his clawed feet sinks into the stone floor, leaving a deep gash as he is pulled across it.

Hope surges in my chest as they pull him, stumbling, forward. But with a shout of pure fury, he pulls back.

Parth approaches from the other side, holding his own megaphone. "What are you?" he demands. "What is a demon?"

They redouble their efforts, and Rex shakes his head back and forth, his eyes rolling back as he struggles to process everything.

"A demon is an arcane construct of the unconscious force of a human's fears," Parth says through his megaphone, giving information in one ear while I shout the words of the code itself into the other.

Seraphex has latched on to Rex's neck with her fangs like a hyena attacking a lion. She hauls his confused form forward, aided by the magical lassos.

They are in front of the portal, and Seraphex turns, half shoving and half pulling Rex toward it. He has descended into an animal state, unable to mount a real defense, but impossibly strong. Still, inch by inch, she maneuvers him. Parth and I, as close as we dare, pour our words into his massive, spiked ears.

Finally, with a great blow, she thrusts him toward the portal. He stumbles toward it for a moment.

But then he howls, letting out a shriek of pure rage and fear. He throws one foot down, his claws scraping deeply into the limestone floor of the museum.

He is trembling, muttering incoherently. But with a shake he pushes Seraphex back. Free for a moment, he falls to the ground. With a mighty blow, he sinks all four of his claws—hands and feet both—into the stone of the floor.

He huddles down, using his inhuman strength to drive the clawed hands and feet deeper and deeper into the stone.

"No!" Seraphex screams, leaping back on him and hauling with all her might. As the colossal form of Rex huddles on the ground, unaware of the world around him, the demon queen and the two sorcerers pull against him. But it's to no avail. His brain has clearly short-circuited, but animal instinct has gotten him too deeply attached to the stone. I can see his massive muscles straining to hold on.

"This isn't working," Liao Ling shouts. "We don't have the power to move him."

Parth gets in too close with the megaphone, trying to keep the verbal assault going, but a sudden twitch from the demon's back smacks into him, sending him sliding on his butt across the floor and smacking into the museum's wall with a dull thump.

"One of the other choppers is down," Dao's voice crackles over the radio. "We were nearly caught in a tornado and have lost control. Going to bail out now, hoping to make it into the river. The other demons are on their way in. I'm sorry I couldn't do more. Give 'em hell, Captain."

CHAPTER 29

I have no idea how Liao Ling managed to inspire such loyalty in her crew in only a few months, but I certainly respect it.

I see Zambrano and Liao Ling share a look.

"I'll go," Liao Ling says. "I'll buy you some time to figure this out." She drops her lasso spell and sprints toward the hallway where Rex entered. I can already feel a wind blowing in through there. I'd have to guess that's Typhoria, mistress of hurricanes.

As Liao Ling leaves, she slams the doors shut.

"She's powerful, but she won't be able to do more than distract and delay them," Zambrano says.

"You think I can't take on a few demons?" Liao Ling's voice comes over the radio.

"No," Zambrano answers matter-of-factly.

"Okay, fair," Liao Ling replies. "I'll try to draw them the other way; just get that big hunk of evil into the portal, okay?"

Parth is back on his feet and continues berating Rex with forbidden demon facts, which is keeping him shuddering on the floor, but he is only digging in farther, his incredibly strong claws half disappeared into the stone of this ground-floor room.

"What is happening to him right now?" I ask. "Is he aware of what's going on?"

"His brain is completely overwhelmed; he's essentially operating on instinct only," Seraphex says.

"Will he remember any of this?" I ask. "When he comes to?"

"He's not supposed to come to," Seraphex answers. "He's supposed to go into the portal before he even understands what's happening."

Outside, we hear massive cracking followed by a deafening avalanche. Whatever Liao Ling is doing out there, it's destroying this wing of the museum. I hope all the most beloved art got out, but it's hard to care too much at this point. If she has to bring the ceiling of the Louvre down on them, so be it.

"If you make the portal invisible, will light pass through it?" I ask, the essence of an idea forming in my head.

"Technically, the light will be bending around it, refracted by an arcane lensing effect," Zambrano explains.

"Will it fool Rex?" I ask. It's a stupid plan. But we don't have any other option. Demons could knock down the door and wreck everything at any moment.

The sorcerer shrugs. "For a few seconds, maybe. No longer."

It's a bad plan. But here goes.

"Seraphex," I say, pointing to the far side of the portal, which Rex is in front of, stubbornly immovable. "Stand here. When he comes to, taunt him. Or entice him. Or something. Get him to come toward you the moment his brain resets and he becomes aware again."

"And if the portal is hidden," Zambrano says, "he charges right into it."

"Exactly," I say.

"We are depending on him to do precisely what we expect," Zambrano complains. "I hate it."

"Do you have a better idea?" I ask.

"I'll prepare the illusion," Zambrano says, letting his lasso disappear and pulling his illusion prism out again.

Seraphex stands in her appointed spot, and Zambrano focuses on his prism. The stele of Hammurabi and the arcane conduit's portal both vanish.

Parth stops with his megaphone and steps away. For a moment, there's relative silence except for some distant crashes and the howling of wind.

Rex continues huddling down in confusion for a moment but then grows still and relaxes.

"What is this?" he demands in a low, rumbling voice. "Where am I?"

Keeping his clawed hands and feet locked into the stone floor, he looks up.

In front of him, Seraphex is preening, moving ever so slightly in a languid pose that screams of both seduction and violence.

"Come, my king, my husband," Seraphex croons, her voice a soft purr with a threatening edge. "Take me if you can."

I'm not sure how she's allowed to call him her husband rather than her former husband, but her ploy is working so far. As if in a trance, Rex stands up to his full, massive height and faces her.

"My queen," his voice thunders. "How I have missed you."

Seraphex shifts her weight invitingly, like a cat that hasn't decided if it's in heat or about to slash your face open.

I had hoped Rex would charge forward immediately, but instead he steps gingerly, body coiled for an attack but not leaping.

Still, he is moving toward the invisible portal and doesn't seem to have noticed yet. Behind him, I see Zambrano tensing up, holding the illusion prism in one hand but gathering a glowing spell in the other. In a moment, the demon king will be close enough to the conduit, and the sorcerer will be able to give him a final magical push.

But instead, the doors to the hallway explode open with a furious gale of wind.

A third massive demonic figure steps through it. This one is a giant demoness, skin a mottled blue and white, with giant wings and tusks protruding from her mouth and wind and hail swirling around her. Typhoria, mistress of hurricanes.

Liao Ling is perched on the demon's back, surrounded by a bubble of protective magic and screaming with rage. She is holding on with both hands to a magical glowing blade that juts out from the demon's shoulder blades—the Caesar Special. Which it turns out is enough to slow down a demon duchess, but not stop her entirely.

"What is this?" Rex says, spinning and taking in the full scene as if suddenly waking up. "What have you done, my queen?"

Liao Ling leaps off Typhoria's back and raises her hands to cast a spell at Rex.

"I have come to your aid, my lord," Typhoria roars and pushes out both her claws. Miniature tornadoes and hurricanes shoot out from them, shaking the entire room. Chunks of ceiling fall down from above, and I dodge backward as one lands where I was standing a moment before.

Zambrano releases his built-up magical energy, but as he does, Typhoria reaches him, swiping at him with the full extent of her clawed arm. His aim is ruined, and the gout of bright purple energy shoots straight up, blasting the ceiling and shaking even more of it loose. The sorcerer scurries backward, desperately throwing up arcane barriers as Typhoria slashes at him.

I can't tell if it's by choice or because of the disruption from Typhoria, but Zambrano drops the illusion hiding both the prism and the stele of Hammurabi. Fortunately, as the spell drops, a massive portion of the ceiling falls on it, covering it in masonry and plaster, hiding it from both Rex and Typhoria.

"The third element—" Parth starts into his megaphone, but the roaring of the tornadoes drowns him out. The room is filled with swirling air and dust, and I'm blinking hard trying to see through it.

Liao Ling raises her hands to cast a spell at the demon king, but he is too fast for her. Rex's arm shoots out, and one of his bolts of red energy smashes into her, clipping her in the hip and sending her to the ground with a scream of pain. Dropping his useless megaphone, Parth runs to her side.

I try to push against the rising winds, but one of the tornadoes catches me, spinning me wildly. It sends me skidding across the room, slamming down onto my behind and up against the wall.

At the same time, from my vantage point on the floor, I see the demon queen make her move. With a dancer's grace, Seraphex pirouettes around the now-visible arcane conduit portal, in a last-ditch attempt to finish our plan.

She smashes a blow at Rex, sending him staggering back, but he lashes out with a powerful kick, which strikes Seraphex square in the chest. The force of it is incredible, and she files backward, sailing across the room and crashing into the wall opposite me.

But Rex is off-balance, and he also teeters backward. I can see him realize with horror what is happening as his tail passes into the flat gray portal. He struggles to regain his balance, waving his arms as he tries to sink his claws into the floor. For one glorious moment, I think he's going to fall backward into the shimmering gray portal, But then he slowly starts to lean forward, balancing. Pulling my gauntlets off, I throw them at the demon, but they bounce off him uselessly as he teeters.

I see a look of joy and rage light up on his face as his weight shifts forward, just starting to regain his balance.

And then a figure flies out of the swirling dust, fearlessly leaping at the demon king.

"*Pyrobolus*, you bastard!" Parth shouts as he jumps into the air. The fireball shoots out from his hands first, blasting Rex right in the eyes. But it's Parth's body that makes the difference, impacting the massive demon dead on his chest as he tries to regain his balance.

As the demon falls backward, Rex grabs at Parth, sinking one claw into my friend. But Parth's maneuver works, and the tiny shove of momentum from his weight is enough to overbalance Rex.

Rex tilts back, and as more parts of his body pass into the gray portal, it pulls on him. Parth tries to yank himself away, but as the demon king falls, his flailing claw still holding Parth and drawing the young man into the portal with him.

"Humans win, asshole!" Parth shouts. "Tell my parents I saved the world!" he adds, a split second before his head is pulled into the swirling energy.

There's a flash of bright white light, and the dual forms of Rex and Parth disappear into the oblivion of the arcane conduit's portal.

CHAPTER 30

Zambrano is still embattled, retreating and trying to maintain a glowing energy barrier as Typhoria steps forward. But, roaring in victory, Seraphex leaps back into the center of the room. Unsteadily, Liao Ling stands to her feet, gathering her magical power.

Typhoria glances between the three and backs away. With a wave of her hand, she sends one more swirl of gusting tornadoes, but she flees with impressive speed, disappearing behind the billowing dust.

Over the course of about fifteen seconds, the floating particles from the wreckage clear, and we're all able to get our breath back slightly.

Numbly, I gather up my gauntlets off the floor as Zambrano goes over to the arcane conduit staff and begins casting a spell.

I take a deep breath as the arcane conduit closes, the shimmering portal evaporating and disappearing before us. Zambrano picks it up, casting a couple detection spells and nodding in satisfaction.

"We got him," he says, grinning madly. "He's cycling in teleportation over and over again, stuck in an infinite loop, unconscious, and unable to do a damn thing about it." He sees my expression, and his joy fades somewhat. "I'm sorry, Bryce."

I'm nowhere near as exultant as Zambrano is, though some small part of me is relieved and celebrating. I knew the moment both he and Parth went into the portal together that with everything we risked to get Rex in there, it would likely be a one-way trip.

"It's good for Parth, but it's a pity Rex won't feel anything, or think anything," Liao Ling says, baring her teeth. "Hopefully at least that bastard's last thought was realizing he'd been defeated. But I hate that Parth is in there too. I was starting to like that kid."

I want to add something meaningful. Some tribute to my friend, who sacrificed himself to save everything. Who's now locked indefinitely in a nonexistent limbo that no one is going to be willing to risk opening up.

"And so, as agreed, my husband is trapped," Seraphex states calmly, ignoring the emotion of our bittersweet victory. "The victory in which I promised to participate is complete." Her voice has a cold edge, like she is putting in effort to exert control.

"Your husband?" I ask, shaking off my thoughts about Parth. Her statement strikes me as odd. "Don't you always call him your former husband?"

"When two demons are wed, as Rex and I are, we make binding promises," Seraphex says, flexing her massive muscular arms and spreading her wings. "There is no divorce court—it is a permanent commitment. You are lucky my marriage vows do not obligate me to rescue my husband from this trap—there is a certain amount of latitude for conflict."

"Uh, okay," I say. "What does this all mean? I don't understand."

"It means bad news for us," Zambrano says, his voice low, filled with fury.

"Correct," Seraphex says. "I referred to him as my former husband because my transformation to that pathetic waterfowl form severed all my prior obligations. The metamorphosis meant I was no longer bound by any previous promises. But this transformation has returned me to that form, and magic recognizes me again in my true form. I am free of *all* commitments made when trapped in that ridiculous waterfowl body. And most importantly, I am not magically compelled by that ridiculous promise of 'friendship' that you extorted out of me."

My heart sinks. I thought we had won. I thought for a moment there that I had made the right call. That I was worthy to make decisions for the team. Not just for the team, but for all of humanity. We beat one demon only to unleash another. She was playing us this whole time.

"Seraphex," Zambrano starts. "I always treated you with respect and companionship. I may have been your jailor, but I could have made your torment a thousand times worse." As he speaks, I can see him backing away, glancing for the exits.

Seraphex advances, a wicked smile on her massive demonic face.

Zambrano braces himself, staring her down.

"Alix died from our first effort to stop you, all those years ago," he shouts. "I won't let it end like this. I can't have failed so badly. You made us a promise!"

"Your love died for nothing in the end," Seraphex taunts him, stepping in his direction, claws raised and wings outstretched behind her.

"*Eye of Jupiter!*" Zambrano shouts and makes a quick motion with his hands, then pushes them forward like he is throwing an invisible ball.

Seraphex barely slows down, her clawed feet cracking the tile floor of the exhibit room as she powers through the increased gravity of Zambrano's spell.

Zambrano leaps backward, but Seraphex pounces, grabbing him like a mountain lion might grab a rabbit.

"*Froststråle!*" Zambrano cries, sending a blast of ice into Seraphex as she grabs him, but she dashes it aside and with a single claw, cuts a gash across his chest. He falls to the ground, groaning in pain and clutching at the wound as blood spreads across his white shirt and suit jacket.

Liao Ling raises herself up on one elbow. "*Léi!*" she calls out, thrusting her hand with her pointed pinky outstretched. There's a sudden thunderclap, and a lance of lightning shoots out from her finger, striking at Seraphex. But the demon queen ignores the spell, not even slowing her stride. Liao Ling, clutching at the injury in her hip from Rex's bolt, collapses back to the floor.

"And you," she says, turning toward me. "My so-called friend, who mercilessly used me for his own selfish purposes."

Every instinct in my body screams for me to turn and run, but I know that would be hopeless. If I show fear, if I fight her, if I run away, that will make it so much easier.

"Seraphex," I say, battling to keep my voice steady as she advances on me. "I was your friend. That was always true."

"What sort of friend would keep me from my true potential?" she asks. "What true friend would allow a queen to be trapped in the body of a waterfowl? You permitted blasphemy."

I stand still, staring at Seraphex.

"You made us a promise," I say. "Of friendship."

"What is friendship, if it is extracted via coercion and force, from an ancient spell meant to bind and control my actions?" Seraphex demands. "Is that friendship or servitude? But that controlling magic is dissolved. I am free of your control."

"I'm your friend," I say, staring up at her as she looms down at me.

"You used me for your purposes," Seraphex says. "You would have me be a servant of humanity, a pawn in your desperate attempt to protect your race of degenerate, short-lived cockroaches."

"We fight together," I say. "You asked for our help, and we made common cause."

Seraphex's grabs at me, wrapping her claws around my neck. I feel the claws dig into my flesh as the strength of her demonic hand compresses around my throat.

"Please," I say, looking up at her eyes, which have gone alien.

"Seraphex! Stop!" Zambrano shouts, and a spell of some sort crashes against her in a shower of sparks, but she is impervious to it.

"Why should I be your friend?" Seraphex demands. "When all you want is my service for your precious world? Give me one good reason I should still be your friend?" Her prismatic skin shimmers with rage, the contained fury of decades trapped in an unfamiliar body.

Her grip is cutting off blood flow to my head, and my vision is starting to contract, like looking through a tunnel that's narrowing by the second.

"There's only one possible reason to be my friend," I croak out. "And that's because you want to be. Not because you made a promise, or because it benefits you or me. Just because you want to, because you care about me, despite everything else. Just because you want me around, the way that I want you around. A thousand reasons, a thousand moments, but in the end no reason at all."

Does what I'm saying make sense? I'm not sure, but everything is swimming, my ears are buzzing, and my vision is a little pinprick of sight, an image of Seraphex's face, miles away.

"Do you want to be my friend?" I rasp, feeling the last bit of my lung capacity used up.

The sound in my ears becomes the roar of the ocean, and I feel my consciousness floating away as my body shuts down. Despite that, I focus on keeping my eyes open, staring up at Seraphex, demanding a proper answer.

Seraphex pauses for a moment, as if calculating her answer. "No," Seraphex answers. I regret asking it, because forcing her to answer makes it a final commitment. Her decision is sealed.

The last bit of my vision disappears, and I feel my body falling to the ground.

In my hazy remnants of consciousness, without sight as I understand it, I have a sort of a sense of Seraphex, towering demon queen, bathed in searing, blinding light.

CHAPTER 31

I don't expect to wake up.

And if I do, I don't expect to wake up, groggily opening my eyes with my vision swimming, to a white-feathered duck sitting amid the dust of the Louvre museum, staring at me with a disconcerting motherly sort of concern. Zambrano is over by Liao Ling, performing one of his healing magic spells on her.

"Seraphex . . . What?"

"I had Zambrano put me back into this form," she says. "It's relatively easy for him to reactivate the spell when I'm inclined to cooperate."

"What happened?" I ask. "You nearly killed me."

"Ah, yes, apologies for that," she says without further elaboration.

"Was this all part of some elaborate plan of yours, some sort of tricky double cross?" I ask. My mind, sluggish though it is, is racing to figure out what quirk of magic lore or demonic promises would have made that make sense. "Was it the only possible path through all the demonic code issues and probabilities for us to win?"

"Could we pretend that that's the case?" Seraphex says. "That would make it much easier for everyone. Let's imagine that I saw that those exact actions, deplorable though they might be, were the only way to victory for our side."

"But they weren't?" I demand as I lever myself up, taking it slowly as my blood flow and breathing resume bit by bit. "What actually happened?"

"I saw your eyes go dead as you passed out. I couldn't take it. So I stopped, and luckily you were unconscious, not dead."

"You said you didn't want to be my friend," I say. "Didn't that commit you to that decision, for your full demon form, at least?"

Seraphex shrugs her little duck shoulders. "I answered 'no,' that I didn't want to be your friend in that moment. And that was true. But I couldn't deny that I was your friend, despite that. Want is a very multifaceted thing, after all. My truest feeling at that moment was that I didn't want to be your friend, but I was in fact your friend despite that. Both of your friends, you and Zambrano. It was more than a demon-code-enforced promise."

"That's very nice," I say, slowly catching my breath as energy returns to my body. "But it would have been great to realize that before you nearly killed me."

"I'm sorry," Seraphex says. Is that her first truly sincere apology? It might be. "I needed to remove all the other elements to understand it. To take away the compulsion, and the promise, and the weakness of being trapped in this form. I don't think real friendship is a promise you can make; it's a process of spending time together, facing challenges, helping each other."

"Thank you," I say.

"I'll admit," Seraphex says, "that it was fun being a fully powered demon and holding the power of your life and death in my hands. It's been far too long since I felt that thrill."

"What a truly wonderful friend you are," I say. "We are so very lucky."

As I recover, I can hear distant sirens wailing. Closer, there is the sound of police radios down the hall.

"It is time to make our escape," Zambrano says, helping Liao Ling to her feet. "It may be time to relax my hard line against French people, but I certainly don't want to spend more of my life than absolutely necessary talking to French cops," Zambrano says, picking up the now-dormant arcane conduit and handing it to me. "Hold on to this, and let's get you next to Liao Ling."

"I have to go see how many of my crew survived, and how much it's going to cost to bribe them out of jail," Liao Ling says. She is standing unsteadily, wincing as she moves, and Zambrano steps over, steadying her and helping her to walk to me.

"You need to heal first," Zambrano insists. "You're not going to be any help to them like this."

"Ugh, fine," Liao Ling answers with a grimace of pain.

Zambrano takes her left hand, I take her right hand, and Seraphex hops up, curling around my neck, connecting all of us. Zambrano has a teleportrait in his other hand, and with a *whoosh*, we are gone.

We reappear in the arrival zone of Liao Ling's island lair. Within a couple minutes, her pirate house staff members who stayed behind help us up to the main building where they dress our wounds.

Zambrano's wounds are less severe than Liao Ling's, so after some bandages are applied, he's able to teleport back to France to try to assess what happened and grab any of the pirates who survived.

Dao and his copilot successfully ditched in the Seine and were able to escape, and Zambrano brings them back with him. A couple of the other pirates landed and were captured and arrested, though Dao assures us that after the situation settles down, we'll be able to break them out. Zambrano, true to form, volunteers to smash into the French jail right now and pull them, but Liao Ling insists they wait. Unfortunately, two more in another helicopter were caught by Typhoria's winds and crashed hard. Neither survived.

I have scrapes and cuts all over but no serious damage, so I recover fairly quickly and spend my time scrolling on my phone, assessing the mood online. That's better than thinking about what happened to Parth at least. I have to stay busy, or my mind will get stuck on it.

The attack on the Louvre has united many countries, and negotiations at the Geneva summit, while dragging on, seem to be resolving a good deal of the chaos Rex was sowing. With the removal of demonic influence, most of the governments have become much more reasonable. Though, naturally, not a single one of them is admitting anything happened or that they were compromised. The whole thing is being swept under the rug.

Media reports are as always completely conflicting. The French government is claiming it repelled the attack, while other sources are reporting on the involvement of Zambrano and a mysterious Asian magic user in helping to stop the demons.

Half the internet thinks Zambrano is the cause of it, while the other half thinks he's the savior. I can't really blame them, it's complicated. And with a number of ironclad demons having fled into the countryside, leaving a trail of destruction as they run for hiding places, blame is shooting around for everyone. And no one is happy a major world museum was wrecked and will be closed for an unknown amount of time while they repair it and try to salvage the damaged art and artifacts.

I also text Mei and confirm she's okay. Slickwad doesn't seem to have any idea that he was played, but she is working like crazy as he tries to stealthily loot some of the magical artifacts from the Louvre. She assures me she's making sure the stele of Hammurabi stays right where it is.

After we've all had a chance to get some rest, we gather again on the incredible balcony overlooking the sea. It's bittersweet, looking out across the stunning seascape. Two of the pirates are dead as well as an unknown number of civilian, police, and other military casualties from the battle and the many demons storming through Paris.

And Parth is . . . I'm not sure what.

"Do we mourn him?" I wonder. "Parth isn't dead. We can't hold a funeral. But we have to tell his parents something." That's the last thing I want to do, but they deserve the story. I guess I'll try to tell them the truth.

But how are you supposed to feel about a friend who isn't dead, but is also completely gone. Possibly never to be seen again, and never to bravely charge into some crazy situation again.

"I'm going to get him out," Liao Ling vows. "There's got to be a way without risking Rex escaping."

"If Rex is back in our world, even for a moment, anything can happen," Seraphex warns. "And I can't risk going back into my demonic form to stuff him back in. I was moments away from forgetting I ever cared about any of you."

"Perhaps with research we can figure out how to reach into the arcane conduit and pluck Mr. Parth out without releasing the demon king," Zambrano says. "But it's more complicated than letting them both out and shoving Rex back in. The spell was not set up with a means to reverse the process and get them out of the loop they're in. Not in a way that a sensitive human body will survive, anyway."

"Like the pocket dimensions we were stuck in," I say, my heart sinking.

"We have time," Zambrano points out. "Neither Liao Ling nor I age. We will figure something out."

That's easy for him to say, with his magically extended life. I'm here without my best friend, the only peer that's still in my life. But I don't say anything. We can't risk global annihilation just because Bryce Alexander is lonely. I also don't know what sort of injuries Parth might have gotten as he and Rex were pulled into the portal.

"It sucks not having him here," I say. "Parth would have wanted to celebrate with us."

"Parth would have chased after one of those ironclad demons to try to see if he could wrestle it into submission, probably dying in the attempt," Liao Ling says wistfully. "What a psycho."

"He was a fun psycho to have around though, wasn't he?" Seraphex says. She's been rather quiet since coming back from her demonic transformation. I'm not sure if she's still adjusting or realizes how close she came to murdering all of us and doesn't want to draw too much attention.

"We'll have time to work on the Parth puzzle," Zambrano says. "But that will have to be a long-term research project. I fear in the nearer term we may have to deal with these new demons that Rex was able to have teleported to Earth. And we will need to reclaim all my property from the MSA. I certainly won't stand for the government futzing around with my precious belongings for long."

"Perhaps we could take, like, I don't know, a couple days off?" I suggest, looking around at all our various injuries.

Dao, his arm in a sling, strolls over, looking out on the waves with a smile. "Normally in the movies, after the big battle or the heist, they go to a tropical island for some of those cocktails with umbrellas in them. Luckily for you, we already live on one. There's a little grotto that is quite lovely and protected from the waves. But please don't go digging too deep in the sand or anything. Wouldn't want you to cut yourself on some, er, wild boar bones or anything."

"Fine," Zambrano says. "For a couple days, we'll let the world take care of itself, and recuperate. But then we are getting my books and artifacts back! And we may need a new base of operations, as nice as this ocean paradise is.

"A couple days is fine," Liao Ling says. "A few weeks if needed, to find you a new location and get your gear. But sorcerers don't share their hideouts for long."

"Don't worry, I have every intention of finding a new home soon," Zambrano says. "I am very particular about how the library is organized."

A million thoughts are racing through my head. There's so much to do with all the demons loose in the world, and who knows what's happening to Agent Crane and the US government. And is Derek okay? Did he get arrested too? And what do we tell Parth's family and friends? Like me, he told them he would be off-grid for a while, but how long can we keep that up?

I feel a bone-deep weariness that one night's sleep has not cleared up. Those concerns will all wait for another day or two. We did save the world, after all.

And I bet the beaches here are a hell of a lot nicer than the ones back in New York City. Though they probably don't have ice cream trucks or fish tacos here on Liao Ling's private island. But you can't have it all, can you?

"Also," Zambrano begins, followed by a long pause, "thank you, Bryce. For helping me stay on this side of the sorcerer's madness. It's nice to still feel sane."

"As sane as you've ever been, at least," Seraphex says.

"Vaguely in the area of sanity," Zambrano answers with a shrug. "I'll take it."

"How do we keep you there?" I ask. It's not a nice question, but it does need to be asked.

"I don't know," Zambrano says. "Maybe a little time off will help. Having all of you around, while infinitely annoying, does seem to be good for me. I categorically refuse to take a corporate HR manager course, if that's what you're thinking."

"We all need a break. I'm going to have to take some time for my hip to heal," Liao Ling says, "even with magical assistance. I'll start the basic research into how we might get Parth back. I have over a thousand years of mathematical progress to catch up on."

"Good. Back in the time of the Sorcerers' Circle," Zambrano says, "some of our members died in battle, or betrayed us. But we

would never tolerate one of us being imprisoned or trapped somewhere for long. Like when Caravello and Zuzanna invented a new
branch of arcane mathematics to pull me out when I was trapped
in one of Merlin's pocket universes. Those were the good old days."

"You know, we've also had our losses," I say, thinking of Parth
trapped in the conduit. At least he's not suffering, just frozen. "But
these days are also pretty good, in their own way."

"Yes, we have built an effective little team," Zambrano admits.
"All of us here, Parth, and even Mei and Agent Crane. The Anti-
Demon All-Stars, were we calling it?"

"That is rather inappropriate given that one of us is, in fact, a
demon," Seraphex notes. "Surely we can be defined by more than
that?"

"Very well," Zambrano says, smiling wistfully. "You know, with
two of us here and Zuzanna out there somewhere, maybe it's just the
Sorcerers' Circle, back in a new form with honorary non-sorcerer
members?"

I hadn't thought much about Susan for the past day. I'm definitely going to have to get in touch with her. She'll want to know
what happened even if she's keeping away from the whole magic
thing. And it'll be nice to have someone to tell the story about Parth
to. Someone else who has a limited lifespan and can't wait around for
a "maybe someday" of him getting out. I miss him already.

I wonder if she'll be terrorizing a new retirement home somewhere. Maybe with the sorcerers' help I could even figure out where
she is and drop by to surprise her, since she spent so many years
secretly tracking me. And it would be nice to have a little more time
to talk about . . . well, everything.

"I'm not sure if Susan wants to be included in a Sorcerers' Circle,"
I say. "But I guess she never officially quit, did she?"

"It's not as if we had a human resources department," Zambrano
says. "Though we did have smart-looking amulets. Another of
my prized possessions that's now in the hands of that infuriating
government."

"Isn't your whole joke that you run a company?" Liao Ling
points out. "With your project manager here, and all that? Didn't
your mother teach you not to mix metaphors?"

"Fine, The Sorcerers' Circle, LLC," Zambrano quips. "Happy now?"

"Sure," Liao Ling says. "But what's an LLC?"

"It stands for limited liability company, a type of corporation that you can form in the United States," Seraphex explains.

"I like it, because I sure as hell am not taking the blame for the nonsense the rest of you get up to!" I say. "Please, please limit my liability!"

"I don't believe you can simply declare yourself an LLC and get away with anything," Seraphex notes.

"Too late," Zambrano says, "we just did. No responsibility! I can abuse my project manager as much as I want with no legal consequences!"

"Whatever," I say. "Where's the path down to this beach, again?"

At your request, we have evaluated the work of Special Agent Angelica Crane, focusing most specifically on her interactions with the Dark Sorcerer Zambrano, his accomplice Bryce Alexander, and their various associates. While the Department of Homeland Security has put a halt to any offensive actions against this group, their classification as potential threats remains in effect.

Extensive interviews with MSA employees under her direct supervision have not yielded conclusive proof of wrongdoing. There is no concrete proof of classified material being shared with the subjects without clearance. It appears this charge was made without sufficient justification.

Additionally, we looked into the case of the missing FGM-148 Javelin missile. While its disappearance was suspicious, there is no evidence of its use by the dark sorcerer, and it was not recovered in the raid on his warehouse.

When reached directly by secure text communication as part of our investigation, Mr. Alexander responded as follows:

"Angelica Crane is an honorable agent, always working to safeguard the country and the world. You are lucky to have her, and she should be returned to her post immediately. Also, could you please return Zambrano's books and stuff? He's starting to get pissy about it, and frankly, I'm tired of his whining. Please, I'm begging you."

Negotiations for the return of the confiscated material are being stalled while the books and artifacts are fully catalogued and examined.

Without substantiation of any of the claimed evidence against Agent Crane, we are unable to recommend disciplinary action at this time. That being said, the volume of suspicious activity is notable, and due to the appearance of a personal relationship with known arcane threats, we suggest that you offer her an early retirement package. While it may decrease her ability to seek private sector work, we recommend against extending her security clearance.

In our interview with her in connection to this investigation, Agent Crane appeared amenable to this resolution. Her exact words as recorded in the interrogation were, "I'm fed up with this goddamn bureaucratic bullshit. I helped save the world a couple times over, and you're all over my ass? I'm done. I'm ready to go live in a cabin somewhere for a few years. Your accusations of me or Bryce or Zambrano being enemies of the state can go [censored] themselves."

While her outburst is a sign of insubordination, at this time we believe pursuing a disciplinary case against her based solely on this interaction would be a waste of department resources.

With her years of service, hazard pay, and history of consistent overtime, Agent Crane should be eligible for a generous separation payment and enhanced pension calculation.

Task Force Officer Derek Kauhane has been promoted to special agent and will be taking on Agent Crane's investigations, to prevent any lapse in coverage. He has been given broad discretion to track the dark sorcerer, Mr. Alexander, and the other suspected members of their group of lawless miscreants.

ABOUT THE AUTHOR

Gavin Brown is a novelist, video game director, and entrepreneur. His books include *Josh Baxter Levels Up*, *Monster Club: Hunters for Hire*, and installments of the 39 Clues and Spirit Animals series. He also created hit indie mobile game *Blindscape* and directed the video games *The 39 Clues, Spirit Animals*, and Scholastic's *Home Base*. Brown lives in a former ice cream factory in New York City.